Kate Evans is a writer of fiction, Donna Morris series is based in North Yorkshire coast where sh Trained as a psychotherapeutic the connection between creativity and mental wellbeing. She has an MA in Creative Writing from Sussex University and has taught creative writing. She currently facilitates creative workshops with an emphasis on wellbeing.

By Kate Evans

A Wake of Crows
Drowning Not Waving
No Justice

No Justice

Kate Evans

CONSTABLE

First published in Great Britain in 2023 by Constable
This paperback edition published in Great Britain in 2024
by Constable

1 3 5 7 9 10 8 6 4 2

Copyright © Kate Evans, 2023

The moral right of the author has been asserted.

A CIP catalogue record for this book
is available from the British Library.

ISBN: 978-1-47213-481-3

Typeset in Caslon by Initial Typesetting Services, Edinburgh
Printed and bound in Great Britain by Clays Ltd, Elcograf S.p.A

Papers used by Constable are from well-managed forests
and other responsible sources

MIX
Paper | Supporting
responsible forestry
FSC
www.fsc.org FSC® C104740

Constable
An imprint of
Little, Brown Book Group
Carmelite House
50 Victoria Embankment
London EC4Y 0DZ

An Hachette UK Company
www.hachette.co.uk

www.littlebrown.co.uk

*After completing this novel, I realised it is also about sisters.
So I dedicate it to my sister Ros, who supports and
loves me through tough times and good.*

*With thanks to Warsan Shire for her incomparable poem 'Home'
and Tanatsei Gambura for her affecting poem 'Things I Have
Forgotten Before'. We can learn a lot from poets.*

And thank you to you the reader who completes the circle.

Prologue

It is a slow afternoon. Possibly because of the weather. Possibly it's the lassitude after the Easter rush. Or the end of month penury. Whatever the reason, the girls are not busy. And this makes Marius Badea furious. 'This isn't a holiday resort,' he tells them. 'You're not here to lie about enjoying yourselves. You have bills to pay. You get me?'

He's short and wide. When he gets wound up, his face bloats and his small nose turns red. The girls call him Mr Pigs and giggle. Amongst themselves. Not in front of him. Those fists are brutish. And not in front of Felka either. Badea is her boyfriend, supposedly, though it doesn't stop him putting her to work like the rest of them. Right now she is finding him his cigarettes, offering to make him some pierogi, the best kind, with mince.

'Why she do that, Sugar?' mutters Marianne. She's too young to have seen what she has. Her skin is so pale it could have been blanched. 'She know we don't have no mince and he mad enough already. And this ain't no hotel.' She rests her head on the older woman's more substantial shoulder and is rewarded by an arm around her own thin ones. They are sitting on the sofa in the waiting room where everyone has been told to congregate. The five girls, who live and work

1

in this meagre second floor to an industrial unit, keep their surroundings clean. More for their own sanity than because of Marius and his colleagues' threats. Even so, the brown carpet is slightly sticky, the furniture flimsy and threadbare and there is a persistent smell of cigarettes, alcohol and sex too easily taken. Marianne carries on: 'If this a hotel, what is it? The Piggy-Ritz.' She gives a snort. Either this or the slight sharpening in her tone attracts Marius's attention.

'What's that?' Marius swings round, pushing Felka roughly away from him. He is looking straight at the sofa. His eyes are what might be called sparkling blue in a romantic novel. 'You, you . . .' His gaze drifts across Marianne's face to the woman sitting next to her. She straightens while the youngster cowers. Badea yells: 'What's that, you black bitch?' He dives forward, grabs her by the arm and pulls her to her feet. He is disconcerted for a second to be reminded that she is as tall as him. Then he punches her hard on the side of the face and kicks her. Her legs cave and she is kneeling before him. 'What's that? Don't you know you owe me everything? You get me? You owe me your life.' His spittle accompanies his words.

She rubs a hand across her face. 'Oruko mi ni Blessing,' she says quietly.

He grabs at her hair. A blonde wig, it is nevertheless held on by pins which drag at her scalp. 'What's that?' he demands. 'Don't speak your dirty, filthy language to me. The queen's English please.' All the vowel sounds over-emphasised.

'I said . . .' Her voice is parched in her throat. It trembles slightly. She levels her gaze on Badea and continues: 'I said, my name is Blessing.'

2

'Brown Sugar, Brown Sugar,' in his mouth the name is neither sweet, nor melodic. He grabs her by the neck and clouts her, leaving her sprawling and breathless on the stinking carpet.

'Don't spoil the merchandise.' The man's entrance makes everyone start, their focus having been so utterly taken by the fight between Marius and Blessing. The girls glance at each other. Is this a punter? He is white and smartly dressed. Maybe too upmarket for their operation and, in any case, he wouldn't have got past the guard on the door. His face is covered by a balaclava. It should look ridiculous. It looks threatening.

Marius takes a breath and turns. All bonhomie, he grasps the man's hand: 'Mr T, my friend, I wasn't expecting you.'

'Clearly.' Mr T's English accent shows up the fault-lines in Marius's Romanian one. There is also something in Mr T's bearing which makes Badea the supplicant.

The girls would cheer if they weren't so afraid. Marianne creeps over to Blessing and helps her to her feet, then they join the other two by the door to the bedrooms. Felka remains apart. Her allegiances split.

Mr T continues: 'We're moving out. Someone's tongue has been wagging.' He lets his stare rest on Marius and then on the hefty henchman who has scrambled to a sort of attention in the corner by the drinks cabinet. Then Mr T shrugs: 'Or perhaps someone just noticed something, a coming or going. In any case, it's about time to move on. Never good to stay in one place for too long. Two cars.' He glances at the girls. 'You,' he points at Blessing. 'And you.' This time it's Felka. 'You're coming with me. You others with him,' he

3

jerks his head towards Marius. Both Felka and Marianne yelp protests, Marianne clinging on to Blessing and Felka taking one step – but no more – towards Badea. The expression on his face makes her retrace it.

Mr T's attention remains on Blessing and Marianne. 'You like each other, huh?' He thrusts his hips. 'I like a bit of babe-on-babe action.' He laughs. 'But not this time. You do as I say or you'll find out what I can do without making a mess. Now get your stuff. We need to be outta here.'

Blessing tries to comfort Marianne as they both scramble to their rooms and throw the few bits of clothing and make-up they have into plastic bags. From the back of a drawer, Blessing retrieves her dhuku. The last one to survive her journey from Nigeria, it has lost much of its lustre. She pulls at it until it cleaves along its length. She hands over one half to Marianne with a promise: 'I will find you. Stay strong, my little one.'

Marius and his henchman come battering down the bedroom doors and the women are herded out into the communal area. Mr T hands Marius a phone. 'Instructions on there. Make sure you throw it in the canal when you're done.' Mr T forces pills into the girls' mouths and water to follow. 'Don't want any travel sickness do we?'

Then he is pushing Blessing and Felka down the fire escape. It's rare for them to see the outside. This evening is foggy and drear. The neighbours – a mix of lock-ups, warehouses and a very few small businesses with employees turning up every day – are indistinct. There are no lights, no people moving around, no obvious place to run to. Even if there were, Blessing and Felka are finding their movements are becoming clumsy, their heads as fuddled as the weather. They are pushed through the tiny back yard into a narrow alley where there is a car waiting. As they shuffle into the back, Mr T says, 'That's right, my sleeping beauties, in you go and wait for your kiss from Prince Charming.' His tone makes it sound more of a curse. It is the last thing they hear as they plunge into a dark vat of nothingness.

Chapter 1

Gordon Yates would hardly be recognisable even to himself. DC Donna Morris hopes no one has given him a mirror. And the pain must be tremendous. The whole right side of his face is a livid mulch of yellow and purple. This and the broken humerus were caused by his fall. After the clout he received, which has closed up and blackened his left eye. Apart from this his white skin looks unlaundered against the starched hospital pillow.

'Mr Yates,' Donna says softly. If he is sleeping, she decides she will leave him to it. But his good eye snaps open and the other one becomes a slit. Donna continues, explaining who she is and why she has come.

At eighty-nine, Gordon Yates probably has the reflex to stand when greeting a woman or someone in authority. He seems determined to try something of the kind.

'There's no need to sit up,' Donna adds hastily. Gordon is linked to various monitoring machines. However, he was lucky to be found so quickly – the postwoman investigating the open front door – he hadn't become too dehydrated and got quick attention. Beyond the usual hospital smells of linoleum and cleaning fluids, there is the slight acidic odour of vomit. The nurse told Donna, they are concerned about concussion. They will keep him in overnight and then will (hopefully) release him into the care of his son.

Donna pulls over a plastic chair and sits. She divests herself of scarf and padded jacket. Outside, a breeze native to the Siberian Steppes – it feels like – is blowing in across the sea and a fog has mobbed the sun. In contrast, the ward is a roasting oven and for Donna one of her internal heat waves is threatening. She brings herself to focus by opening her notepad: 'I wonder if you could tell me what happened, Mr Yates?'

'I was attacked,' he says gruffly. 'It was that Khalil. I shouldn't have trusted him.' He said much the same to the paramedics as he went in and out of consciousness.

'Perhaps you could give me some more details?' prompts Donna as Gordon does not appear to be about to carry on.

'What more do you want? You should be out there arresting him.'

'And we will, Mr Yates, we will arrest whoever has done this to you—'

'It was Khalil. Are you saying I'm a liar?' Once again he tries to pull himself more upright and his face screws up in agony. 'Dammit,' he says in a weakened voice.

'Please, Mr Yates, I know this has all been very distressing, but I do need some more information.'

After several stuttering breaths, Gordon growls, 'What do you want to know?'

'Why don't you start at lunchtime today and move forward from there?' With some reluctance, Gordon Yates agrees. He slowly, precisely, answers Donna's questions and she pieces together his story. Lunch was at twelve-thirty, as it always is. It consisted of pea soup which he had made earlier from scratch, with a ham and mustard sandwich. He washed up and set the tea tray ready. This was found by the attending PC, untouched, in the kitchen – two cups and saucers, milk in a jug, sugar in a bowl, ginger biscuits on a plate and the pot a quarter full of water which had once been warming. After making his preparations for his visitor, Gordon Yates sat and read for thirty minutes. By then it was one forty-five and Khalil was late. Gordon went to the front door to look up and down his road. Nothing was stirring. On returning to his chair, he decided to leave the door on the latch. 'I take a bit longer these days to get up on the old pins,' he explains to Donna. 'I thought Khalil could let himself in and bring in the tea tray without me having to bother.' He closes both his eyes, liquid seeps from the bulging slit. 'Why did I do that? Why? If I hadn't been surprised, I could have defended myself.' He contracts the fist at the end of his unbroken arm.

Donna waits for him to settle a bit, then asks him what happened next.

His eyes remain shut. 'I don't know, I think I dropped off, I must have, because I woke up and there was someone in the room. Well, of course, it was Khalil and he was rummaging through the drawers in the sideboard behind me. I stood up, I asked him what the hell he was doing. Pardon my French. I turned and then . . .' He stops. Breaths gutter like sobs.

Donna would take his hand and squeeze it, if it wasn't unprofessional. Instead, she gently pats his arm.

'He hit me,' Gordon says finally. 'And I went down.'

'And it was Khalil?'

'Yes, I've said so haven't I?' His agitation turns quickly fiery.

'Tell me about Khalil.'

'What do you want to know?'

'A family name would help and contact details?'

'Family name? Oh. you mean surname. I could never get my tongue round it. But it's written down, in my address book under K, with his phone number. I don't know his address.'

'How did you meet him?'

'He came round one day, about ten months ago, said he could help with the garden. I told him I wasn't that old, I could manage. But really, after all these years, who wants to keep doing all the weeding? Betty, my wife, it was her domain. I haven't kept up with it properly, I have to admit. And I like it when people try to do something for themselves, don't always sit there waiting for handouts. So I gave him a chance. And he was very hard working. Very. He started to do small bits around the house. Things I was finding it difficult to manage. And then I'd give him a cuppa and he'd ask me things. He was a good listener. Kids these days, they don't care what an old codger like me has done with my life. No curiosity. But Khalil, he always had the time to listen. And he remembered what I'd said. He was interested. Bah,' Gordon pauses. 'I should never have trusted him. My son warned me. They are always up to no good.'

'They?' She steels herself for disappointment. Disappointment for what she is about to hear. Disappointment that she won't challenge it.

'Those people who come here on those boats. They've no right to come here and expect everything handed to them on a plate.' This last harsh statement seems to drain him. He puts his hand up to his mouth. His skin, if possible, goes a further shade of grey.

'Are you OK, Mr Yates?'

'Not really, lass. I wonder if you could find a nurse for me?' he says very softly as if it pains him to push out the words.

'Of course. And, rest assured, we will find whoever has perpetrated this attack against you.' She stands.

'Khalil, it was Khalil. And he'll be long gone, lass, long gone. I won't see him again.' He says it as if this thought tortures him the most.

Chapter 2

'It's his smell, I can't get rid of it. Some fancy, poncy . . . what do they call it? Men's perfume? Christian Dior or what the fuck. It makes me feel sick, literally physically sick.' Kelsey Geraty has screwed herself up, arms around body, legs around each other.

Hannah Poole feels a parallel tightening and twisting inside herself. She's aware this is not merely a mirroring of her client's distress, there's a resonance in this story for her. Twenty-year-old Kelsey is chunky. Brash and brassy with her platinum-dyed hair and mask of make-up – *warpaint*, Hannah had observed to herself during the first session – she favours tight tops, short skirts and high heels. She'd spent the first two weeks explaining in language littered with expletives how she's 'gonna deal' with her attacker herself, since the police 'fucked the case up'. And now they only have six sessions left after this one, six hours to unravel it all.

Hannah senses the ooze of her frustration. Primarily at the government, doling out therapy sessions as if they were rationed favours at a wedding for thousands and then patting itself on the back for its supposed generosity. Then there's her frustration at . . . herself. Because she can't fix this, for Kelsey. *I'm not good enough*, the thought ambushes her. *Ah, there's the rub, isn't it, Hannah?* 'We're not here to fix, we can't fix,' the words of her supervisor come to mind. 'We're here to listen.'

Hannah refocuses herself on the youngster in front of her. 'Kelsey,' she says gently. 'I believe you. I believe he dragged you to the edge of the park, away from anyone who could see or help you, and he raped you.'

'Everyone says, everyone says I asked for it,' the words come out as hiccups. She sounds about five.

Hannah wonders again whether this is the first time Kelsey has been raped. *Six weeks is not enough time to unwrap all that*, she cautions herself. *Work with what is in front of you.* 'No one asks to be raped.'

'The porkers think I did.'

'The police have to be guided by the Crown Prosecution Service and they felt a conviction would be unlikely.' Hannah doesn't tell her client the DI in charge, Theo, is a close friend, and she knows he would have done everything in his power to get the case to court. 'It's not about belief, or even truth, it's about the amount of evidence available.' *And what a defence lawyer would do to you, my love: tear you to pieces. Would that have been better?* 'Take a breath, Kelsey, that's it, and another.'

Kelsey's voice is stronger as she continues, her feet flat on the ground, her elbows resting on her knees, 'I see him, he's fucking everywhere, fucking everywhere I go.'

'Has he approached you? Is Nathaniel Withenshaw harassing you? You can get a restraining order.'

Kelsey's head rears upwards, 'I'll fucking kill him, I'll get a knife and fucking put it in his heart—'

'Kelsey, are you following him around?'

The youngster drops forward again, face partially hidden behind hair.

'Kelsey, don't do this to yourself.'

'He's having such a great time,' the words are muffled. 'Like, like nothing fucking happened, got girls all ova 'im. Why should he fucking get away with it? Have his life when I . . .' The plump hands, the colour of daisy petals, are held out, beseeching, empty. Then she says, 'I have to know where he is.'

Hannah takes a moment to compose herself; anger, sadness, defeat all competing with each other. She lets her eyes rove around the room, an elegantly appointed, high-ceilinged room in an elegantly appointed Victorian town house on the south side of town. In the mid-nineteenth century an up-and-coming destination for the rich. The coving remains, as does the extravagant marble fireplace and tall arched windows. Now that it's owned by the Scarborough Centre for Therapy Excellence (SC4TE), however, the furnishings are bland, comfortable, practical. Hannah trained here and now she practises from here. She hears a colleague ushering a client down the graceful sweep of the stairs. Not for the first time, she wonders what tales these old walls might tell. Kelsey's being added like another skim of plaster. 'It's not fair,' Hannah says quietly. 'It's not fair, Kelsey. Tell me, tell me what's going on for you, right now.'

The fists form, the hair sways back. 'I'm fucking angry, that's what, I'm going to get him.'

Cushion hitting? Punch the anger out? Something stays Hannah's suggestion, she sees it in Kelsey's eyes. She's not noticed them before, had always been distracted by the make-up, they are a tincture of forget-me-nots. *Fear? Yes.* 'He won't hurt you again.'

'How do you know?'

Good question. And which 'him' are we talking about? The one when you were a kid? The one who raped you eighteen months ago? Or the future hims who are going to misuse you? Her shoulders click painfully, she's been holding herself too still, she tries to stretch her back without being too obvious about it and to snatch a glance at the clock. *What can we do in ten minutes?* She breathes slowly. 'You're right, I don't know. You're right, I can't keep you safe from everyone and everything. I want to but I can't. One thing I do know, though, is that following him around and getting yourself armed with a knife are going to put you in danger. You know enough kids around you who've been hurt by knives or arrested for possession to be sure of that yourself. What's going to keep you safe, Kelsey? Who can support you?' It's stuff they've already been through and it sounds lame even to Hannah, but it fills the time and maybe, just maybe, it'll get Kelsey through another week.

Chapter 3

'Sometimes cases just are that straightforward,' says DS Harrie Shilling. The younger woman is slighter than Donna has been for some twenty years. Her dark trouser suit is sharp. As she glances at Donna sitting beside her, Harrie raises a tweezered eyebrow. The acute contours of her white-skinned cheeks are ferociously blushered.

'What's bothering you, Donna?' asks DI Theo Akande. They are gathered in his small office. He is a black man in his mid-forties. There is a neatness about his medium build which belies his athleticism. His hair is in orderly cornrows. His navy suit is as dapper as it was at the beginning of this long day. The pinstripe in his tie matches the green of his shirt and rims of his glasses. Through the small square office window, a daylight which hardly got ignited is dimming into dusk. Both Theo and Harrie have waited beyond the end of their shifts to hear the report from Donna's interview with Gordon Yates.

And now they have heard it, why should I keep them longer? she wonders. *A gut feeling? Or is it just that I didn't like Gordon Yates's racism?* 'I don't think we should rush to conclusions, that's all,' she says carefully.

'We've certainly got to identify, find and speak to this Khalil,' says Theo. 'And review the forensic evidence. We won't take Mr Yates's ID of the perpetrator as the end of the matter, if that's what you are worried about.' He sounds mildly affronted.

Donna rushes in to say, of course, she knows this. Harrie suggests they do a handover to the night shift to 'move things along'. There's a weariness in her tone and she stands. But Donna isn't ready to stop. At the very least she wants to find out something more about Khalil. Theo agrees she can go to Yates's house to unearth his address book and talk to the crime scene manager. However, if she can't immediately locate their suspect, she must let the duty DS take the next steps. 'It's too early in the financial year for me to blow my overtime budget,' he says, pulling on his knee-length wool coat. Donna recognises this is mostly – though not completely – a joke. The robbery at Gordon Yates's house had been audacious and violent. None of them wants the perpetrator free to act again.

Donna takes a short cut through a corner of the Dean Road cemetery which, for the last two centuries, has scored a green swathe between the South and North Bays. It is nearly eight months since Donna arrived in the town for her probationary year as detective constable, choosing to come to follow her daughter, Elizabeth. As a relative newcomer, Donna has explored many of the ways to the sea. And this is one she has come to know well. Despite the gathering darkness over the graves, it is a familiar route, the path is wide and still populated by dog walkers. As she hurries past, she, nevertheless, glances at what has fast become one of her favourite graves. It's difficult to miss. A memorial to Adelaide, born

Arras in 1852. The same question always presents itself: *What had brought her to this country? Was it a story of happenchance? Like my own?* This evening, she adds Khalil to her thoughts. What had washed him up on these shores? If indeed, Gordon Yates's prejudices are accurate, and Khalil doesn't turn out to be a native of Manchester or somewhere else in the UK. Donna tells herself off for jumping to the conclusions she had wanted them all to avoid.

Gordon Yates's house stands on a pleasant residential street next to the cemetery and the wooded glen which leads into Peasholm Park. It is a detached 1930s property with its modest bay windows downstairs at the front and pebble-dashed brickwork. *Well maintained but in need of some renewal,* Donna imagines an estate agent's kindly appraisal.

There is a young PC sentinel at the gate who is receiving some advice from PC Trevor Trench. He greets Donna warmly. He is a big man made bulkier by his uniform jacket with all its accoutrements and a yellow hi-vis. He makes Donna think of a bee. A bee which has spent the afternoon gathering honey, albeit rather ponderously and slowly. He has been leading the house-to-house. There's not much to report. Most residents were out at work or too busy with childcare to notice much. Just one, watching for the postie, said she thought she saw a young man running towards the cemetery around two-ten in the afternoon. Trev describes their witness as an 'elderly lady', which makes Donna wonder about her eyesight – Trev is no spring chicken. Once they have a photograph, they'll check back with the woman. Meanwhile, however, Donna says Trev can get off home.

17

She walks up the path to the house. There's a slightly tipsy, small, glazed porch protecting the front door, which had allowed Gordon Yates to leave it unlocked even with the less than clement weather. Donna stands in the porch and calls through the hall. The CSM, Ethan Buckle, comes to meet her. Squat and ex-military, he is still swaddled in his white suit, but the hood is pulled back to show his bald domed head. They are packing up. She can come in. There is a short hall with both the kitchen and sitting room branching off it at the back. The sitting room is stuffed to bursting with dark wood furniture: sofa, armchairs, TV, occasional tables, sideboard, chest of drawers, bookshelves. Every surface covered with something: an ornament, a book, clutches of photographs. Donna can see how Gordon Yates gathered most of his life around the chair positioned with the best view of the TV, its fading upholstering sagging and covered by a dark blue throw. On the table nearest are the phone, a hardback history of the Second World War, a framed photo of a smiling woman in her seventies, a glass of water, a small digital radio and a TV listings magazine. Behind the chair is a narrow gap and then the chest of drawers. Ethan is demonstrating how Gordon Yates could have got up from the chair, turned, been hit by the person rifling through the drawers and then fallen onto the sharp corners of the sideboard.

Donna watches closely for the angles. 'Did he turn enough to see his attacker?'

Ethan shrugs. 'It's difficult to be absolutely certain. He could have.'

Donna asks about fingerprints and DNA traces.

'We've got some to send to the lab. Mr Yates kept the place pretty clean. We've only been able to lift one set from the chest of drawers.'

'Which could be Mr Yates's?'

'We will have to see.'

'Our suspect, Khalil, apparently visited Mr Yates regularly.'

'We won't necessarily be able to tell when a trace was left,' says Ethan. 'We've no blood from the assault.'

A fingerprint of a perpetrator in the blood of a victim would put them there at the time of the attack. 'I'm looking for an address book.'

Ethan points to under the phone. 'As far as we can tell, no one went upstairs. It all looks orderly up there. However, we've lifted some more samples and fingerprints. We'll need Mr Yates to tell us what has been taken from the drawers. They haven't been emptied by any means.'

She nods as she finds what she is looking for. The entry reads: Khalil Qasim, with a mobile number beside it. *Qasim doesn't seem that hard to say nor remember.* She dials the number. She is unsurprised when it rings out.

Ethan asks whether she has seen enough and if they can depart.

She nods. She feels able to hand over what she has to the duty DS and IT forensics. She doesn't expect there to be any further answers until morning anyway. She glances out the back window. Even in the shadows, she can see Khalil did a good job tending the garden. 'Is there a back entrance?'

Ethan nods. 'The back door was closed but not locked. We've got fingerprints from the handle. Garden gate and fence are sturdy. The gate has a bolt on the inside. It wasn't shot.'

'And where does the gate exit?'

'Barrowedge Fields.'

Barrowedge. Gordon Yates's respectable house had its back robustly set against the estate known for the delinquency of its young and not so young. Is it likely Gordon Yates would not have kept the gate firmly bolted?

Chapter 4

As she always does, to settle herself, Hannah walks. She strides along the Esplanade which traces the top of the south cliff gardens. Below, at the base of the cliff, the Gothic cupolas of the Victorian spa building come into view. Then the wedding-cake-curve of its sun court lit by foggy-white lighting, as if for an ethereal ball. The sea stretching out to the horizon is the cracked skin of a reptilian creature breathing in deeply and then exhaling. Hannah can hear its remorseful sighs. They still her. She grasps the iron railing. She is at the level of the tops of the oak and beech trees which are rooted several feet below. At first they look black and skeletal. But no, they are not bone. They are alive with little whorls of green. This cheers Hannah as she carries on going, slowly, to the care home.

It is a modern brick two-storey building set back from the road in luxuriant gardens, trimmed and colourful. Daffodils have followed snowdrops and now there is a rug of bluebells under the birch with its shawl of budding lime-hued leaves. Inside all is warmth and activity. Hannah is greeted by staff, who she finds ceaselessly and inexplicably patient, cheerful and kind. Inexplicably, because she merely has to cross the threshold to feel the tension twist into her guts. She manages to plaster on a smile which fools neither her nor her mother.

Val Poole would rather be visited by her son (a rare occurrence). Her daughter would rather be elsewhere. Yet Hannah continues to stop by regularly and receive updates. Her mother is doing well, the staff and residents appear to like her, which surprises Hannah no end. She is in constant fear of being asked to remove her mother. There had been a shaky diagnosis of dementia which brought Val to the care home in the first place. Hannah now suspects it was more a reaction to the death of Stan Poole and all that exposed. Her mother has certain chronic physical ailments brought on by a lifetime of relying on alcohol to deal with emotion. Despite these, if Hannah ever chooses to be honest with herself, she knows Val could be cared for at home. In the house her husband's will bequeathed to their daughter. Though this could be considered a compensation of a sort, it continues to evoke a prickle of guilt. But if Val did come home, Hannah does not want to contemplate the detrimental effect on their joint wellbeing. Besides, Stan Poole also left enough money for his widow to live comfortably in a care home.

Val Poole is sitting in the communal lounge. Since coming to the care home she has been treated to decent dyes and cuts for her fading brown hair, plus she has facials and manicures and she's always dressed in clean clothes. She's short and her waistline is spreading with the food she eats; she has a triple chin. Even so she is looking pretty smart in trousers and blouse with a turquoise cardigan Hannah bought her for Christmas and was dismissed at the time as not being 'my colour'. As Hannah sits beside her she catches a whiff of alcohol. Val has several bottles of sherry stashed up in her room, presumably obtained through bribery and deception. Hannah had questioned whether she should bring this to the attention of Val's care-plan manager (her olfactory capacity obviously stunted by the smells she encounters on a daily basis). Then Hannah decided if her mother wanted to drink herself to death it was her choice and it wasn't her daughter's business to stand in the way of free will.

Val motors into some tale about a trip to Whitby and the flattering attentions of a fellow resident. Then she stops, 'What are you moping about?' Her fingers with their bright red talons drum on the arm of her chair.

Hannah realises her smile must have slipped – she re-applies it.

'What's that sly grin?' snaps Val Poole. 'You don't believe I could be of interest to any gentleman, is that it? Not that I'd look at anyone after my dear Stan. If he was here now he'd see me right. You got everything you ever wanted. Saw me out of my house as soon as you could. Abandoned me here. I know you're waiting for me to die, wouldn't surprise me if you'd help me on my way.'

Don't tempt me. 'You like it here. Look at you, they've done wonders with your hair. You've got people cleaning and cooking for you and there's always loads of entertainment.' There is a noisy game of Scrabble going on around a nearby table.

Val touches her hair with some satisfaction. 'Cooking and cleaning, looking after me, these should be your jobs, missie.' Her gaze is always wandering around the room looking for someone more interesting than her daughter.

She sees someone and gives a little wave. 'There's Stella. Now she's a child who knows her duty.'

Stella Horsham joins them. She is a tall woman – though most people appear tall to Hannah – who dresses and holds herself elegantly. Her white hair cut into a bob and a slight rippling in the skin around her throat suggest to Hannah she could be a couple of decades older than her, perhaps in her fifties.

Val immediately grabs Stella's hand and gushes, 'And how is your wonderful mother, how is Eileen?'

'Mummy's having a little lie down upstairs. Thank you, Val.' Stella turns to Hannah, 'Your mother has been an absolute brick, such a support since I had to bring Mummy in here. She had a little fall and the hospital said she couldn't come straight home, but we'll get her back there just as soon as we're able. I hate being in the house without Mummy.'

Hannah is having great difficulty deciding what to do with her face. She hopes it is showing just the right amount of concern and friendliness, despite her discomfort. *Mummy? Really? Val a support?*

Val is making sympathetic noises. 'It's a scandal how elderly people are just shunted hither and thither . . .'

Hither and thither? Hannah recognises the posh tone which has crept into her mother's voice. It's the one she uses when she wants to impress. Generally she and her daughter share the same accent, dully middle-class.

'. . . no one cares,' she finishes with melodrama.

'Oh but everyone has been very lovely to Mummy,' says Stella. 'Very caring indeed. Mummy and I are so grateful.

Having her here means I can continue with my job at the hospital. And this is such a lovely place. You must be very glad, Hannah, that you are able to have your mother here. So close you can visit her every day.'

Val gives a snorted 'hah'.

Stella does not seem to notice. She continues, 'Yes, a very lovely place, a very caring place, though, of course, I shall be very glad when Mummy can leave.'

Mummy six times? What is she trying to prove?

'But oh . . .' Stella loses momentum, her chin falls forward and worry marks her brow.

'What is it, my dear?' Val hasn't let go of Stella's hand and now she pumps it up and down.

'You're so kind.' Stella gives a winsome smile. 'I don't want to make a fuss.'

'You, make a fuss? I'm sure that's not possible.' There's nothing Val Poole loves more than a fuss and she teases out of Stella her concern that the medical staff have missed something more serious.

'I really don't know what I would do if Mummy were to die.' She puts her hand to her mouth.

'Oh, my dear,' says Val. 'And they do miss things. I am always saying to Hannah about my heart.' She puts her hand to her sternum.

You're as strong as an ox. Unfortunately. Hannah suggests more evenly that Stella take up her concerns with the care-home manager and the GP.

Stella nods, agrees with Hannah's good sense. 'It's just when I think of Mummy suffering, well, I can't think straight.'

Val glares at her daughter.

Hannah struggles to force a sentence out, the word mummy has been so expertly rammed down her throat. Finally she suggests she could go with Stella to talk to the care-home manager now, if she wants. Stella demurs, but asks whether she might have Hannah's phone number in case she needs more advice. Once she has this, with effusive thanks, she departs.

She leaves behind her a kind of void, one which Hannah and her mother stare into, unable to bridge it and connect with each other again. It was as if Stella had been a super-conductor for them and now she's gone their contacts hang uselessly in mid-air. 'Stella is something high up in personnel,' mutters Val at one point.

Hannah takes this as a dig at her for her underachieving and doesn't reply. Finally she says she has to be going.

'Yes, off you go, Hannah, leave me here on my own. Lonely, you have no idea how lonely it is here. But you don't care. You killed your father and now you'll be the death of me.'

Hannah hears her mother's voice rumble across the abyss and then crash, a tsunami of words and accusations, over her head. They keep coming as she stands, turns, goes.

She stomps back through the night, up the Esplanade, the noise of the roiling waves matching the thoughts smashing around her skull. How she would like to get home and retreat to her bedroom in the attic without further human contact. It is not to be. Her lodger, Zlota, comes out into the hall to greet her. Normally, Hannah would be able to deflect her, say she needs a bit of quiet and Zlota would be understanding. Not tonight. 'Hannah, I have someone I want you to meet.'

A young man appears from behind her. He sticks out his hand and says, 'My name is Khalil Qasim. I am very pleased to meet you.'

Chapter 5

Donna spends the morning pulling together the information coming in concerning Khalil Qasim and his phone, and from the fingerprint expert. She updates Harrie and Theo in the DI's office over spicy falafel pittas smothered in cool minty sauce.

Despite what Gordon Yates inferred, twenty-eight-year-old Khalil Qasim did not arrive to the UK, or even Europe, in an overcrowded inflatable dinghy. A year ago, he took a short bus ride into Turkey from his native Syria, then a flight to Manchester and immediately claimed asylum. He and his brother were involved in an organisation opposing (peacefully, at least initially) the president, Bashar al-Assad. They also found themselves in conflict with the various other factions – domestic and international – which piled into the Syrian civil war. When his brother was gunned down by a gang of indeterminate origin eighteen months ago, Qasim decided it was time to get out. Though it is slow, he is going through the asylum process relatively smoothly. His claim has not raised any red flags for the Home Office and he should have his final decision within the month. A refugee charity had offered him housing in Scarborough. They report he is 'no trouble', a quiet and kind man. With his qualifications in botany and garden design (not to mention computer science), the charity got him some volunteer work at a care home doing gardening projects with residents, and they know he has been helping out some individuals. He never asks for money, and if he is given any, it goes straight to the charity. 'His housemates, the charity, manager of the care home, even the Home Office, no one has a bad word to say about him,' finishes Donna.

'What about his movements yesterday?' asks Harrie. She has polished off her lunch and removes the swathes of paper towel she has been wearing to avoid her cream blouse being splattered.

Donna takes a few quick bites, enjoying the mingle of piquant and mild, then swigs some water. Qasim lives in a small terrace house, one of the many which were built for railway workers in the nineteenth century. The street it is on fans out from the old Cinder Track closed down in the Beeching cuts of the 1960s. The house has two bedrooms, however, the lounge has also been converted, which means there are three young men, all asylum seekers, sharing the space. The other two headed out mid-morning yesterday, with no grand plans, just wanting to be going somewhere and in search of a decent strong coffee, which they got on the seafront. Qasim had told them he was expected by Gordon Yates and would not join them. They were the last people to see him for sure. There is the sighting by Gordon's neighbour. She has been shown the photo of Qasim the Home Office provided and said she thought it might have been the same person she saw running away.

'What about CCTV and Qasim's phone?' asks Theo.

'The quickest route between Qasim's house and Gordon's

is via the graveyard and glen so there's not much coverage. We're checking for any private cameras. Qasim's phone puts him in the vicinity at three minutes past two but then it's switched off and hasn't been on since.'

'Forensics?' Theo has also finished up his falafel roll. He sets about making coffee for him and Harrie and a fruit tea for Donna.

'The Home Office furnished fingerprints. These have been matched to various found in the house. The only ones on the chest of drawers were Gordon Yates's.'

'Or the perpetrator wore gloves?' suggests Harrie.

'The back door was unlocked. There's a partial found there which so far doesn't match anyone known to be in the house nor on our databases. The back gate was unbolted. No fingerprint lifted.'

'Partials are hard to match. Could be Mr Yates's. He leaves his back door and gate unsecured. Unwise, but not unheard of.' Harrie takes her coffee from her DI and sips with a contented sigh.

Donna tries to feel as pleased with her tea. Coffee would likely bring on one of her torturous headaches. 'Or someone else went out that way, someone wearing gloves.'

'We have Mr Yates identifying Qasim. We have him in the vicinity. We have his fingerprints—'

'Which could have been left at any time, on previous visits,' cuts in Donna through a mouthful. She realises, too late, she is undoubtedly dripping sauce down her front and won't be staying as pristine as her colleague.

Harrie shrugs. 'We have him seen running away.'

'Maybe seen,' Donna mumbles.

'And now he has disappeared.'

Donna swallows the last of her pitta. 'Why would he do it, though? He's so close to getting the decision on his claim. It puts everything in jeopardy.'

'Mr Yates's son has said there was upward of three-hundred pounds in that drawer and a box of antique silver spoons is missing,' says Harrie. 'We've all read it, people fleeing a war zone have to pay to get out. Maybe Qasim's debt was due.'

Donna is slightly mollified that Harrie is showing some empathy.

Theo has taken his seat again. He looks from one to the other as if to ask, 'Finished?' Then he says, 'Mr Yates's property exits onto Barrowedge doesn't it? Ask Trev to organise a house-to-house there and also see what he can do about retrieving any useful CCTV. However, what we really need is to talk to Khalil Qasim. Any thoughts?'

Donna nods. 'The manager at the care home thinks Khalil had become friends with one of the care workers, a Zlota Warszawska. I've tried calling her, no answer. But I've got an address.'

'What are you two waiting for then?' says Theo.

'This is Hannah Poole's house,' Harrie says as Donna parks. 'She's a friend of Theo's.'

Donna rechecks the address and insists it is the right one. The house is a semi at the end of a street which halts at the edge of a cliff on the southernmost reaches of the South Bay. The property is rendered in white with a long, tinted glass window on what is probably the stairwell. With its smooth lines, it is reminiscent of a 1920s liner. As they walk up the path, Harrie explains that Hannah's father had once been a 'big cheese' in the town, the editor of the local paper. After he died several years back, however, his name popped up in an investigation into a paedophile ring. 'Nothing proven. But I reckon there was something in it,' she says as she pushes the bell button.

It takes a while for Hannah to answer. Her greeting is warm, though she does not invite them in. She holds onto the edge of the door as if she is afraid they might force entry. When Donna asks if Zlota Warszawska is a resident in the house, Hannah's nod is hesitant. 'Is she in?' Donna pursues.

Hannah glances over her shoulder. 'Wait here, I'll go and see.'

'Don't you know?' bursts out Harrie. 'Come on, Hannah, let us in, will you? It's proper nesh out here.'

Harrie is right – low cloud mixed with a fret rising from the beach is supping up the spring sunshine. However, Donna recognises Harrie's ploy – her colleague would not normally admit to being affected by the cold.

Hannah's fingers grasp the wood as if it is a plank saving her from drowning. She is a short woman, generously proportioned, perhaps in her late thirties. She is wearing grey wide-leg trousers plus a collarless top patterned with small red and yellow and green diamond shapes. The combination suits her and the house. Her hair is auburn and thickly curled. Her freckled skin is pale. Her eyes, which skim from Harrie to Donna and back, are an unusual hazel colour.

'What's going on?' Harrie's tone is now serious and quieter. 'You in trouble?'

Donna's thoughts catch up with Harrie's. Is there someone threatening Hannah? Is Khalil Qasim here? And is he dangerous? Donna steps back when she hears someone else coming up behind Hannah. She recalls the names of women police officers shot on what were considered routine call outs.

Chapter 6

Hannah lets go of the door and reveals a slight man with a mop of dark hair, dressed in jeans and sweatshirt. 'You are police?' he asks. When they nod, he holds out his arms as if expecting to be manacled. 'I am Khalil Qasim.'

Harrie says genially, 'It's good to have eventually caught up with you, Mr Qasim. Unfortunately, we have to arrest you on suspicion of robbery and ask you to come down to the station.'

Once she has finished with the caution, Khalil asks, 'Is Mr Yates . . . How is Mr Yates?'

'He's in hospital,' says Harrie.

Another woman appears at the doorway and says forcefully, 'You can't take him. He has done nothing.'

Harrie raises a tweezered eyebrow; 'And you are?'

'My name is Zlota Warszawska.' She is a more robust, more muscular presence than the other two. She has high Slav cheekbones in a creamy-skinned face. Her long hair is dyed a bright rosehip and is pulled back into a complicated braid.

'Zlota lives here with me,' offers Hannah.

'We'll need both of you to come down to the station to make a statement,' says Harrie.

Zlota begins to protest, but Hannah links arms with her

and says, with a grin – a forced one – for the officers, 'We'll come straight away. And Khalil, talk to the duty solicitor before you are interviewed.'

Harrie appears to swallow down her retort and turns her attention to Khalil. However, once they are down the path and their suspect is in the back of the car, she mutters to Donna, 'Hannah should know better – she is this close to finding herself arrested for assisting an offender.'

Despite his consultation with the duty solicitor, Reggie Harvey, who has undoubtedly advised a 'no comment' interview, Khalil is fulsome in his explanation. He came to know Gordon Yates through offering to help him in the garden. 'I was passing one day and I saw him struggling to get up from weeding,' Khalil says. He is sitting across the scarred table from Donna and Harrie, gazing directly at them, his hands open and relaxed in his lap. Beside him sits Reggie in his trademark tweed suit and natty bow tie, rather like an amiable teddy bear. Donna isn't fooled. Harvey has a reputation for rescuing lost causes, even when they really should fail.

Khalil's description of how his relationship with Yates developed concurs with the older man's. Except Khalil says, 'We became friends.' Gordon had not admitted to a friendship with his visitor, despite his actions alluding to it. Donna interrogates him on how often he visited Mr Yates – about once a fortnight – and what he knows about the contents of the chest of drawers – nothing. He answers easily.

However, when Donna asks him about what happened the previous day, Qasim's fingers clasp each other and his shoulders hunch. He doesn't look away. He pauses, as if to gather himself, and says: 'I was expected at Mr Yates at thirty minutes past one and I was late.' He shakes his head, 'It was stupid, my housemate was given a computer tablet which wasn't working properly and I was trying to improve its functionality. I misplaced time.'

Donna notes the idiosyncratic use of idiom. Something she is prone to. She warms to the young man further. *He doesn't look like he can swat a fly,* she thinks to herself. And then cautions, *we're all capable of violence.*

'If I was on time, perhaps I could have prevented what happened to Mr Yates,' Khalil continues sadly.

'What did happen?' prompts Donna.

He goes on slowly, as if piecing it together himself, 'I come quickly across the graveyard. The porch door is unlocked. This is normal. But the front door is open. This is not normal.'

'It was open or unlocked?' asks Donna.

'Open. Very much open.'

Could it have swung open on its own? She nods to encourage him on with his story.

'I go down the hallway. I am shouting, "Hello, Mr Yates." No answer. Then I step into the sitting room. I expect to see him in his chair asleep. Only he is not,' he ends in a whisper and his face screws up as if he is in sudden pain. 'He is lying on the floor. Very still. Blood, I saw blood . . .'

There wasn't any blood.

'And, I am ashamed, I ran.' He brings up his hands, his face dropping into them.

'What did you do next?'

36

'I . . . I am not exactly . . . I ran back to the graveyard and walked around for a bit. It's stupid, stupid, I know . . .' He lifts up his head. 'I was thinking of my brother. He was killed. I was thinking someone has killed Mr Yates. I sit for some moments, then I think, maybe he is not dead. Mr Yates is not dead. So I run back. I see police car, ambulance. And I am afraid again. I know I should have stayed and talked to them. But I am running away again.' He looks down at the table top. He is gripping the edge of it. 'I am sorry. I am very sorry. Please tell me, will Mr Yates recover?'

Donna nods, 'We expect him to.'

'This is a relief.' Some of the tension does seem to go out of his body. He lifts his face again.

Donna notices his eyes appear large for his face; the irises are a deep brown. 'Mr Qasim, just so we can be very clear about what happened, you were expected at Mr Yates's at one-thirty?'

'Yes.'

'What time did you get there?'

'It was three minutes after two. I was so late. Mr Yates cannot abide lateness,' he finishes with a groan.

'How can you be so sure of the time?'

'I turned off my phone when I reached the front gate. Mr Yates cannot abide mobiles either.'

The witness has Khalil running away at ten past two. Or about ten past two. That's seven minutes for Khalil to go in, see Mr Yates and run out again. Is it too long? Was he up to something else in the house during those seven minutes? The questions churn through her as she carries on with the interview: 'And you spent how long in the graveyard before returning?'

37

He shrugs. 'I must apologise, DC Morris, I did not see a clock. Maybe ten minutes?'

The postie called 999 at fourteen minutes past two. First response took about ten minutes. Meaning if Khalil is telling the truth, he spent more like fifteen minutes in the graveyard. 'Did anyone see you there?'

Another lifting and dropping of the shoulders. 'I am sorry, I was not aware of anything, just my heart going bam-bam-bam.' He strikes his chest with his fist.

We can ask for sightings, thinks Donna, making a note of this.

As she does so, Harrie asks, 'And when you ran away the second time, Mr Qasim, what did you do then?'

He straightens in his chair and turns to his new interrogator: 'I walked down to North Bay and then up onto cliffs, along the path—'

'The Cleveland Way?'

He nods.

'For the tape, Mr Qasim is agreeing. Why did you go there?'

'I needed to work out what to do.' He pauses. 'I was scared, DS Shilling.' He brings his hands together on the table top as if in prayer. 'You have to understand, in my country the police are not . . .' He searches for a word. 'They are not kind, DS Shilling, especially in my experience. And there is my asylum claim. I thought if I can help Mr Yates, I must go back. But the police and ambulance were there. He had help.' Another pause. 'I did not know what to do. I thought I would get some advice from my friend.'

'Zlota Warszawska?'

'Yes. Her shift end is at five p.m. I went to meet her.'

'And you told her everything?'

Donna can see the realisation dawning on Kahlil. He looks up at the corner behind Harrie's head. 'No.' He swallows. 'I was cold and hungry. I was still scared. I thought I would . . . How do you say? Sleep on it.'

'And she took you back to Hannah Poole's house for the night?'

'This is correct.'

'And you told no one what had happened?'

'This is correct.' He now cannot meet either of the officers' gazes. 'I am thirsty,' he adds quietly.

As if this is a cue – which it may be – Reggie Harvey leans forwards. 'Are there more questions, DS Shilling? I think my client has been very frank and open.'

'Indeed,' says Harrie. Looking her fiercest, she says to Khalil, 'We have your fingerprints in the house and Mr Yates identifying you as the person who attacked him.'

'No,' Khalil slams himself back against the chair.

Harrie continues: 'I put it to you that you arrived at Mr Yates's house, found him asleep, decided to help yourself to the money and silver you knew were in the chest of drawers in the sitting room—'

'I did not know. I said I did not,' his voice is rising in octaves.

'And when Mr Yates suddenly woke to discover what you were doing, you hit him – you appear to have grazed your knuckles—'

'I fell, I fell going up those steps in the cliff.'

39

'And you ran, not caring whether Mr Yates was alive or dead.'

'No, no, no,' Khalil shouts. 'I have told you what happened. I have told you the truth.'

'I repeat, Mr Yates identified you as his attacker.'

Khalil collapses in on himself, shaking his head vigorously.

Reggie Harvey puts a hand gently on his client's shoulder and moves as if to interpose himself between Khalil and the detectives. 'I suggest that is enough for now, DS Shilling. Mr Qasim has been fully cooperative and he is in need of a break and to consult with his solicitor. Isn't this so, Mr Qasim?'

Khalil gives a sad nod of the head and Harrie agrees to end the interview.

Chapter 7

Since Harrie knows Hannah, it is Donna who takes her statement and Harrie who talks to Zlota. They reconvene to compare notes. Hannah had explained she met Zlota Warszawska because she worked at the care home where Hannah's mother is resident. Zlota came to the UK at the beginning of 2013, to reinstate contact with her younger sister who had followed her boyfriend to Sicily and then to the UK. They are now in touch, intermittently, and Zlota is trying to persuade her sister to return to their homeland.

Zlota became Hannah's tenant about eight months previously. 'The house is too big for one person,' Hannah said. 'And the rent helps too, means I don't have to take on more clients than I can support.' This business arrangement has become a friendship. Zlota is free to bring anyone she likes to the house, however, she rarely does. Hannah was, therefore, surprised to find Khalil and to discover Zlota had invited him to stay the night. But Hannah was exhausted by her day and did not ask any questions. During the morning she went to her Pilates class and saw her supervisor. She met Zlota and Khalil again over lunch. 'He told me he was an asylum seeker and had done some gardening at the care home where he met Zlota. I asked him what had brought him to stay with us. I didn't want to sound unwelcoming or anything, but I could see there was nothing going on between him and Zlota, so it wasn't that, and I was curious.' Hannah paused. 'The atmosphere changed, as soon as he began to talk I thought something is wrong here. I thought it best to warn him if there was anything, you know, criminal, I would have to involve the police. I felt bad. And Zlota was furious. Said she thought because I am a counsellor it could all be confidential. I was trying to explain Khalil isn't my client and anyway, if it's a crime ... Well, you know. And then you and Harrie turned up.'

Harrie says, 'So Hannah wasn't told anything by Khalil.' She sounds relieved.

'What about Zlota?' asks Donna.

'A tough cookie,' says Harrie, scanning her notes. 'I had to remind her that withholding evidence is a criminal offence, as is knowingly harbouring a suspect. But it seems Khalil's account to her of what happened at Gordon Yates's house was the same as it was to us.'

'It was obvious he was lying when he said he hadn't told her anything.'

Harrie agrees. 'Which doesn't mean he has told the truth about everything else.'

'No. But it would mean he's a bloody good actor.'

'Maybe he was a leading light in the Syrian national theatre,' says Harrie testily. 'You don't know. In fact, isn't that the problem? He could have been the Moriarty of Damascus and there would be no way we could get that information.'

'Or he could be a young lad trying to make his way in the world who has got caught up in something beyond his control.'

'What does Theo say? What do we know? We know he was in the house in the right timeframe. Mr Yates says it was him. He has contusions on his knuckles consistent with hitting someone. He ran.'

'And what do we also know? His prints were not on the drawer with the money and spoons in.'

'He put on gloves.'

'So why take them off to wop Mr Yates? And where are the money and spoons?'

Harrie wags her head from side to side. 'He has had plenty of time to hide them or get rid of them. I am not saying there isn't more work to do. But you know there is enough evidence to charge him. And he's a flight risk. We're going to have to remand him. Cuppa?' She stands up. She gives Donna a gentle nudge. 'Cheer up, this'll improve our clear-up stats – the DCI will be pleased.' When Donna doesn't return her grin, Harrie continues, 'We all know what desperation can lead people to do.'

This Donna understands. True of her daughter Elizabeth. *And me*, she reminds herself.

Chapter 8

It has been eight months since Donna moved to the sea. It has been almost two months since she started swimming in it. In this time, Donna has come to appreciate the sea's moods which are often indifferent to the disposition of the land. Leaving her house, this Saturday morning was grey. Here at the water's edge, the sun has squeezed a wedge through the cloud, drizzling gold and garnets across the rippling surface.

There are three of them. Donna's neighbour, Rose Short, and another woman. Rose had persuaded Donna to try sea swimming. Rose's stature matches her surname. Her long grey plait is tucked into her cap; she wears a swimming costume, her only concession to the season being gloves and boots. Donna and the other woman are in full wetsuits. They are nodding acquaintances. Donna always swims with Rose and sometimes there is someone else, but there's little chat and no one has ever asked what Donna does for a living. They probably assume an office job, most people do. The anonymity suits her. An anonymity mixed with a peculiar fellowship, as together they walk towards the water.

The beach shelves gently at first, the sand in hard ridges, the memory of the recent tide. It is just on the turn, the water slack. As Donna moves forwards, it creeps from feet, to ankle, to knee, to thigh. The three of them keep up their steady pace. The cold is registering through every nerve in Donna's body, yet she is lured on, until there is no point in going back – she lets herself drop to be caught immediately by the waves.

She floats on her back. The sea slips frosty fingers across her shoulders and between her breasts. She rolls onto her front. Despite rebecoming a strong pool swimmer, she does not make much headway towards the pillar-of-salt lighthouse at the end of the harbour pier. She's not bothered. She feels buoyed by the gleaming sea. The South Bay curves its protective arm around her. A cormorant hardly acknowledges her presence, as if they are of the same stuff.

She turns back towards her comrades. The sunlight is beginning to dwindle. Shadows punch at the many-roomed façade of the Grand Hotel turning its windows into pockmarks. Clouds plummet off the cliffs of Cornelian and Cayton Bays only a few miles to the south, and shroud anything further away. The water inside her suit is coming to body temperature, only her face remains exposed. A lively breeze scrapes ice from the waves and tosses it into her face. It disorientates her. She stops. Finds herself in deeper than she thought. Makes for the shore, only to feel as if it is getting further away. Then she is caught up by a wave and tossed spluttering into the shallows. She stands quickly, not wanting to be dragged out again. The other two ask if she is OK. She reassures them. She turns back to the horizon. It has closed its maw, swallowing the sun whole. Out there she was a selkie slipped into a new skin. Now she is a fifty-two-year-old tending-to-portly woman on shaky legs.

'You're brave,' is her daughter's verdict on her mother's early morning dip.

'Or foolhardy.' In the stuffy confines of HMP North Yorkshire's (miserably misnamed) 'visitors' suite', everything is dull and hard surfaces. Her sea swim shifts further into the realms of dreams.

'That sounds like Dad talking.'

Donna was not aware of parroting her husband. However, now she comes to think of it, he had used the word when she told him of her first venture into the waves. She has not mentioned it again in their weekly phone calls. Jim still lives in the house they lovingly tended as a couple for thirty years. 'Foolhardy' was probably also the word he had used in their disagreements over whether Donna should come to Scarborough to do her probationary year as DC and to be close to their wayward daughter, just moved to the more open Yorkshire prison. Donna stuck with her decision, stubborn in the face of Jim's counter-arguments as she had never been before with him. She is glad she did. Not only has she been able to begin to heal her relationship with Elizabeth, but she has also felt herself flourishing professionally under Theo's – and Harrie's – guidance. Where it has left her marriage is another question. They still talk as if Donna will return to Kenilworth when her probationary year is over in September. She wants to be with Jim – *don't I? – of course I do!* And yet, and yet, there's so much she doesn't want to leave behind here: the sea; Elizabeth (she will still have time to serve); the friendships she is forging; her work. Can she abandon all that and go back to being

– what Donna? – merely Jim's wife? Not merely. I'd carry on working, wouldn't I? But she knows it wouldn't be the same.

'Mum?'

Elizabeth's strident exclamation breaks through Donna's thoughts.

'I knew it, you haven't been listening.' Elizabeth sits back. Her jaw is set, making her look more like her father. Now she is no longer using and is eating properly, she has regained weight and the sturdiness she inherited from Jim. Her height and her brown hair, Elizabeth has from her mother.

'Sorry, love,' says Donna wanting to avoid aggravating her daughter further, knowing this is a familiar pattern. Previously, the apology might have fuelled Elizabeth's petulance further. However, not giving it was equally hazardous. 'Tell me.'

'You tell me. You've obviously got a lot on your mind.' Elizabeth's tone is a step back from her usual simmering rage.

Where does all the fury come from? It's a question Donna has often interrogated. She can't help but think it has come from something she has done. Or not done. Today she is surprised, and pleased, by her daughter's control. On the other hand, she doesn't really want to share her thoughts on her marriage. Relations between Jim and his daughter are fraught at the best of times. 'Just a case I've been working on,' she says. Not wholly untrue, thoughts of Khalil now on remand in HMP Hull were with her as she drove over the moors this morning to see her own daughter. At least Elizabeth is in her native country, has family here, and when

47

she gets out, well, there are possibilities. For Khalil, whatever happens, his future is more ominous than ever. Harrie said this was not their concern. However, Donna could see it troubled her too.

Elizabeth knows not to push for details of her mother's work if they are not forthcoming. She says, teasingly, 'Hope it doesn't concern any of my new mates.' She glances around the room.

Donna does the same. Their space is suddenly intruded on by others: mothers, fathers, children, siblings, aunts, uncles, friends, even a grandparent or two, gathered in fragile groups around the bare utilitarian tables. She brings her attention back to her daughter and sees her smile fade. 'What's up?'

Iris, the one buddy Elizabeth has in this institution, someone she has come to rely on a lot, is going home. 'I should be glad for her. I am glad for her. Only I'll miss her.'

Donna can hear the grief in her voice. 'Course you will. You'll keep in touch.'

'Maybe she won't want to. Maybe she won't want to be reminded of this place. Of me.'

'Elizabeth, why wouldn't she? You've been a good friend to her.' Elizabeth had used her fists more than once to defend Iris from racist abuse. Donna has not openly condoned it, though she can't help but be proud of her daughter's fierceness.

'She should never have been here, would never have been here if she'd had my skin colour, my background.' Elizabeth pauses. 'I do know what I've thrown away, Mum,' she says quietly. 'Iris told me straight, many a time. But I've always known, really. In the end, I think it's why I took the drugs. To start with it was a laugh and, yeah,' her grin is edged with sadness, 'I wanted to stick two fingers up at Dad, pop his pomposity. Stupid. Of me, I mean. Though Dad is, can be, stupid too.' She takes a breath. 'But he didn't make me. No one made me. I did it to myself, and after a bit, it was easier to keep going than face up to it. Know what I mean, Mum?' Her hands are tightly clenched on the table top. Her eyes glance up, though her head is lowered.

Easier to keep going than remember. 'Yes, I do, Elizabeth. I spent thirty years not facing up to what I'd done.'

'What?' For a moment she looks confused. Then she says, 'Oh that. Well it's not quite the same. You didn't smash someone over the head, did you?'

I shot someone. I shot at someone. She still can't articulate it. *He didn't die.* Her way of shoving it away. 'I lied to you, your brother and your father, about where I came from. How I got here. I said I was West German when I wasn't.' Neither her son, Christopher, nor Jim had reacted much to her news. Neither of them had asked her much since. Not so, Elizabeth. She is always desperate for details. Some details Donna does not have. She can give a teenage version of her parents: her dad working in the post office, her mum as the chef in a hospital. They were kind, if trammelled by their loyalty to the party. Or so it seemed to Donna's younger self. Now she thinks they were probably just doing what they needed to get by. But what of Donna's own grandparents? Elizabeth wants to know. Donna only remembers one, her mother's mother, Eva, with the long dark hair. Donna's mother was constantly trying to get her to eat. In the end she didn't, not enough, and she faded away, or so it appeared to her five-year-old granddaughter. Donna does not remember much interaction with her father's parents, especially after their move from Dresden to Berlin when she was thirteen.

Elizabeth is constantly urging Donna, as she does now, to search for her parents. 'It's easy, Mum, put something out on social media. Wait for my day release, Mum, we'll do it together.'

Donna nods. However, it is not the practicalities which are putting her off. It's what she might find. It's how her history might unravel itself. She'd vowed to herself never to lie to her daughter again, yet, here she is once more, withholding the truth.

As is her way, Elizabeth has moved on – supported by Iris, she crafted a letter to her brother. She has had a response, not from him exactly, from his wife. It has renewed her hope that this is another fence she can fix. If his wife can forgive Elizabeth for stealing from her parents on hers and Christopher's wedding day, surely Christopher can do so too. Donna isn't so certain. Besides he is wrapped up in his architect work and the property business he is setting up with his dad to the extent that he barely speaks to his mum. However, Donna readily agrees with her daughter's assessment, meaning this visit, at any rate, can end on a positive note.

On the way back, though it has only been forty minutes since she used the facilities at the prison, she has to stop on the North Promenade at Whitby to find toilets. The bleeding started this morning as she had breakfast. And it is epic. Again.

To cheer herself up, she buys a hot chocolate and a bacon butty at the café at the base of the cliffs. The mix of sweet and salt revives her somewhat. In the preceding weeks she has had many an investigation into her body – endoscopy; colonoscopy; hysteroscopy; ultrasound – many an undignified examination and scraping. The final diagnosis is her chronic anaemia – now being controlled by iron tablets – is being caused by menorrhagia. A neat word for a very untidy condition, Donna feels. And what she wants to know is when it will stop. When will she become menopausal instead of peri-menopausal? No medical person is prepared to put a date on it. It could be in an hour. It could be tomorrow. It could be next month. It could be in five years. *Five years?* She knows she will go insane. It's no surprise to Donna that hysteria was once thought to originate in the womb. *I have to do something,* she decides. Again. *But what?* HRT (she has to keep reminding Jim) is not applicable. The various mixes of oestrogen and progesterone have proved ineffective. As has a coil, which unceremoniously fell out after three days. Surgery appears extreme for something which, on some days, bothers her not. Except for the anxiety which has skulked into her thinking. When she's not bleeding, she thinks about it and wonders when it will come on once more. She's noticed how this robs her of her confidence. She is always second guessing whether she is up to doing things she took in her stride. She wonders whether to mention it to her GP or the force's occupational health worker Theo has pulled in to support her. She doesn't want to have it written down, on her record. She fears, whatever the official rhetoric, in the police, admitting to anxiety remains a sign of weakness.

She tells herself now is not the time. Monday she is finally being interviewed in an Independent Office for Police Conduct inquiry kicked off by a complaint made by Theo about the actions of some traffic officers back in January. Now would not be a great time to raise questions about her competence, not to mention her lapses in memory. Her statement has to be solid. For Theo's sake. No one is going to weasel out of what they did to him. Not because of her.

She stares out the café window. The sea is battered pewter. *I was out there,* she tells herself. It doesn't feel possible. *And yet I was.* It's why she finally agreed to Rose's urging to swim in the sea. *To prove to myself I am still capable.* Then she remembers Elizabeth's words. With a grin, she says softly to herself, 'And brave.'

Chapter 9

Once the greening begins, it comes on a pace. Leaf buds unfurl overnight it seems. This Sunday morning, the skies have cleared sufficiently for Hannah to come out into her garden with her mug of tea. She wanders across the lawn and inspects the borders. Her mother (in her more sober moments) used to keep them in order and the grass trim. Not so Hannah. It's better for the wildlife, she argues (to herself and anyone who comments), though really it's apathy. She likes to be out in nature, but gets bored at the thought of picking up a trowel. Dandelions snuggle up with daffodils – their trumpets browning at the edge – daisies with the loose-lipped tulips when they push through.

Hannah watches a blackbird hop down from the raggedy copper beech hedge to gather nesting material. It soothes her. Zlota has always had a brusque side. But generally her sharpness has been directed at 'incompetent box-tickers' who do not understand what a day's work in a care home is like. Or at companies which provide a 'pathetic' service. Zlota is not persuaded that behind it all are people often trying to do their best under pressure. 'I could do better in my sleep,' is her damning estimation. Since Friday, however, her ire has been turned on Hannah. She should never have let them take Khalil. She should have hidden him. She should have made those two 'porkie-sows' go away, given time for Khalil to escape.

Hannah winced at the insult to Harrie and her colleague, what was her name? DC Donna Morris. Theo had mentioned the probationer joining the force last autumn. Hannah hadn't expected an older woman, white speckling the brown in her close-cropped hair. To the fuming Zlota Hannah pointed out it was Khalil who came to the door.

There's a part of her that does feel guilty. Khalil seemed like a nice young man, a gentle young man. Though this, she knows from her work, is no guarantee that he couldn't have turned to violence. *Maybe I should have let him talk? I would have got a better sense of him.* And she's aware going to prison, even on remand, will doubtless be disastrous for him. On the other hand, she firmly believes in Theo's probity. There would have been enough evidence to charge. *And, perhaps, Khalil is just a bloody good liar.* A blue tit is now trying to grasp a twig as long as its body and carry it up to the bird box on the wall above the hebe. Hannah admires her perseverance.

The argument continued at points during yesterday, with Zlota adamant that she and Hannah should not have spoken to the 'porkie-sows' either. Hannah countered that Zlota's story had been supportive of Khalil's. 'Didn't do him any good though, did it?' Zlota said, pacing the room. 'I should have said he was with me all day. I should have given him a . . . what do you call it?'

'An alibi,' said Hannah quietly, trying to bring down the angry energy around her. 'And that would be lying, not to mention easy to disprove: you were at work on Friday. You'd have been in trouble.'

'Better I go to prison than him. This means they will send him back to die!' was Zlota's parting shot.

Now, twenty-four hours later, she appears at the French windows which lead from the garden into the kitchen. She too has a beverage in a mug, along with a plate of the almond cookies she baked during what she says was essentially a sleepless night. She offers some to Hannah. They both sit on the step warmed by the sun, relishing Zlota's latest culinary triumph. Another reason Hannah has been glad of her house guest. Hannah thinks of cooking much as she does gardening – she wants the product without having to engage with the process.

Zlota is subdued today. Maybe she has simply run out of fuel. However, Hannah guesses there is something more and she is right. After being in regular contact with her sister for almost a year, and meeting her several times in Manchester on days out, Zlota is suddenly unable to raise her. 'Phone, WhatsApp, Facebook, all nothing.'

The sisters' relationship is not easy. 'That man is no good for her,' is Zlota's oft-repeated opinion of her sister's boyfriend. An opinion she frequently imparts forcefully to her sister. Hannah has heard her do so over the phone and has (gently) suggested to Zlota she try to listen and negotiate more with her sister. 'She will only get more defensive,' Hannah has warned. Zlota hasn't much time for what she considers is Hannah's softly-softly counsellor approach.

Yet it is obvious how much she loves her younger sister and is worried about her. With the early death of their mother, Zlota stepped into that role and has never been able to let it go. Hannah rests her hand tenderly on Zlota's shoulder, 'How long has it been?'

'A week. And it's Sunday, we always talk on Sunday.'

'We could go to Manchester together, go to her address.'

'She never told me where she was staying,' Zlota hangs her head. 'I should have made her . . .'

'You've done your best,' Hannah reassures her. 'And she's probably just lost her phone or out having fun or gone off on an adventure somewhere. She'll pop up again.'

'I don't know, I have a bad feeling here,' she rubs her stomach. 'When she went to Sicily with that man without telling me, I knew she had gone. We are, you know, joined.' She puts her clenched fist to her chest and then moves it outwards as if it is following a length of twine.

Hannah puts her arm around Zlota who allows herself to be pulled into a sideways hug. Hannah says, 'Don't you worry, we'll find her, we'll find Felka.'

Chapter 10

'I don't want to die.' The voice is frail at the other end of the connection. A ghost's voice. It hardly penetrates the thick expectant air of the CID office as it comes over the speaker phone. Donna strains to hear something from the background, anything which would tell them where Abi Davis is. That's her job, for now. Harrie is on a separate line to IT forensics. Theo is doing the talking.

'I don't want you to die,' he says.

His tone is measured, however, Donna can see the tension he has banished from his words has sunk into his joints.

'It's too late,' says the almost-ghost.

'It's not too late,' Theo replies with more conviction than Donna feels. 'But you need to tell me where you are Abi.' There's a silence and then the fragile connection is cut. 'Fuck!' He redials several times. Each time it clicks to an automated message saying the phone number is currently unobtainable. 'Fuck!' He turns: 'Harrie?'

Shilling shakes her head, 'She's probably got her mobile data turned off or her phone on flight mode.'

Theo turns to Donna, 'Get anything?'

She shakes her head. 'I'd say she was outside,' she says hesitantly.

'That narrows it down. Great!'

Donna is momentarily destabilised by his vehemence. She had decided they would pinpoint Abi's signal or Theo would persuade her to say where she is. Either way, they would get to her before it is too late. Now both options are closed, her mind is temporarily empty of others. *Think, Donna, think,* she tells herself. *Was there something else?*

Unusually for him, Theo is looking distinctly worn. His forehead deeply creased. His tie – with pinstripes to match the red frames of his glasses – yanked away from his collar. With an obvious display of effort he collects himself and says less harshly: 'We functioned before mobiles and IT forensics. We can do so again. We have to. Let's run through what we know.'

Shilling's ferociously blushered cheeks are white underneath. A blonde tress has strayed from its ponytail. She tucks it back in and summarises the case so far. Initially it did not appear to be a 'case' at all. Abi's friend rang in at 3.37 p.m. saying she was worried; Abi had been acting strangely since the weekend and had now not turned up for her shift. However, Abi Davis is a twenty-seven-year-old nurse and, apart from the acting strangely, could not really be considered a vulnerable adult. PC Trevor Trench was sent over to speak to Abi's friend, plus he gained access to Abi's room in the staff accommodation. It was there he found a note suggesting she intended suicide.

Scarborough is a small town of sixty-thousand souls, however, it's not so small that there are no places to hide. 'Where would Abi choose?' Theo poses the question, again, the one they've been wrangling with for hours.

'Church bells,' Donna blurts out. 'There were church bells in the background.'

'Are you sure?' ask Theo and Harrie in unison.

No. 'Yes, pretty sure.'

'How many churches are there around here?'

'Quite a few, I reckon,' says Harrie. 'But not many which chime. Perhaps she attended one?'

Theo speaks to Abi's friend again. The conversation is once more on speaker. Abi didn't go to church, is not particularly religious even. Theo asks: 'Where would she go if she were afraid?'

'I don't know, I don't know,' the young woman is sounding more and more panicky. 'She's never afraid. She's dependable, normally. She's been so weird these last few days, she could be anywhere.'

'But she's not anywhere,' says Theo authoritatively, evidently trying to keep Abi's friend thinking clearly. 'She's somewhere and you can help us find her. Tell me what she does, what she likes to do.'

'Read, she reads. She reads almost anything but recently she's been on about the Brontës . . .'

St Mary's? Donna has done some of the tourist trails on her days off. She writes her query on a piece of paper and Theo asks it:

'Which Brontë?'

'Which . . . ?' The woman breathes heavily into the mouthpiece.

Theo throws Donna a questioning glance. She writes again and he says:

'Charlotte? Emily? Anne?'

'Anne, Anne, yes, the tenant of some hall or other, is that it? Is this helping?'

Donna nods.

'Yes it is. You sit tight there with Trevor. I'll keep you updated.' Theo ends the call. Then he demands an answer from his DC. When Donna explains, he says slowly, 'I suppose it's a place to start.' And they all want a place to start.

The castle headland hunkers down between the North and South Bays. On its collarbone above the harbour and Old Town is the stolid structure of St Mary's with its squat tower and blue-faced clock. Dusk is being ushered in from across the waves. Lights from houses huddled on the slopes are piercing it, as well as the coloured bulbs which mark the curve of the foreshore below. Up here, however, there is only the wreck of the castle keep and a graveyard for company.

In daylight, when Donna visited this place before, she marvelled at the view across the glittering sea 'fair down to Flamborough', as an old fisherman once said to her. In this moment, she notices only hulking shadows. And the isolation. She is glad of the presence of her fellow officers. Even if they are turning into wraiths as the daylight fails. Theo has ordered them to spread out to start searching. They have shouted out Abi's name several times in the hope she would answer. Nothing has come back to them, except the buffet of the breeze made sharper by its climb over the headland. Now they have been told to keep quiet and listen. Donna feels as if she is stretching her ears in all directions, trying to pick up a tell-tale sound which would be an indication that Abi is still alive. *If she is here.* Donna is beginning to doubt the connections she made. Did she hear the church bells? Were they really this church's bells? So what if Abi is an Anne Brontë fan? Would she really choose to come to her grave to die?

She circles round to the remnants of the old church destroyed in the Civil War. The sandstone stacks – which used to be a wall, the frame of a stained-glass window – are the knobbly backbone of a petrified animal. Here the grass is less kempt, and the current chancel throws a wide swathe of deep gloom. Her feet brushing through the undergrowth are spectres whispering. No one as yet has shouted out what they all want to hear: 'Found her.' Maybe this is because she's not here. *I've brought them all on a wild goose chase.* For once Donna can't enjoy the deliciousness of the idiom. *Abi is going to die somewhere else. Lost and alone.*

Chapter 11

'He's been up to something, I can tell.' Kelsey is sitting comfortably on the sofa opposite Hannah. She appears less anxious today. She's wearing jeans and a pretty blouse which covers and flatters her chest. She has – or rather, she told Hannah, her sister has for her – curled her hair. A few ringlets fall fetchingly across her plump cheek. There is less 'warpaint'. Consequently her forget-me-not blue eyes are more noticeable.

And Hannah does notice them, she notices how bright they are. She says, 'Who?' Hoping her guess proves incorrect.

It doesn't. 'Nate. Nathaniel. Nathaniel Withenshaw.' For the last rendition of the name, she puts on an accent which wouldn't be out of place in a TV period drama.

'I thought we'd agreed you wouldn't follow him. You'd give him a wide berth.

'I'm keeping an eye on him. To keep other women safe. Remember, Hannah, my cloak of strength?' She grins. 'I'm like one of them super-heroes, heroines, whatever.'

It's a metaphor, the cloak of strength, they're weaving it together, metaphorically, so Kelsey can put it on when she is feeling apprehensive. It is a way of helping her to keep stepping out into the world when it is the last thing she wants to do. In that it appears to have been successful.

'Anyway, I wasn't following him. I was up at the hospital Friday, me mate's having a baby and she was taken in, high blood pressure, or summat. The dad's not around, not any more, streak of yella he is. And what do you know, there's Nate bloody Withenshaw walking across the car park. There's those flats, on the edge of the site, he'd come over from there, or at least that direction, we kind of met on the zebra crossing to the bus stop. I looked him straight in the eye, wanted him to know he didn't scare me any more. He looked through me, like I wasn't there, only there was something, something about him.' She trails off.

A part of Hannah is curious about what the something might be. On the other hand, she doesn't want to encourage Kelsey to keep obsessing over Withenshaw. What they've been working on is ways for Kelsey to hold onto the truth of what happened to her while also re-engaging with her life. What Kelsey says is she doesn't want her old life back. 'I'm not like I was, Hannah, I'm different, in here,' Kelsey's palm went to her sternum. 'So I'm gonna be different out here, out there too.' She pointed to the window. There are moments in her work when Hannah's own paltry reserves of hope are boosted by her clients' resilience. This was one of them. She had wanted to give Kelsey a big hug – she did not, she hoped her warm smile said enough.

Kelsey has plans, to get some qualifications, 'Maybe I'll get to be like you, Hannah, helping people.'

I hope not entirely like me, Hannah's critical voice was loud inside herself, though she was encouraging to the younger woman. *Why not? Why bloody not train to be a counsellor?* But if she is going down that road, Hannah knows Kelsey has

63

her past to confront. *Like I had to do with mine. Is now the time for Kelsey?*

Hannah discussed this with her supervisor. He was cautious. They batted the consequences backwards and forwards. At one point, he said, 'Who are you trying to save, Hannah, you or Kelsey? You need to watch your rescuer tendencies, especially when you're dealing with young, vulnerable, abused girls.'

Hannah gave him assurances which neither truly believed. *Me, of course me, I'm rescuing me, constantly, because no one did when I needed it,* the words sing in her mind even as she decides to take the next tentative step. Besides, Nathaniel Withenshaw has had plenty airtime, he tends to suck the oxygen out of the room. Hannah says gently: 'That cloak of strength seems to work for you, Kelsey, you appear less tense, more comfortable in yourself. And that's really good. However, we mustn't forget the hurt part of you, she needs looking after too, and maybe this is one of the few places where that part of you can get attention? Does she want some attention right now in here?'

Whoosh. Sometimes in a therapy session Hannah feels as if she and her client have been transported to another dimension. Suddenly. Without warning. She and Kelsey are back several years in the kitchen of one of Kelsey's cousins. It is the cousin's husband who has the eleven-year-old Kelsey cornered, stroking her cheek, telling her how pretty she is. Then his fingers slip to where her breasts are budding and linger, before moving down to lift her dress and insinuate their way into her pants. 'I didn't want it, I didn't want him to,' Kelsey is bent forwards, her hands clutching at her knees. She is rocking slightly. 'But I couldn't get him off.'

'You were a child, Kelsey, it wasn't your fault. He raped you.'

'Not properly, only stuck his fingers . . .' She pauses and swallows.

'He raped you. It was rape. Did you tell anyone?'

'I said to my cousin I didn't want to be left with her husband again and she went mad. She was doing me mam a favour keeping me after school. She'd only gone down the shops for summat. I didn't say nothing more.'

'Did he do it again?'

She shakes her head, 'I made bloody sure I offered to run the errands when need be.'

'Did you tell your mum?'

She folds again, 'She was taken up with me dad leaving, she was working two jobs. Me sister said, he was always like that and I shouldn't have let him get me.'

'You, both of you, were too young to know what to do. Your cousin should have listened properly.'

'She wouldn't believe me against him.' Her tone is that of a little girl's who is afraid.

As with Nathaniel Withenshaw.

Kelsey sits up, says more boldly, 'Nate. It's my cousin's husband all over again.'

'Yes.' *Smart girl.* Hannah feels vindicated. Her instincts have been right. The pain and the shame of what had just happened to Kelsey is merely another layer on old unhealed pain and shame. *We need to be working on both.* She says as much to Kelsey and the younger woman nods slowly.

Hannah continues, 'You were a little kid then, you were not to blame for what happened, but there was no one to tell you, really make you believe that the blame was with your cousin's husband.'

'I felt dirty, wanted baths all the time, sent Mam mad with the bills.'

'You've carried that blame with you all these years. It makes it harder for you to now give it to your rapist, where it truly lies.'

'I feel it must be my fault, cos it's happened twice.' Kelsey is tearful.

'It's not your fault. Those two men are to blame. You've taken on the shame and the blame for them. Give it back to them, give it back to them.'

'But I let it happen twice—'

'No, Kelsey, it happened twice. Is your cousin still married to this man?'

'He died, heart attack or summat. I never thought he had a working heart in the first place. There was talk when he copped it, but my cousin alus defends him.'

'It is the perpetrators who decide what they are going to do and then do it. Let them feel the shame, let them take the blame.'

'I tried, didn't I, with bloody Withenshaw?' Kelsey's tone is scornful. 'Didn't work, though, did it? Thrown back at me.'

The truth of this gives Hannah pause. Gently she reminds Kelsey of her bravery in going to the police, telling her story. 'You did all you could. It was the system which let you down.'

Kelsey chews on her lip.

'Your two rapists, give them the blame,' Hannah says, hoping her conviction will be enough for both of them.

After the session with Kelsey, Hannah has to sit very still, very quietly, to pull the fractured parts of herself together again. The words she had said to Kelsey could equally have applied to herself; she has to continually work at knowing the blame for what happened to her lies with her father and his cronies.

As she slowly packs up to go home, her mobile rings. It's not a number she recognises and she debates whether to let it go to voicemail. At the last minute she picks up. It is Stella Horsham. The phone accentuates her cut-crystal timbre – it sounds particularly breakable this evening. Unsurprisingly, for her mother has died in her own bed, last Saturday night only shortly after leaving the care home. Hannah expresses her condolences as she silently wishes she hadn't answered the call. To Stella she promises to let Val know. The funeral is apparently postponed for a post-mortem. 'They have to be so careful these days,' says Stella in taut whisper. 'Since Shipman.' There's a pause, then Stella says, 'Hannah, I hate to ask, your mother said you know a police officer. If they become involved, I would very much welcome your advice.'

'The police?' Hannah manages to squeak. 'Why would—?'

'Oh, I don't know, I've just been told it might be a possibility. Thank you so much,' as if Hannah had agreed. It takes a while for the exchanged promises to keep in touch to come to a final 'bye then'. For a moment, Hannah sits on the edge of her chair staring at her phone, trying to fathom Stella Horsham. Then she realises someone else might be waiting for the room, and she gets ready to leave.

Outside she is glad of the cool air. She walks along Prince of Wales Terrace with its tall, white-fronted Victorian town houses to where the horizon dramatically opens up at the edge of the Esplanade. She lets her gaze travel across the sea to where it meets the sky. It had been a blue day, tolerably warm. Now the darkness is sifting through the scrapes of cloud to reach down to the flat sea. It is like molten silver alloy. The moon is a delicate sickle beyond the ruins of the castle keep standing on its headland, above the harbour, between the two bays. She sees the rhythmic sweep of a looping blue light by St Mary's Church and wonders if Theo is involved. *I hope he's OK*, she thinks as she turns for home. *And no one is in too much trouble.*

Chapter 12

With the night comes the cold. The breeze is now bitter. There's only a thin peel of moon. Under its spectral glow, the blackthorn blossom transforms into the furls of phantoms.

The officers continue quietly walking, stopping, listening. Donna hears rustling, the click of pebble on rock, a cry even. In each case it turns out not to be Abi, not to be anything at all. She imagines it is the same for everyone else. And yet they keep going. *She's not here*, the nagging doubt grows louder. *And while we're wasting our time here, she's dying somewhere else.*

The main church door is locked. Theo sends an officer off to hunt down a key. Though how could Abi be inside a locked church? It's evident he's not going to leave anything un-investigated. His flashlight allows Donna to see the building more clearly. The stones glow honey-coloured – some are hollowed out, some brushed with brown or jade curves, by the action of the rain and the wind. In the corner created by the protruding transept, there are mossy-green patches where water has seeped from a drainpipe instead of being spat forth through the mouth of a welded gargoyle.

The night is not tranquil. Donna and her colleagues continue on their methodical way. A crow tightrope walks the roof ridge. There is the noise of a car accelerating around the foreshore road. Theo shouts for everyone to stop and for absolute silence. He turns. He swings round again. The crow hops down to a lower level, claws around the gutter. Everybody's breath is held. Nothing.

The officer returns with the key to the church as well as a man in a donkey jacket who turns out to be the verger. There's now commotion around the main door, a lightening of the mood, this is another possibility being opened up. But no, she can't be in there, it was locked.

Donna moves away towards the corner, tries to blank out the hubbub behind her, strains once again to listen, to hear. She finds Theo beside her. The crow tilts its head downwards, gives a triumphant 'caw' and lifts itself up on black wings to fly into the darkness.

'Sir, sir,' Theo is being called back. He doesn't turn, he keeps level with Donna, sweeping his torchlight to and fro. There are bushes in the lee of the church wall which have stretched forward to lean on a raised tomb with a cracked carved stone across its top. 'Abi, Abi are you there?' Donna croaks. She and Theo push at the branches, which scratch and tear as if to hold them back. Then, at last, there on the patch of bald earth before them lies a young woman folded into a foetal position.

'We've found her,' Theo shouts over his shoulder. 'We need the ambulance.'

Donna drops to her knees into the mud beside the body. There's the sharp smell of vomit rising from the blanket the young woman has wrapped herself in. Her long dark hair is hanging limply over her white face. Her skin is clammy as Donna touches her neck and presses to find a pulse. *It has to be there. Come on Abi.* She holds herself very still for a moment, seeking with her fingers this tiny sign of life, and, yes, there it is.

'Yes,' she says quickly to Theo who is now kneeling beside her. Together they check the woman's airways, and, finding her mouth partially blocked with regurgitated matter, Donna clears it out. Harrie arrives, tells them the paramedics, who have been standing by, are on their way. She has a clean blanket to wrap the woman in as they put her in the recovery position. Theo finds a purse which confirms they have found Abi Davis. Donna sits by her head, her hand gently stroking Abi's forehead. She wakes, coughs, half-chokes. She mews softly, like a lost kitten. Theo gives Donna a wipe to clean up Abi's lips and chin. Donna is reminded for a moment of doing the same for Elizabeth – both as a child eating too much chocolate, as well as a teenager imbibing too much alcohol. Donna says gently, 'It's OK, Abi, we're here now and it's not too late.'

Chapter 13

Abi Davis is in no state to speak to Donna and Harrie, but at least she is safe, warm and under medical observation. The doctor suggests the officers come back the following afternoon. Then she pauses, as if uncertain whether to carry on.

'Is there something worrying you?' asks Donna.

She grins grimly. 'The lack of beds. The disintegration of the NHS. Whether my eldest is doing enough work for his exams.'

'I meant about Abi Davis,' says Donna, smiling encouragingly in return.

'Course you did. I'm surprised you're that interested, to be honest – an attempted suicide, hardly a crime is it?'

'We have a report to write,' explains Harrie. Though this is certainly not the only reason they are here. All that time worrying about Abi, they can't just pass her along.

'Course you do.' Again she stops, compressing her lips together. Then she says, 'OK, well I don't know if this is worth noting in your report, but Abi Davis has significant bruising on the tops of her arms, she's had a nasty bump on the head and some injuries to the vaginal area.'

'Commensurate with non-consensual sex?'

The doctor wags her head sideways. In the land of her ancestors, it would be a yes, but in the land of her birth, it

72

indicates uncertainty. 'Perhaps. Or Ms Davis liked sex more than a bit rough.'

'When did these injuries occur?'

'Last weekend probably.' The doctor snaps the cover over her clipboard. As far as she is concerned, the conversation is over.

'There may be no link,' says Theo. It is Friday mid-morning. He has joined Donna and Harrie in the screened-off DS section in the corner of the open-plan CID room. 'We don't even know it was rape.'

'But you've been thinking about it too,' says Harrie flatly.

There's an intensity to this exchange which Donna is finding hard to interpret.

'I don't need Abi's injuries to remind me,' responds Theo.

'Nor do I,' says Harrie. She turns to Donna, 'Fifth of November 2012 a young lass, Kelsey Geraty, was raped. She accused a certain Nathaniel Withenshaw. However, we couldn't get enough evidence together to charge.'

'There was another suspect, Tony Finch,' says Theo.

'Connected.' They say in unison.

'Nathaniel Withenshaw,' says Donna. 'Do I know that name? It's not one you'd forget.'

'You may have heard it,' replies Harrie. 'He owns the bar and nightclub in the town centre and has some property he rents out to NHS staff. Tony Finch is his right-hand man, security for the nightclub, maintenance for the flats, Tony sorts it all. He's a Wesie.'

From the part of Yorkshire which is the other side of York, Donna decodes. 'And Withenshaw?'

'He was born in this country, but most recently Sicily.'

'Sicily? Why'd he come here?' Despite her love for her adopted town, Donna would think blue skies and blue sea would trump it every time.

Theo leans back on the window ledge and takes up the story. Nathaniel (or Nate) Withenshaw is in his mid-forties. He was brought up by his father and a stepmother in Surrey. In his twenties, he went to Spain and then Italy on various business ventures involving road haulage. He came to Scarborough in March 2012. He took over a failing pub and turned it into a commercially successful enterprise and started a property business, also going well.

'He's a sharp operator, that's for sure,' says Harrie.

'You didn't take to Nathaniel Withenshaw?' asks Donna. She lets the old-fashioned syllables roll over her tongue.

Harrie shrugs. 'What I don't like is not nailing a perpetrator. There's no doubt Kelsey was raped.'

'What happened to her?' asks Donna..

Harrie explains how, Bonfire night eighteen months ago, Kelsey Geraty went to the beach with her mates to watch the fireworks and then to Withenshaw's establishment where there were half-priced Guy Fawkes themed cocktails. Around eleven, Nate approached the group of girls with a free round. He started chatting to them. When most of them drifted away to dance or speak with other friends, it became just Nate and Kelsey. He offered to show her the VIP suite and she went with him to the plush room upstairs.

'Wait a minute,' interrupts Donna. 'You said Kelsey is young and Nate in his forties?'

74

'He's blond, brown-eyed, well dressed,' says Harrie. 'Some would find him attractive.'

It doesn't sound like Harrie does. In the eight months she has known her, Donna hasn't ascertained Harrie's 'type'.

'In any case,' Harrie continues, 'Kelsey admits to being drunk and to being curious. Girls from her side of town don't often get invites to VIP anythings.'

Surrounded by crimson and gold furnishings and decor, with a tank of exotic fish forming the window overlooking the downstairs, Nate began to fondle, caress and kiss her. At first, Kelsey did not object. She enjoyed the attention. But when she realised Nate was intending on sex, she pulled back, said no. He let her go. He apologised if he had offended her and escorted her back to her pals. The incident had taken the gloss off the evening, and Kelsey soon headed home. She didn't have enough money for a taxi and anyway wanted a walk to sober up. She stuck her earphones in and set off determinedly with music blocking out any other sound. She reached the edge of Falsgrave Park where evergreen bushes were still thick on the banks rising from the pavement and obscured the street light. Then someone grabbed Kelsey, dragged her on a narrow path through the bushes, held her around her neck, pulled a woollen hat over her face, before turning her around, hitting her hard and repeatedly, while forcing her to the ground and raping her.

Harrie falls silent. She and Theo exchange glances.

Hearing a first disclosure of sexual violence, it never leaves you, thinks Donna. She waits.

Eventually Theo goes on, Kelsey Geraty practically walked in front of a taxi. The driver described her as being in a terrible state: disoriented, her skirt and top muddied and torn. He took her to hospital. The police were called. Both Theo and Harrie attended. All the correct procedures were followed. Kelsey named Nate immediately. She hadn't seen her attacker, it was his smell, the feel of his hands on her, which made her so certain. And she never wavered.

'And Withenshaw?

'He was seen leaving the club shortly after Kelsey,' says Harrie. 'He turned up at a friend's party maybe thirty or forty minutes later. He said thirty, the other party goers couldn't be sure, said maybe forty or even fifty. He could have raped Kelsey on the way. Only he's one cool customer if he did. None of his friends noticed anything odd.'

'Forensics?' asks Donna.

'Nate washed his clothes before we could get to them. His DNA was on Kelsey's clothing, however, it could have been transferred during their encounter earlier in the evening. Kelsey's rapist used a condom. This and the woollen hat were never found. We searched the park, the surrounding area, Nate's flat and Nate's mate's house. Nothing. Nate had "forgotten" his phone at the club, so there was no digital trail either.'

Donna notices the quote marks. Maybe Nathaniel Withenshaw hadn't done it. Or maybe the attack had been well thought through. Harrie obviously has her doubts about Withenshaw's story. Donna asks: 'You said there was another suspect? Tony Finch?'

Theo nods, 'He'd been on the door and had said something along the lines of, "Cheerio, darling" to Kelsey as she left. Finch had gone off shortly afterwards saying he felt unwell. He said he'd gone straight home, where he lives alone. CCTV put him in the general area of the park within the timeframe but nothing more.'

'In any case, Kelsey Geraty was adamant Nathaniel Withenshaw was our man. It meant we couldn't really pursue Finch,' says Harrie. 'And now we have another rape.'

'Possible rape,' says Theo.

After a moment of gloomy silence, Donna works out what is niggling her. An identification, this time by a woman of her rapist, ignored, whereas Gordon Yates's is taken at face value. Before she really thinks it through, she says as much. 'So Nathaniel Withenshaw gets off—'

'Donna,' Theo cautions.

She finishes anyway: 'And Khalil Qasim ends up in prison.' Because he isn't white, she could add. She leaves it hanging. She is sure this thought has occurred to Theo at least.

Her colleagues greet this with stony expressions. She can feel them bristling. She regrets her outburst. Partially.

'We work each case as best we can,' says Theo abruptly.

'And no one ever said we're always on the side of fairness,' says Harrie, like she is the school teacher and Donna the teenager.

Neither look content with these assessments. Then, as if by silent mutual agreement, they appear to shove aside contemplation and turn quickly to what tasks there are to be actioned.

Chapter 14

Abi is not good at lying. She's not used to it. Donna is talking to her in a single room at the hospital. Abi's face is the same hue as the pillow; it is framed by her long dark hair, now glossy as a crow's feather. Her short fingers fidget with the bedclothes as if she is playing the piano. She keeps glancing out of the window. The view is unprepossessing: there is the brick incinerator chimney and, on a muddy mini-roundabout, one rowan is gamely budding leaves.

'So things just got on top of you?' Donna says gently.

Abi nods.

'And that's what you meant in your note when you wrote you couldn't stand it any more?'

Another nod.

'What did you mean by "it"?'

In the corridor outside, someone clatters past with a trolley. There are voices slightly raised – whether in anger or in jest, it's difficult to say. Abi glances around. 'Work,' she mumbles. 'There's a lot of pressure to get things right.'

'Your friend said you love your work. She said it all changed last weekend. What happened last weekend, Abi?'

She shakes her head and focuses on the chimney again.

'No one is going to blame you for anything, we just want to know what happened.'

Again she says nothing.

Once more, Donna is taken back to her daughter's bedroom. Elizabeth curled up in her bed, her back to her mother, Donna trying to get to the bottom of another unexplained 'all-nighter' or job lost. Only Abi is much more fragile than Elizabeth ever was. Even so, Donna realises she will have to take the direct approach. 'Do you have a boyfriend?'

Abi's stare turns to a glare, however, she says nothing.

'Did he hurt you last weekend? Make you do something you didn't want to do? Abi?'

Her head swivels round, she clutches the blanket up to her chin, 'None of your business. And don't think I'm grateful you saved me. I'm not.' There is a ferocity in her words which is not huge and yet is startling. She's not used to shouting either.

'You said you didn't want to die.'

'I've changed my mind. Now will you go please, I've had enough.' She closes her eyes.

Donna stands. She knows she can't outstay her welcome. She checks her notebook and remembers what Theo asked her to do. *Dem Himmel sei Dank for pens and paper.* 'Abi, would you mind if we had a look in your room?'

Her lids snap open, there's a pinkening to her wan-ness, 'Yes I bloody would. You can't go in there if I don't say you can.'

'Yes, you're right I can't. That's why I was asking. Abi, I only want to help you.'

'Well don't bother. I don't even know why you're here, suicide hasn't been a crime since the 1960s.' She turns over and buries her head under her sheets with an audible yelp of discomfort.

'But assaulting someone is a crime, Abi, as is non-consensual sex and if that's what happened to you, I will do everything I can to bring the perpetrator to justice.'

Abi mumbles something. It could be: 'It won't be enough.' It might be something else.

Donna waits for a moment, willing Abi to turn back to her, to be ready to speak. Then she puts her card on the bed-side table. 'I'll leave this here for you, Abi. If you want me, phone me, you'll get directly to my mobile.' She goes to find the nurse to tell him she's leaving and to ask how long Abi is going to be kept in.

'She could have been gone by now, but we need someone to discharge her to. Her sister is turning up later today to take her home with her.'

'In Scarborough?'

The nurse looks up from the computer terminal he's been scanning, inspects Donna, probably decides that, after all, she's trustworthy. 'Newcastle, I think. Probably do her good to get away for a bit,' he adds, immediately becoming less of an automaton. Donna hands him one of her cards to give to Abi's sister. It gets left on the desk next to the computer keyboard. Donna hopes it won't end up in the bin.

Chapter 15

Donna updates the log with her visit to see Abi Davis. She doesn't have much to add to PC Trevor Trench's initial report. He spoke to Abi's friend who had reported her disappearance, plus a few of her colleagues who lived in the same complex of flats. They were all distressed about what happened and said similar things. Abi is a good nurse and a cheery character. She changed after the weekend of 26 and 27 April. She became distant and distracted. None of them knew why. Abi was quieter than usual and did not share what was troubling her.

On the afternoon Abi went missing, Trench did get access to her room. He did a cursory search. There was a red dress discarded under the bed. Trench notes Abi's friend saying this was unusual, Abi is normally a tidy person. Trench also photographed the farewell note left by Abi on her dressing table, alongside a plastic tub. This contained the pills Abi took to attempt her suicide. Donna zooms in on the label on the tub. The medication is a sleeping tablet, temazepam, and it was issued by the hospital pharmacy on 19 February 2014. During his conversations with Abi's friend (also a nurse), Trench established the usual hospital protocol would have made it difficult for Abi simply to walk out with the tub of pills. Ordinarily it would be prescribed for a particular person and then there is a process whereby it is tracked to the patient or back to the pharmacy. It is odd that someone like Abi would be in possession of drugs which must have been obtained by subterfuge.

However, there is nothing more Donna can do. Abi has gone to Newcastle with her sister, Una, without saying anything further. Despite DCI Sewell's misgivings about an unsolved case which might not even be a crime, Theo has successfully argued for the log to remain open. Though for now, it is NFA-ed – No Further Action.

Donna was barely eighteen when she came to the UK from Berlin on papers which falsified her name and birthdate. She was under the wing of a family returning after the father finished a stint at the British embassy. She spent a year helping with their kids and with the renovation of the house they purchased in Ludlow. All Donna wanted to do was blend in, shake off the otherness bred of a life behind the iron curtain. The family she worked for seemed to understand this, they assisted her reinvention. She resurfaced herself so well, now people rarely pick up on her accent, they accept her presentation as a housewife from the posh side of the West Midlands come late into a career. And for over thirty years, she gladly took on that mantle, subsuming what she was into what she thought she wanted to be. Until her first case in Scarborough upturned everything. Brought back buried memories. She knows how it feels to be different, to be lumped into a stereotype just because of where you come from. She is certain she never experienced any abuse or racial slurring to the level Khalil most likely has. Even so, their shared movement across borders gives a certain kinship.

It is with zeal, therefore, that Donna applies herself to working out what has happened to the goods stolen from Gordon Yates's house. She has confirmation – from Mr Yates's son, bank and insurance company – that the cash and spoons do exist and were probably in the chest of drawers in the living room at the time of the attack. Neither have turned up in searches of Qasim's house, nor of Hannah's. The money might have been easy to stash somewhere. But the spoons? To be useful they would have to be turned into currency. Donna is contacting the town's pawn shops and organising for a photo (which was taken of them for insurance purposes) to be released to them, the local press and on social media. She hopes someone will come forward either claiming to have found them stowed behind a gravestone, or to have innocently acquired them from an eBay sale. If the spoons could be found and the provenance confirmed, Donna feels sure this would exonerate Khalil. Or not. Either way, she would feel easier about his fate.

She is glad to be distracted by Theo coming over to her desk. The coroner has asked for an investigation into a sudden death. Theo gives Donna a summary of what he knows. Stella Horsham called an ambulance at 8.57 a.m. on Sunday 27 April for her mother, who had died in her own bed during the night. The doctor at the hospital, in discussion with Mrs Horsham's GP, decided not to sign the death certificate without a referral to the coroner and a post-mortem. Although Eileen was ninety years old, and had recently received some treatment for a fall down the steps outside a local chemist, she was not expected to die. Theo has read the report from the pathologist, Professor Hari Jayasundera. He identified some narrowing of the heart arteries, which had almost certainly been putting strain on the heart muscles for some while. This could have been exacerbated by the shock of the fall. There are small blood spots in the lung tissues. These could be due to a number of conditions, but the prof has raised the suspicious-death flag because they might be an indication of suffocation. However, there is no bruising or signs of a struggle. Though this could be due to the traces of sleeping pills in Mrs Horsham's system.

Theo suggests Donna accompanies him to the Horsham household and she agrees readily. He drives to a long avenue overlooking the golf course and the North Bay. The Horsham residence is a 1930s brick detached house, with bay windows to either side of the door. It stands square behind its thick privet and leylandii hedges.

Donna rings the bell, there is a pause before movement from inside becomes evident. The door is opened as far as a security chain allows and a woman peers out. Donna explains who they are and when she asks if the woman is Stella Horsham, she nods. Donna goes on to say they would like to speak to her about her mother and asks if they can come in. Stella slowly unhooks the chain and allows them access to the hall.

She leads them through to the back of the house. The decor is heavy and dark, with wooden panelling in the hall-way and stolid wooden furniture. The room they are taken to is very lived in. There is a gas fire (unlit) surrounded by a sturdy mantel, shelves of books, a low table and two arm-chairs with faded cushions and blankets thrown onto them. Stella turns off the radio playing opera and indicates they should take the chairs, saying she'll get herself 'a perch' from the kitchen for herself. Theo insists she sits in the chair she has obviously recently vacated and says he'll fetch some-thing for himself. Stella settles herself down and waits. Her pale silver hair hangs loosely. She is wearing slacks and a blouse, a light shawl around her bony shoulders. At fifty-two, Donna knows Stella is the same age as her, yet the other woman appears to belong to a different era.

Donna attempts to get comfortable in the chair she has been assigned, shifting between the sagging and lumpy upholstery. She notices the pile of stationery on the table. Stella has obviously been in the middle of writing on some black-edged cards. Her handwriting is an exquisite copper-plate. 'People have been so kind,' she says softly.

Theo returns with a stool and manages – with the grace of a heron – to prop himself against it. He says gently, 'I am very sorry to have to tell you, Mrs Horsham, that the coroner has asked us to investigate your mother's death as suspicious.'

It takes a moment for Stella's face to react and then it collects into a frown. 'I don't understand, what does that mean?'

'It means the pathologist has found some indications which suggest your mother may have suffocated.'

'Suffocated? Oh poor Mummy. How did she manage that?' There's a little-girl quality to Stella's tone.

Theo doesn't respond to her question, only asks her if she could tell them what happened the previous weekend, on Saturday 26 and Sunday 27 April.

Stella settles her hands neatly into her lap and begins. Theo lets her tell her tale without interruption, though it meanders somewhat; she details, for instance, the shopping she 'nipped out' for during the day of the twenty-sixth. Stella says she was with her mother all of the Saturday, they did the crossword together, listened to some music show on Radio 3 which they never missed. Then Stella went away for the night, not far, to a hotel at Hackness. She's taken to going there every so often, she explains. 'They've a spa, I have a room overlooking the hills, the food is good, it's never too raucous. I must have got there about six I suppose, I left Mummy with Mrs King from next door. They were having such a lovely chat. I'd prepared a meal for Mummy – all Nate had to do was pop it in the oven for her when he arrived.'

Now Theo does break in, 'Nate?'

'Yes, Nathaniel Withenshaw. He comes and stays the night when I have my little trips.'

Nathaniel Withenshaw? How has he come into the picture? Again? Donna can see Theo is puzzling over it too even as Stella continues, a tad more slowly as she comes to the crux of the matter.

'I was due back Sunday about ten in the morning, but for some reason I felt called home. I arrived at just before nine, I suppose, and went to see Mummy. I saw immediately she had passed.' Stella's voice peters out, her eyes turn glassy, she searches and finds a handkerchief and dabs at them. 'I'm sorry, it's all been such a shock. Mummy was fine when I left. Well, not exactly fine, but not ill either, not exactly, otherwise I wouldn't have left her. You don't know how many times I've said to myself, what if I hadn't gone? Only she said I ought to, she said I should go.' She lifts her chin, studs in her ears flash diamond-like in the light from the floor lamp. She puts her long-fingered hand to her neck – it is a fine white-skinned neck, like a swan's. 'And now you're telling me Mummy suffocated herself. It's just too horrible.' Stella sounds genuinely distraught.

Donna offers to get her some tea, she wouldn't mind a cuppa herself, but Stella asks for a glass of water. The kitchen must have looked splendid when it was new. The tap grinds and judders as Donna turns it on and off. Back in the lounge, she hands the glass over. Stella takes a delicate sip and sets it on the floor. Then she turns her attention to Theo, waiting for him to speak.

'And Nathaniel Withenshaw was with your mother all night?' he asks.

'Yes, of course. He wouldn't leave her.'

'Ms Horsham,' Theo pauses as if considering his next words. 'Ms Horsham, what is your relationship with Mr Withenshaw?'

'Relationship?' surprise injects Stella's voice. 'Oh, you mean . . . ? Oh, no nothing like that, Detective Inspector.' She smiles briefly. 'No, Nate helps me out, that's all.'

How did they even meet – the handsome entrepreneur from Sicily and this small-town personnel officer? Donna finds her voice, 'You know Mr Withenshaw well then?

'Oh, yes, since he came to Scarborough.' Stella is not being forthcoming.

Deliberately so? Donna wonders if she should push, is it germane to the case? She glances over at Theo.

He says, 'How did you meet?'

'Oh, now, well it's not such a big place is it, Scarborough?' Her gaze hasn't wavered from Theo, even when answering Donna. Now she says quietly, 'Are you Hannah's friend? Hannah Poole's?'

Theo retains his composed expression, though Donna can hear the caution in his answer: 'How do you know?'

'We met when Mummy was in that care home after her fall. I'm sure Mummy would have done much better if she had come straight home. But there . . .' She swallows and continues, 'Mrs Poole said Hannah has a police officer who is— I mean, is a detective, who could perhaps help me. But I didn't want to make a fuss then, and now, oh, it's all too late.' Her fingers clutch at her handkerchief.

A caged bird. Stella Horsham reminds Donna of a caged bird gripping its roost while flapping.

'What was it, Ms Horsham?' asks Theo. 'What did you want to talk to me about?'

'Oh, well, I did think . . . I did think they were missing something, the doctors at the hospital. I know, of course I do, how pressured they are, and I just think, maybe they weren't as careful as they might have been, you know, because Mummy was, well, she was in her ninetieth year.' She shakes her head. 'Our doctors would never, of course . . . only it was some agency staff and I just didn't think they took the time they should have,' she finishes and deflates as if she has no energy left.

'And you consider this is a police matter?' asks Theo.

'Isn't it?' Stella's voice has that little-girl quality again. 'You're here now, aren't you? A suspicious death, you said – couldn't it be something they didn't do at the hospital? I'm sorry, Inspector, I don't really understand these things, I am sure you know best.'

'And I am sure you know how to instigate an inquiry at the hospital,' says Theo. 'Or at least ask some questions.'

'You'll mention it in your report, though, won't you?'

She nods when he asks if they could look around the house, especially at Eileen Horsham's bedroom. 'You'd be very welcome to, Detective Inspector, but I'm afraid I've been doing a lot of clearing out. I'm expecting to sell as soon as I can. They're only objects, anyway. Mummy's in here,' she touches her clavicle lightly with her fingers.

Stella has certainly been efficient with her clearing out. Her mother's room is empty. This disconcerts Donna for a moment. It's as if Eileen Horsham never existed corporally, only in her daughter's account. Stella's bedroom is sparse, containing a single bed, a bedside cabinet and a wardrobe. There is a further box room almost completely filled by an empty, dark wood wardrobe. There is a folded camp bed leaning against it. The bathroom has the minimum of accoutrements: toothbrush and paste, soap, shampoo, towels, talc scented with tea rose, a hot-water bottle and a couple of boxes of aspirin. Downstairs the two front rooms contain no furniture, only the indentations in the carpets and the outlines on the wallpaper to show where it had been, along with a fair few pictures. There are boxes which contain books, some china ornaments and the paintings which once graced the walls. These have Post-its with either 'auction' or 'charity' written on them. There are also a couple of suitcases of clothes which Donna assumes are Eileen's. From these she can tell Mrs Horsham was as tall as her daughter and of the same build. There are some flowing dresses made from real silk, their labels faded. But mostly the suitcases contain comfortable slacks, blouses and pullovers in varying shades of green and blue. According to the Post-it these are all destined to 'charity'.

Donna and Theo return via the hall to the back of the house and find Stella in the kitchen. She is drying-up the one plate, mug, knife, fork, wooden spoon and small pan which had been sitting on the draining board. She turns. Perhaps it is the harsh fluorescent lighting which makes her face ashen. Theo asks about the suitcases and is told they are Mrs Horsham's. He asks about any medication she was on.

Slowly Stella pulls a shoebox off one of the shelves of a dresser, which takes up one wall and a lot of floorspace. 'I was getting round to taking them to the chemist, they're all Mummy's pills.'

Donna has a shufty through. There are antacid pills, three containers of different drugs for high blood pressure and some multivitamins. Then she picks it up: a squat plastic tub with the hospital's label on detailing the contents as temazepam. It looks exactly the same as the one in the photo from Abi's room. Is she sure? Fairly. She would have to compare the dates on them. She asks Stella about the tub. Stella stares at it for a moment, then says, yes, of course they were prescribed by the hospital. 'Mummy was finding it hard to sleep, with the pain.' She leans her back against the sink and crosses her arms. 'I've been thinking, Detective Inspector, you said there were "indications" of suffocation. So nothing is proven?'

Theo shakes his head.

Stella carries on: 'I really don't know how Mummy could have done that to herself. She was lying on her back when I saw her, her pillows in place, she looked so peaceful. I really do think there must be another explanation for those "indications".' Her tone is more business-like than before – Donna can finally imagine her managing an office. 'Mummy was more poorly than any of us thought, bless her.'

'We are merely making preliminary enquiries, to establish what happened as best we can,' says Theo.

'And these enquiries, how long are you expecting them to take? Without a death certificate, I can't bury Mummy. And I'm stuck.' She tosses a glance around the small room. 'Please, Detective Inspector, please help get this resolved as quickly as you can. It's all been an incredible strain.'

Theo nods and asks whether there is anyone they can call to come and be with her.

She shakes her head, 'I wouldn't want to trouble anyone. Anyway, I don't feel alone, Mummy is here. Oh, I don't mean her ghost.' Her lips smile. 'I don't believe in them. But, you know, my memories, they keep me company.'

Chapter 16

The call comes five-thirty Sunday morning. Donna is up, preparing to leave for an overnight trip to see Jim since she has the Bank Holiday Monday off. She answers automatically as she deliberates over what clothes to take. In Kenilworth, she still has half a wardrobe full in the house – *my home*, she reminds herself – but when she takes them out, they seem to belong to another woman. As soon as she hears the voice, Donna's attention snaps to the phone. She recognises the intonation, though the caller does not identify herself. The words come out as they did on the speakerphone in the CID office two days ago – desperate and desperately sad – 'I need to talk to you.'

Donna sits on the edge of her bed. 'I'm listening.' Not getting a response from the other end of the line, she says, 'Go on, Abi, I'm here, tell me what it is you want to say.'

'I was raped,' Abi whispers. Then cuts the connection.

Déjà vu. Only this time, Donna hopes Abi has not taken an overdose and is not alone somewhere waiting for death. She checks her phone log: Abi's number has registered. However, before she can dial it, the phone rings again. It is Abi's sister, Una. Abi is safe with her, she is ready to make a statement. 'Naturally, she's very distressed.' The woman comes over as competent, calm. 'Can you come here? Today?'

Donna promptly agrees and takes down the address. She only thinks about the consequences once she has hung up. *What will Jim say?*

She decides on speaking to a man who she is finding increasingly easier to communicate with than her own husband. Theo offers her a way out: he will go with Harrie. 'But she asked for me,' the thought comes out of her mouth before she can stop it. *Perhaps it is only because she had my card?* Donna is conflicted. She should keep on with her plans with Jim, and yet she wants to support Abi so she can say what happened to her. Donna notices the positioning of the 'should' and the 'want'. It makes up her mind.

'Didn't you have plans?' Theo is driving them over the moors. It is a route familiar to Donna, as it is the one she takes to see Elizabeth. She has watched the tops as they changed their palette through the seasons – from autumn rust to winter monochrome to this unrolling of varying tones of jade and pale amber across the tumps and as a frosting in the tree branches. To their right the flimsy patchwork of land butts into the solid stretch of mica etched by the spindrift. The road turns westward, away from the sea; it is a moment of parting Donna has come to acknowledge with a breath. 'It wasn't a problem to change them,' she says. And, indeed, Jim did take it well. *A bit too well?* 'Did you?' She hopes her nosiness isn't obvious. Donna was with Theo when he met his current partner, DS Gus Spinelli, as they worked a case which took them into Humberside's jurisdiction.

Theo answers with a smile of recognition at her interest, and, perhaps, the fittingness of it. 'We did. Gus is trying out a firm of respite carers for his dad, so we had today and tomorrow together. Now we'll probably only have this evening.' He doesn't sound resentful, just a bit wistful.

'How is his dad?'

'His dementia's not getting any better. As for the rest of him, he's in good shape.'

'Not easy.' It's in conversations like these that Donna thinks about her own parents, the ones she left – *abandoned* – when she was just shy of eighteen. She wonders how they are faring.

'No.' After a pause, he adds, 'He can be a cantankerous old goat sometimes, and not entirely accepting . . .' He negotiates his way around a tractor and doesn't finish his sentence.

Donna does so for him, 'Of you and Gus?'

Theo nods.

As their two-hour road trip continues and the route becomes more industrial when they hit Teesside, their conversation touches on many things. Theo asks how Donna is, knowing she had a GP appointment earlier in the week. She forces herself to say the words 'heavy bleeding' when explaining that this has been established as the cause of her anaemia. She can't catch him flinching, so she plunges on, she may have to consider a hysterectomy. She watches him carefully.

'You need to do what is best for you,' Theo says.

Donna waits for the 'but'. Surgery equals time off, lots of time off.

The 'but' does not come, Theo merely asks, 'And how are you feeling in yourself?'

Rubbish! she wants to scream. She doesn't, of course. 'I'm OK.'

'I know anxiety and a lack of confidence can come with the menopause.'

Bloody new men, think they know everything. The anger surges through her, *you can't know, you can't know what it's like to have the best part of yourself pickaxed out of you.* She can't form a sentence. She stares at the steel structures rising from the banks of the Tees. Metal cages suspended between earth and sky. She feels the heat rising and cracks open the car window to breathe diesel-perfumed air.

'You're a good officer,' says Theo.

Again she waits for the negative conjunction. It doesn't come.

'Have you thought what you might do after your probationary year?'

She shakes her head.

'I suppose you will want to go back to Kenilworth?'

She doesn't respond, because she doesn't know how to.

'But—

The 'but' at last.

'As you know we've got a DC vacancy.' Neither will mention the reason for the vacancy, a colleague's betrayal. However, Theo does swallow before saying: 'And I'd like to keep you.'

What? She catches the exclamation before it tumbles out.

He glances quickly at her, then back at the motorway with its corridor of thundering artics. 'Will you think about it anyway?'

'Yes,' she says quickly. *Apply for the DC vacancy? Or consider it?*

'Good,' he says.

Once they have sunk in properly, his words bolster her. She tells him what she has discovered about the tub of temazepam found at the Horshams'. As she suspected, the label is similar to the one on the container found in Abi's room. It has a different patient number, however, it has the same prescribing pharmacist and, more interestingly, date. This is 19 February 2014. Eileen Horsham was in hospital from 13 to 16 April. They both agree there must be something in this coincidence. 'Abi probably knows Stella through her role as personnel officer at the hospital,' says Donna slowly. 'Perhaps, Stella asked Abi to get the pills to help her mother sleep.'

'Why didn't Stella just ask the GP? Abi would be risking a lot to smuggle out medication Stella could get hold of legitimately.'

'It's like there're these pieces in a kaleidoscope – Abi, the Horshams, Nathaniel Withenshaw, Tony Finch, Kelsey Geraty – and there's no light coming through, I can't see the pattern.'

'Mm, I'd still like to know exactly how Stella got to know Nate.'

'Perhaps it is just because we live in a small town.'

'Not that small. Today is about Abi, and, hopefully, we will know more after speaking to her, but I would like you to see what you can dig up about a link between Ms Horsham and Mr Withenshaw.'

Donna pulls out her notebook. *A short pencil is better than a long memory*, is a new phrase she has come across. Well, she hasn't got a long memory any more, just copious 'to do' lists. Theo puts on the satnav for the final approach into Newcastle. The journey is coming to an end and there is one thing they haven't discussed. Donna wonders if Theo has been skirting around it as well: her interview by the IOPC. They are not supposed to talk about it, so maybe it is just as well. Though Donna would like to know how Theo is weathering it all.

Una provides coffees for Donna and Theo. They are sitting in the open-plan sitting-room-kitchen of her flat. The view is breathtaking. The Millennium Bridge over the Tyne reminds Donna of a giant's egg slicer with its slender arch and suspension cables attached to it. Beyond the khaki green water of the river is the Sage concert hall, its metallic surfaces catching flashes of the sun; it could be a monster armadillo nesting on the further bank.

Despite summoning them up there. Despite her revelation. Despite saying she wanted to talk. Abi is not immediately forthcoming. Theo is encouraging her to tell them what happened to her or talk about whatever she wants, but she only manages a greeting and a few 'um's and 'I don't knows' and 'I'm not sures'.

'You don't have to be sure,' says Donna. 'Just tell us what you recollect.'

'I don't know what I remember,' says Abi crossly.

Her sister is sat quietly to one side. She says gently, 'Come on, hinny, tell 'em what you told me.' Her Newcastle accent is stronger than Abi's. She's bigger than her sister, more robust, though they share the same dark hair and very pale skin.

Abi shakes her head, her long hair falling to cover most of her face. Unlike her sister, she is still in pyjamas and a very fluffy bathrobe.

The sun slanting through the window is making Donna warm. Theo obviously feels the same as he takes off his lime-green linen jacket. He leans forward. 'Let's not worry for now about what you remember or what you're sure about, we can sort it out later. Tell me a bit about the week running up to the weekend of the twenty-sixth and twenty-seventh of April. Were you working?'

Abi nods.

'Tell me a bit about it, then, about your work.'

She starts off hesitantly and then grows more enthusiastic. While not being exactly fluent, she is saying enough for Donna to see she does indeed enjoy her work and is conscientious. She was on night shift when an elderly lady she had come to know over various stays in hospital had died.

'A tough week then,' says Donna.

'No more than usual. It's sad when anyone dies, of course, but her family was with her and I was around, you know, to help her, them. Many people are scared of dying, but, usually, it really is a slipping away. It's worse for the families.'

'I'm sure you were a great support,' says Theo. 'Then along came the weekend. You had plans for the weekend? To see friends maybe?'

'I . . . I . . . It's silly, I thought, well I thought someone liked me . . .'

'Who?' asks Theo.

She shakes her head. 'It doesn't matter. He didn't turn up.'

We still need to know who. Donna thinks about Trench's description of Abi's room. She says, 'You got all smart in your lovely new red dress and went out to meet this someone and he wasn't there?'

She nods. 'Stupid,' she says quietly.

'Not stupid, we've all been stood up at one time or another. Where were you to meet?'

'Weatherspoon's at nine-thirty p.m. But he didn't turn up. I waited an hour,' she says as if she herself cannot believe it. 'I called him, of course, and he said, oh, he said, he'd forgotten, hadn't thought it was an arrangement, exactly.' She gives emphasis to the last two words. Abi puts her hands to her face. 'I'd got it all wrong.'

'It's all right, love,' murmurs her sister.

Theo prompts gently, 'Can you tell us what happened then?'

Between hiccupping sobs Abi goes on. She was making her way back to her room in the flats next to the hospital, walking along the edge of Falsgrave Park, when she was grabbed from behind, punched, a woollen hat put over her head. She was pushed along a narrow path through the hedgerow, into the park, then forced onto the ground and raped. They all have to wait while she weeps, her sister goes to sit next to her on the couch, finds her a clean hanky, strokes her shoulder. Finally Abi is able to finish, 'I thought he was going to kill me.'

'Did he say he would?' asks Theo.

'Yes, yes, maybe he did, I'm not sure, I don't remember his voice. When he got off me, I just lay there, I couldn't make myself move, couldn't make myself open my eyes.

When I did I was on my own, it was almost, almost like nothing had ever happened. But it had,' she says with some ferocity. 'It had.'

'And you did what?' asks Theo.

'Went home, went back to my flat, had a shower, took that fucking dress off. It was all torn and dirty anyway.'

Like you feel, thinks Donna.

Theo asks: 'Can you recall anything about your attacker? His build?'

She shakes her head, 'Big, he felt big, powerful.'

Abi appears particularly diminutive today – big could mean average. Theo continues asking if there are any details which come to her mind. 'Did he say anything? His smell?'

She's been shaking her head, only at 'smell' does she stop for a second, then she says quite definitely, 'No.'

'Did you meet anyone on your way home? Did you speak to anyone? Did anyone see you?'

She sighs. 'I don't know. It wasn't late, just past eleven I think, there could have been other people around. Does it matter? He'd gone and I got rid of any evidence that it had happened. I wanted to make it like it hadn't happened. I thought I could forget it ever did. I hardly remember Sunday, I think I stayed in bed most of it. I . . . I . . . it was all so painful everywhere.' Her hand stops clutching at the bathrobe and flutters up and down her body. 'On Monday I went back to work.'

'It must have been very difficult for you,' says Donna. 'Not being able to tell anyone.'

'I couldn't forget, the physical pain kept reminding me and in my head it all kept going round and round and I felt horrible inside, violated.' She pauses, seems pleased, or maybe amazed, she has found the right word. 'Violated.' She looks up at Theo. 'I didn't want to die, I just wanted all the pain and the feelings to go away.'

He nods. They wait while her sister fetches Abi a glass of water and she sips some down. In this moment, Donna notices how taut she herself has become, clutching her mug. She puts it down and breathes deeply to bring some looseness to her shoulders and spine. When Abi sits back, Donna asks her about the pills, where did she get them?

She looks and sounds enormously tired. 'I work in a hospital.'

'I understand there are procedures, it's not easy to walk out with a tub of sleeping pills.'

'The procedures are not foolproof.'

'Can you tell us how you did it?'

She shakes her head and gazes at her hands. 'I 'spect there will be an investigation now,' she says quietly.

Donna recalls once again Trench's report. 'You say you got rid of all the evidence – that's not quite true, your dress is in your room. If we could have access to it and your phone—'

'No!' The exclamation explodes forth. Abi wraps her arms firmly around her chest.

Theo says, 'The dress will give us vital information which could help us find your attacker.'

She considers this and then says she will ask her nurse friend to let Donna in to take the dress. Abi does not give permission for anything else.

'And the phone?' prompts Theo.

'There's nothing on it,' she says quickly. Then she turns to her sister, 'I don't feel well, I'm going to be sick.' She doesn't look ill, just angry.

'Oh hinny.' The older sister hurries the younger one out presumably towards the bathroom.

Left to themselves, Theo and Donna go to the windows. It's busy down on the river quayside. The Lilliputians are strolling by in bright costumes, a sleek model Mercedes pulls up at the toytown swanky hotel. Donna feels soothed by the flow of the water. She would like to feel the breeze which is ruffling its smooth surface. She says, 'She must be doing a bit of all right to live here.'

'Financial adviser, I think,' says Theo.

The she they are referring to comes back at this point, says her sister has gone to bed. 'I'm sorry, I think she needs to rest.'

'Of course,' says Theo turning to her. 'I can see what a support you're being to her. Is she getting any professional help?'

'She's agreed to go and see a counsellor at Rape Crisis.' She lets out her breath. 'She's agreed to Mam and Dad coming down this afternoon from Byker. Mam's been going spare, but Abi just refused to have them come. I think she was, you know, embarrassed.'

'Has she told you more than she did us?' asks Donna.

'She didn't say as much.' Then she appears to rally a little, even smiles. 'Once everything gets back to normal, she'll feel better.'

Donna hopes the impulsion to normality won't run roughshod over Abi's need for time to heal.

Chapter 17

It might be mid-morning on a Bank Holiday Monday, but the CID office is full of officers prepared to forego their leave to push forward the investigation into the rape reported by Abi Davis. Theo explains there has already been some progress. A CSI team has been searching the corner of the park where Abi said she was attacked. It's obviously over a week on, which will complicate things, however, a haul of detritus has been taken off for analysis. A Northumbrian force officer is going to get a DNA swab from Abi for comparisons.

CCTV and statements from bar staff have confirmed Abi's story of going to the city-centre pub, waiting and then leaving around 10.30 p.m. She is also picked up by a hospital camera at 11.34 walking towards the flats. She is hurrying with her head down, her coat held tight around her. The red dress is just visible and it looks like it could be torn. Yesterday, Trev and Donna accessed Abi's room. No dress. Abi's friend said she had not touched anything and had not been aware of anyone going into the room, which had been locked. When asked who has keys to the flats, she gave two familiar names: Tony Finch and Nathaniel Withenshaw. A quick internet search confirmed the flats are part of Withenshaw's property portfolio.

In all honesty, Donna would have left it at that. But

Trev is nothing if he isn't thorough. And an hour later, a red dress was disinterred from a rubbish bag full of kitchen waste thrown into the dumpster at the back of the flats. It is now with forensics. If it yields anything, it will be a slog to prove incontrovertibly it is Abi's and that it isn't unacceptably contaminated.

The corner of the park being investigated is a CCTV blind spot. However, footage from surrounding streets is being sought and examined for men heading towards or away from the area in the right timeframe. It will be a frustrating and protracted task.

Follow-up tasks assigned, Theo meets with Harrie and Donna in the DS's alcove to discuss speaking with Nathaniel Withenshaw. The MO for the rape is the same. On the other hand, if he didn't rape Kelsey, then there is no reason why the similarities should lead to him. Rapes are most often carried out by someone known to the victim. The date who never showed? More pressure needs to be applied to Abi to say who he was. But how much pressure can she take? None of them relish it, however, if she doesn't yield, a warrant for her phone will have to be sought.

'We have to talk to Withenshaw about Eileen Horsham anyway,' says Theo. 'At least we have a probable link between him and Stella, if hospital staff are being housed in his accommodation.'

'And he has keys to Abi's room,' says Donna. 'He could have removed the dress.'

'Or Tony could have,' says Harrie.

Theo nods. 'You two talk to Mr Withenshaw and Mr Finch, both about their whereabouts on the twenty-sixth of

April, and whether they have done any clearing out of Abi's room. And Donna, please substantiate Stella's movements on the weekend her mother died.'

'Boots and braces,' says Donna in all seriousness. When the others chuckle she remembers, *it's belts*. She smiles, confident she is being laughed with, not at.

Walking down through the busy pedestrian precinct, Donna is glad she is no longer in uniform. She enjoyed her several years as a Special and then ten more as a police constable. She liked the protection her uniform afforded – most (not all) people would think twice before giving her more than a bit of lip. However, today, in the warm spring weather, she knows she would be overheating in the heavy fabric and well on the way to a headache. She has on light leggings and a cotton dress – rather too akin to a tent for her taste, but practical for keeping her cool. They take the steep street which plunges into the Valley. Once a stream big enough to power fulling mills, now one of the main traffic arteries to the beach. Its steep slopes retain the remnants of Victorian pleasure gardens, dotted with trees whipped in candy-floss blossom. Turning to the sea, Donna is hit by the cacophony of the kittiwakes. They are nesting – as if they are on the high cliffs – in the girders of the nineteenth-century footbridge leading to the Spa. Then comes the acidic hint of ammonia, as Donna and Harrie pass underneath.

Today, in contrast with the rowdy birds, the sea is languid. A silvery frill at the bottom edge of the expanse of sand, which is full of people in holiday outfits and mood. The colours of the clothes, the beach balls, the wind breaks, of a kite rising into the blue sky, spark against the dun backdrop. Donkeys, sleek now they are shorn of their winter coats, sport pink pompoms on their bridles as they meander back and forth. All the foreshore amusements and shops are open creating a ragged symphony of their own. The mechanical Zoltan in his plastic box leaps into life as Harrie and Donna go by, exalting them to have their fortunes read. The jolt it gives to Donna makes both her and Harrie chortle.

Nathaniel Withenshaw has agreed to meet them at one of his latest acquisitions, a four-storey building right by the harbour. Downstairs used to be a gift shop. Upstairs was holiday accommodation which hadn't seen much maintenance since the 1970s, when cheap flights began to take the town's usual clientele to the sunny climes of Spain. The shop will become a bijou café, Withenshaw explains as they climb the flights of stairs denuded of carpet, and 'here' and 'here', he indicates, will be upmarket self-catering apartments. He takes them to a large room on the third floor with an impressive arched window. It is high enough above the hubbub of the street to be relatively peaceful and has a sweeping view of the fishing boats, the yachts, the lighthouse and the sparkling water beyond. The place has been gutted, but Nate has the gift of invention, summoning up for Donna visions of a high-spec bedsitting room with a balcony on which to sup an oat milk latte and vegan breakfast purchased from the café below.

Now, though, all that is on offer are three hard wooden chairs and the possibility of instant coffee in chipped mugs, which both Donna and Harrie decline. For different reasons: Donna regretfully forgoes the caffeine; Harrie turns her nose up at the state of the crockery. The kettle and accoutrements stand on a table by a tap dripping into a stained basin on a cracked pedestal. There is another desk to the other side of the window along with a squat, lockable portable filing cabinet.

Nathaniel Withenshaw manages to lounge in his chair, legs wide, hands resting on his thighs. He is wearing work-aday jeans, a dark blue polo shirt. His thatch of hair is unruly and more white than blond. His skin has a deeper tan than would be expected at this time of year on the North Yorkshire coast. 'What can I do for you, Detective Sergeant Shilling and Detective Constable Morris?' he says with a bland expression.

Donna starts, 'We understand you were with Mrs Eileen Horsham on the night of Saturday the twenty-sixth of April when she died. Could you tell us what happened?'

'Sure. I turned up at Eileen's house around seven, I guess. Mrs King was there. She left shortly afterwards. Stella had prepared a dinner for me and Eileen – I heated it up.' His tone is measured, as if he is walking himself through an evening which held no surprises. They ate together, watched some TV and Eileen went to bed about nine-thirty. He explains that when he stays over he 'camps out' in the box room which looks onto the street. He spent the rest of the night in there, listening to music, dealing with some emails, reading for a while. He checked on Eileen at around mid-night and then went to sleep himself. 'I woke about eight or a bit after. I had just got myself up and dressed when Stella arrived.' Here he pauses, rubs his forehead, 'It was she who found Eileen. Poor Stella.'

'You didn't check on Eileen between midnight and Stella coming home?'

'No, there was no reason to. Eileen said she felt fine, Stella had not given me any cause to worry and Eileen keeps . . . kept a bell by her bed. She would always ring if she needed anything. Not that she ever did. I thought . . . well we both did, me and Stella . . . that Eileen had drifted off in her sleep. But now Stella tells me it's a suspicious death, and you've come to talk to me. I can't get my head round it.' He looks at Donna straight in the eye, seeking an explanation from her.

Donna continues, 'Mr Withenshaw, how did you come to know Stella and her mother?'

Nate doesn't answer immediately. He offers coffee again and then ambles over to pour himself a mug of water. Once more sitting, he replies, 'The flats I bought, the ones on the boundary of the hospital? They mainly accommodate NHS staff, so, of course, Stella and my paths crossed, especially when she was placing junior doctors coming to Scarborough on rotation. We became friends.'

It chimes with Donna's expectations. *But then why didn't Stella explain it like that?*

'Must have been quite a friendship,' says Harrie with an edge to her voice. Withenshaw had greeted her as if their last encounter had been as pals rather than during a rape investigation. Harrie's response was only fractionally the correct side of polite. 'For Ms Horsham to entrust her ailing mother to you?'

Nate gives her a wide smile. 'I have some paramedic training. I think this was the main attraction.'

'Where?' asks Donna.

'What?' Nate appears slightly disconcerted by the query.

'Where did you do the paramedic training?'

'Oh, a spell in the Territorials,' he responds quickly.

Donna makes a note to herself to check.

Nate continues, 'I am really very sorry about Eileen Horsham, she was a fine old lady. But I don't think I can help you further.'

'You didn't go out at all that night?'

He shakes his head.

In the clear for the rape then?

He says, looking from one to the other, 'Is there anything else I can help you with?'

Harrie says, 'You have keys to each of the flats in the block by the hospital?'

He nods. 'Of course, in case of emergencies.'

'Did you access the rooms of Abi Davis between the first of May and today?'

'I don't believe so.'

'It's only been in the last five days, surely you would recall,' snaps Harrie.

Then it's as if something occurs to him. 'So that's what all this is about? A woman is raped and you come knocking on my door again? I don't rape women, Detective Sergeant Shilling,' he says leaning forward.

'Someone went into Ms Davis's flat and removed a vital piece of evidence,' says Harrie. 'You have keys. It's reasonable we would pose the question.'

'How do you know what happened to Ms Davis?' asks Donna.

For a moment, Nate appears disconcerted as he peels his attention from one officer to the other. 'What?'

Donna repeats herself.

'I must have heard,' says Nate standing and moving to the window. 'Stella, Stella told me.'

Abi only told us yesterday. Would she have told Stella? Donna turns it over in her mind. *If so, it means they know each other personally? Stella must be off work with her bereavement.*

'Yes, she told me what had happened to the unfortunate Ms Davis. I did not go into her room and, therefore, I did not remove anything from it.'

'But you did go into Eileen Horsham's bedroom on the twenty-sixth of April,' Harrie starts slowly and gains momentum. 'Was it an accident or did you mean to suffocate her?'

Donna is astonished. She holds her breath.

Withenshaw turns and rests against the sill. 'That is ridiculous, Detective Sergeant Shilling, and you know it. What possible reason would I have for killing her? You're trying to provoke me and it really won't do.' There is a silence between them all into which a child's screech (possibly) of delight penetrates. Then Nate smiles again genially. 'Anything further?'

Donna finds she can breathe.

'We'd like to speak to Tony Finch,' says Harrie briskly.

'I'll find him for you.' Nate strides out.

As he passes, Donna gets a waft of aftershave. She tries to place it. An advert comes to mind of a man in the desert and wolves, everything subtly lit. But the strapline just won't come. Meanwhile, Harrie is pacing the floor, glowering.

'He's got an answer for everything that man,' she mutters. She only comes to a halt when Tony Finch enters.

He is not as tall, nor as handsome as his boss, though he swaggers as if he hasn't noticed and he has a fine head of thick, overly black hair. His 'What can I do for you two ladies?' riles Harrie further.

She snaps her questions. Firstly, where was he on 26 April? Security at the nightclub until 2 a.m. He even had to summon a couple of Special Constables to deal with an incident. When he says the Specials were with him between ten-thirty and midnight, Harrie looks even more disgruntled. She asks whether he has been to Abi Davis's room in the last five days? He gives a quick and categorical denial, accompanied by a grin which sets Donna's teeth on edge. He does not admit to knowing Stella nor Eileen Horsham and there don't seem to be any more pertinent questions.

Once they are in the bustle of the street, Harrie announces her desire for a proper coffee. They fetch up at the Tea Pot café at the furthest reach of the South Bay. Once they have their beverages, Donna and Harrie climb the steps onto the sea wall. Up here there is a tickle of a fresh breeze. The waves sloosh against the rock armour. A cormorant stands just beyond their reach, hanging its black wings out to dry. Donna finds it all calming after the frenetic foreshore and her recent encounter with Nate Withenshaw and Tony Finch. Perhaps Harrie does too. Her tone is more composed as she says: 'Theo always claims interview time is never wasted.' She lets out a long breath. 'I don't know if I agree with him.'

Chapter 18

Scarborough, Thursday 8 May 2014

Hannah's spirits are low after two difficult sessions. Earlier that day she had said goodbye to a long-term client. In many ways a positive occurrence; they had both agreed it was the right time to end and Hannah could see how much distance they had covered together. 'They can't stay with us for ever,' her supervisor would say. Even so, Hannah knows she will miss her client and there will be times when she will suddenly be invaded by her, wondering how she is coping. Hannah had not expected to become attached to her clients. Attachment being something she's not practised at. However, there are few she forgets, few who don't abruptly come to mind or creep into her heart at some time or other.

Of course, in a small town, there's plenty to remind her: sightings; accidental meetings; the mention of a road name or place of work; a reference in casual conversation to an issue which had come up in the therapy. Maybe a hairstyle seen at a distance or a food or a scrap of music. Hannah sometimes feels like a book, each page scribbled on by a client. Does she have any more pages to be written on? Today she feels at capacity. Her supervisor says she has to work harder at holding onto her own ego. The scrap left to her after her childhood and over subsequent years has been getting stronger. It is a narrow blade of steel within her which remains overly flexible, blighted by the propensity to be bent and twisted.

Her route takes her down through the gardens, the air scented with garlic, towards the meringue-white curve of the sun court attached to the honeycomb spa buildings. At the base of the cliffs, the sea is easing up the tawny sand. She can smell the salt in the air and the tincture of bladderwrack where it garlands the rockpools.

She walks around the South Bay. There's still the Bank Holiday overspill of visitors, enjoying the balmy weather. Once past the harbour, the pubs and the seafood stalls, the Marine Drive skirts the bottom of the castle headland. Here there's the late afternoon shadow and a tartness to the breeze rubbing across her skin. The waves rut against each other, snowy-headed stags. A black-headed gull launches itself gracefully off the sea wall, surfing the uplift. *I wish I had your facility*, she tells it silently.

The session with Kelsey, which Hannah has not long left, had also been tough. Kelsey is taking classes, hoping to resit, and pass this time, her English and Maths GCSEs. She is finding the work harder than she expected. It would be easier for her to walk away. Indeed, several friends are urging her to do so, to go out with them, have some fun. Be like the old Kelsey used to be. 'How can I ever be like her again?' Kelsey said. 'I'm nearly twenty. I feel forty.' She'd been alternately tearful and belligerent. She'd been angry at Hannah: 'You said I'd feel better. I don't feel any better. I'm never going to feel any better. I feel shit inside, like I'm full of shit.'

Hannah couldn't remember promising Kelsey would feel better, but she didn't argue. Kelsey needed to be angry, she had a right to be angry. 'His shit,' Hannah said quietly. 'Not yours. You're not full of shit. I know you feel that way, but it's not true, you are not full of shit.'

'Yeah well, you keep making me remember it all. You're the one who's supposed to be taking it all away.'

I can't do that Kelsey, Hannah now explains to the compact black-headed gull hanging over the turbulent sea. *No one can.* A wave splashes up and she tastes salty ice on her lips. *It's about learning to live with it, but it never goes away, it'll always be there to bite you on the bum.*

She reaches the café in the curve of the North Bay and enters the cosy interior. Theo and Gus have bagged one of the coveted tables by the window. She goes to join them. The next little while is taken up with greetings, both men giving her a comforting hug, and explanations of why Gus is here. When Theo was pulled into work over the Bank Holiday, Gus swapped his days, which has given him some lieu time allowing him to drive up for this evening. Hannah briefly wonders if moulding his life around Theo's work is causing tensions for Gus, but he appears comfortable enough. DS Gus Spinelli is a trim man of average height, with Mediterranean skin tones and a head of unruly dark curls. In the few months she has got to know him through Theo, Hannah has come to appreciate his relaxed manner, especially when it comes to being flexible around plans made with his boyfriend. *But everyone has their limits. Right?*

They all decide they are ravenous enough for fried egg

sandwiches with their coffee. They are meeting in order to head to the cinema. They discuss which film to go to. There's a choice of an arthouse film about a Greek doctor mourning his wife after her suicide. 'Ultimately uplifting', the reviews said. Or there's the new *Star Trek* movie. Actually there's not much debate. They all agree they need something which will take them to another galaxy.

Apart from her work day, Hannah is worried about Zlota. Relations with her have eased, though Hannah hadn't dared say who she is meeting tonight, but Zlota is more on edge because there is still nothing from her sister. Hannah might have mentioned this to Theo if they were on their own. Gus's presence holds her back, plus the thought of trampling the boundaries Theo and she have to take care to maintain. The one thing Zlota is pleased about is that she and Hannah will be able to see Khalil at the weekend. Another off limits discussion with Theo.

Even so, the conversation flows around subjects such as music, films, travelling they want to do (Hannah notices how Gus hangs back in this one, perhaps because of his concerns around his father). There's news from mutual friends to share – especially an erstwhile boyfriend of Hannah's who has taken himself off to Australia. She feels Theo's gaze on her as she speaks, measuring her upset, which she herself cannot entirely calculate. 'At least he's having a good time,' she finishes, her lowness threatening to creep right back in.

Gus looks from Theo to Hannah, then proposes cake. 'Do we have time?'

'We always have time for cake,' say Hannah and Theo at the same time. Hannah dissolves into welcome giggles – she feels a little lighter as if, maybe, she could almost glide with the gull.

Stella Horsham is odd. It is the conclusion Donna comes to after spending fifteen minutes on the phone with her. Donna rang up with two simple questions: how did Stella find out about Abi's rape, and did Stella tell Nate Withenshaw about it? There was a lot of prevarication on Stella's part, more words than substance. However, what Donna thinks she has understood is that Abi did ring Stella at home and, for a reason which still escapes Donna, Stella told Withenshaw. Donna realises she will also have to verify this timeline with Abi, but decides to check in with Theo first. He likes to be across things, especially since one of his officers went rogue during a case a few months back.

The previous day, Donna went to the swanky hotel where Stella spent 26 April. The staff know her there and it seems she spoke to most of them on that particular Saturday night. Their account of her movements matches hers. On the other hand, her room – the one she always stays in – has an exit into the gardens and the car park CCTV is recorded over every seven days. Meaning Stella Horsham could have left at any time between 10 p.m. (when she said goodnight to the bar staff) and 8.30 a.m. (when she said goodbye to the receptionist). Donna has found that Stella's route home would not trigger any ANPR. Trev has done some house-to-house. Mrs King has confirmed she sat with Eileen, who seemed on good form, until Withenshaw arrived. Beyond that, no neighbour (safely ensconced behind their substantial hedges) could say more about anything going on at the

Horsham house. Donna does note a teenage daughter from down the street arriving home in a taxi around 11.30 p.m. She doesn't remember anything much, having had a couple too many and being intent on her phone as she toddled towards the front door. *But the taxi driver? He or she might have been more observant?* Donna calls the relevant company and asks for details on the driver. She is told they will get back to her.

She then decides she can head home. There has been no response to her request to the Territorials for more information on Nate. But she's achieved one thing. After many hours reviewing CCTV with another officer, Tony Finch has been caught out in at least one lie.

If she had not decided she needed a trip to the toilets, to staunch the flow of blood until she gets home, someone else would have answered the call, because Donna would have been gone. However, the phone rings when she is packing up and she picks up. Initially it seems innocuous: a person reporting on a house in their neighbourhood which has been empty and used for storage for many a year suddenly becoming a centre of activity. Folks – men, yes all men – coming and going late at night and in the early hours. Then there appear to be occupants of the house – women, yes, maybe two women – but you only catch sight of them very occasionally. The curtains are mainly shut or the windows boarded up. 'I wouldn't have thought anything of it,' says the caller. 'Only my daughter has done this project on slave labour in the UK and she said I should do something.'

Or rather, hand the responsibility over to Donna. Once she has taken down the details, thanked the informant and cut the connection, Donna sits feeling the weight of it. *It could be something or nothing*, she tells herself. She debates whether it could be left until the morning. Then decides it's not her decision. With relief she dials her DI.

Theo's phone sounds while they are eating cake. Hannah sees immediately it is work. Theo asks for an address, which he writes on a paper napkin, and then says, 'OK, I'll meet you there.' Then, almost as an afterthought, 'Get Trench, if he's on, and bring stabbies. Spare ones.' Turning to Gus and Hannah he apologises, maybe no film tonight, he has to check out a property. Gus says he will go with him. Hannah watches the internal tussle before Theo (gratefully) agrees.

'Well, I'll bring up the rear,' she says resolutely enough to cover her nerves. *Excitement, fear, the same pump of adrenalin*, she reminds herself. Both Theo and Gus try to talk her out of it. Hannah points at the serviette, 'It's only round the corner, if this doesn't take you too long, we might still make the film. Don't worry, I'll keep well out the way.'

With the sun rimming the moors to the west, its darker and cooler than they expect when they step out of the café. Woollen gloves and hats are retrieved from pockets as they ascend the narrow path which takes them to the street running along the top of the cliffs above North Bay. At its furthest reach is the dilapidated castle with its walls girding the promontory. To their right are the backs and car parks for bed and breakfasts. To their left the steep drop to the sea. About 80 metres ahead is a strange afterthought of a terrace which is almost pitching itself down the incline to the beach below. These used to be shops and small workspaces – a sign still hangs above one door advertising 'quality tailoring'. The board is wind-battered and salt-water scraped. Each narrow building has two floors and an attic. None looks occupied. Hannah can see beds and other bits of furniture stacked against the windows of one. She looks along the row: the middle one has boarded-up windows downstairs; upstairs, however, appears to have new curtains – at least they are thick and heavy and in one piece. Then she sees her, briefly, a black woman pulling the edge of the fabric to one side. She slams her palm against the pane of glass, as if to catch their attention.

'Do you see her?' breathes Hannah. Without fully thinking about it, she waves. Is the woman being pulled back? The curtain falls. 'What are we going to do?'

'You're staying here,' says Theo firmly. 'In fact, move further back, and keep to this side of the road.'

In that moment, a car draws up. Hannah recognises DC Donna Morris and the stolid PC Trevor Trench as they step out and come over to their huddle. A tad disappointed to be left out, she does as she is told and sits on a bench at the corner of the promenade.

Corseted in her stab vest and with colleagues as focused as she is, Donna is assured. Theo sends Trench and Gus to the back of the terrace to assess, while he and Donna will concentrate on the front. No one will make an approach until they have a proper idea of what they are dealing with. Donna did a quick information sweep before leaving the police station. All she could find was that the ownership of the building was in the name of a company based in Sicily.

119

According to council records, it should be unoccupied. *But Theo saw the woman at the window,* she reminds herself. *And he describes her as looking desperate.*

They approach slowly. Darkness falls quickly at this time of year on this part of the coast. Unlike its southern sister, the foreshore of North Bay has few businesses to spill out light. At the bottom of the cliffs, the sea is a leisurely spreading ink stain. The moon is a misshapen smudge on the horizon. Up here, the street lamps are unequal to the encroaching night. Donna steps cautiously between the puddles of feeble glow. The light in front of the house they are interested in has fizzled out completely. Donna searches the frontage for any signs of life or of what might be going on behind its nondescript exterior. Theo scans over it with a torch beam. Nothing untoward is exposed. Donna wonders if, under his composure, he has the same questions and doubts as her.

The explosion, when it comes, spins Donna's heart and grips at her stomach. It takes her more than a few seconds to work out what has happened: one of the planks has been wrenched from the inside of the downstairs window and hurled through it. Shards of glass and a woman are following it. The woman hurls herself clear. She runs. She is running down the street towards Hannah. Theo sets off after her.

Donna catches a movement in the corner of her eye. She twists round, so her back is to Theo and the woman. A young man in a dark hoody and trousers has turned tail and is scarpering. Believing Theo can look after himself, Donna attempts to follow the youngster. However, by the time she has reached the T-junction at the end of the street, he has disappeared from sight. Perhaps into the maze of streets which descend from St Mary's Church into the Old Town and then to the harbour. Or maybe into the equally circuitous Castle Dykes. She searches in one direction and then in the other. All she finds is a dumped plastic bag containing a pizza box still warmed by its contents. Was the fugitive carrying this? She brings her first image of him to mind. *Yes,* she thinks triumphantly, *he was.*

Running. The woman is running towards her. Hannah automatically moves in her direction. *She needs my help.* It is the woman she saw at the window. She is tall, skinny, her hair is shorn. As the gap between them closes, Hannah can see the blood on the woman's face and arms. The woman is gasping now. She stumbles. Is on her knees, face in her hands. Theo reaches her just before Hannah. He squats down, puts his coat around her shoulders. Hannah joins them, her knees thumping into the tarmac. She's breathing hard. Anyway, she can't marshal her thoughts to say anything. *Is this woman a victim? A perpetrator? Desperate? Dangerous? Or both?*

The woman whispers. Hannah can hardly hear the words, they sound something like: 'Oruko mi ni Blessing.'

Theo leans in, he says softly: 'Oruko mi ni Theo.'

The woman suddenly laughs: 'Your accent. So damned English.' She begins to sob.

Having slowed down to this moment crouched with the distraught woman, time now begins to whirl. With his hand still protectively on the woman's back, Theo is summoning an ambulance, a CSI team and further police officers. Then Donna arrives back, a huge grin on her face, bearing a pizza box in a plastic bag. *What, does she think we are hungry?*

121

Hannah feels dazed. Finally, Gus comes up towing a reluctant young woman. Dark hair in a scraggy ponytail and dark eyes against a chalk-white skin, she is smaller than her sister and looks painfully thin. Hannah recognises her from the photos she has seen.

'She won't say what her name is,' says Gus.

'It's Felka, Felka Warszawska.' It jumps out of her. She wonders whether Zlota would approve of her giving this information to the very police officers she thinks so badly of. Felka certainly doesn't. Her scowl is the exact twin of her sister's.

Chapter 19

Donna joins Harrie and Theo in his office. He tells them DCI Sewell has called in the National Crime Agency.

'Oh great,' says Harrie dismally. 'Londoners who think we all own whippets or racing pigeons, wear flat caps and have brains the consistency of Yorkshire puddings. Not the ones I make,' she adds with a grin. 'The ones my mother does, they have more air in them.'

Theo responds genially, 'You know as well as I do, the NCA's involvement was inevitable. These gangs work across borders and have financial tricks our resources couldn't hope to untangle. We need them.' He becomes more serious: 'And they need us and our local knowledge. Don't ever forget that. Or let them forget it either.' He goes on to explain, after a night in hospital, Blessing Okokon has been taken to the women's refuge. He and Donna will talk to her there. The NCA agreed they could undertake the first interview.

'Very decent of them,' Harrie mutters, 'before they stomp their big shoes all over our patch.'

'Grumble away, DS Shilling,' Theo teases. 'I'll expect complete collaboration when needed.'

She nods, taking the gentle reminder on the chin. 'What about the other woman we picked up? Felka War . . . Wuz . . .' She searches her notebook.

'Felka Warszawska,' says Donna. The name rolls off her tongue, it tastes sweet. She spent a good part of her childhood not a spit away from Poland.

'Still in hospital. Suspected concussion.' Last night, the young woman twisted out of Gus's grip and pelted towards the cliffs, slipping and slamming her head against a kerbstone. 'In any case she appears less inclined to speak to us than Ms Okokon. Harrie, please can you pull everything we have so far on this investigation and also on Abi Davis's report of rape? And we'll reconvene for an update on both inquiries later this afternoon.'

'What about Eileen Horsham?' asks Donna.

'The DCI thinks we can't go any further with that, it's being handed back to the coroner for her to review.'

'And the taxi driver?'

'Have you found them yet?'

She shakes her head.

'If we come up with something further, we can always pass it on,' says Theo. 'The coroner won't complete her deliberations until next week. Sewell doesn't want Eileen Horsham lingering in the morgue longer than absolutely necessary.' He gets up.

The other two do the same. As Harrie reaches the door, Theo calls out her name. With a wide grin, he says, 'The NCA officers will be with us by midday. You can organise the welcome.'

They all know he has been deliberate about his timing. Harrie snorts, then says with feigned obsequiousness, 'Yes, sir.'

***

The women's refuge is in a quiet residential area. It is a couple of unassuming semi-detached houses knocked through to form one building. There's space for nine women, one half having been totally converted into bedrooms and the other half having bedrooms upstairs with kitchen, lounge and dining room downstairs. There's a small extension which accommodates an office and a meeting room. It is here Hannah brings Theo and Donna. The walls are a dove grey and a soft lilac. There is a seascape on one wall. There are several comfortable chairs, a sofa and a low table plus a large wooden cabinet. The window looks out over a small garden where shrubs are flourishing. It is enclosed by the strong high fence which runs around the whole of the property. Donna and Theo have already gone through a security system which includes a video-intercom. *Cosy,* thinks Donna sitting in one of the chairs. The day's sun is creeping round and peeping over the fence, she can feel its warmth on her shoulders. *Cosy and safe.*

Hannah offers refreshments, her dress – green and clinched at the waist – would not look out of place at a 1950s tea party. However, she is here in her professional capacity. She is on the founding committee for the refuge and Blessing has asked her to be present. Donna notices the easiness between Hannah and Theo. Her DI is looking more informal than usual, in jeans and a dark blue casual long-sleeve shirt.

After a bit of chit chat, Hannah goes upstairs and returns about five minutes later with Blessing. Donna and Theo stand to greet her. She is taller than either of them. She is wearing an odd assortment of rollnecks and jumpers with a pair of baggy jogging pants. Her feet are in fluffy slippers. There is something about the hollowness under her eyes and the breadth of her shoulders which suggests she was once more filled out. There are patches where her dark skin has almost lost its pigment. The scratches from the window glass are conspicuous across her face, as if it has been stitched by some unpractised giant's needle. Both her lower arms are bandaged since she had used them to batter her way out into the street.

Theo says something which Donna cannot interpret, though she knows it is the Yoruba language, learnt from his father. Blessing appears delighted in her response as they all sit. Then she glances at Hannah and Donna. 'I will speak English. In any case, your Akande detective inspector sounds like he is colonial . . .' She pauses. Her accent is heavy on the consonants and she can roll her 'r's impressively, which she now does: 'Aristocracy, yes? When he speaks his father's tongue. What is it you want to know?'

'Your story,' says Theo gently.

'My story? Then that is a long one. Hannah I will have some water, please. I will need it.'

'Take your time,' says Theo. 'We can stop at any point.'

She nods. 'But if you are to prevent the abuse of more women like me, then I must tell you everything.' She takes a sip from the glass Hannah hands her. 'Then I will begin.' She explains she grew up in Lagos. Both her parents are teachers – her mother of English – and education was important to them. However, public employees were not always paid and schools were not always well resourced, so there were times when the family went into debt and Blessing's schooling was

126

interrupted. Despite this she went to college to train to be a science teacher like her father. Here she met the man who would become her husband. She leans forward, elbows on her knees, 'The problem was my parents are very Christian and he was Hausa. Yes,' she looks at Theo. 'You understand.' She blows out a breath. 'I had to choose between my family and my heart. I regret some things I have done, but not following my heart. Though if I had not, then maybe I would not be here.

'I moved with my husband to the north and we had five happy years. Then he died and his family, well, they were never accepting. At first, I tried to stay on.' She shakes her head. 'It was not easy with them and what you call the rebels, what others call freedom fighters. They want everyone to convert to Islam, they want a Muslim government. I was safe with my husband; without him, I was not safe. They came one night – maybe rebels, maybe government troops, maybe my husband's family – I don't know. The house was burnt down. I would have died if it was not for my neighbour. She was Hausa too, she wanted a Muslim government. She was poor. She said the south took all their riches. Maybe she was right. But she would not tolerate violence. She took me in.

'I knew I would bring danger to her, so I could not stay. I had to make a choice. Go back and try to mend things with my family. Or go on an adventure. Or so it seemed at the time. I have good English. I have teaching qualifications. Britain, the old motherland, would want me, she has no teachers. That's what I heard. I was so tired, tired of being scared, I thought I will go. I have a bit of money and I will go. I did not know what being scared is.' She falls silent and her gaze drops to the carpet. She shakes her head. 'I did not know.'

No one speaks. Donna can feel the anticipation in the room. They want to hear more. And yet they can all see the toll it is taking on Blessing. Hannah suggests a break and another round of tea and coffee. She asks Blessing to come and help her. They depart, leaving a silence behind them which Donna finds difficult to break. She also ran away from a difficult situation when she was in her teens, but she expects her journey to the UK will seem like a walk in the park besides what they are going to hear from Blessing.

Activity and a serving of strong coffee revive Blessing enough for her to go on. She describes handing over money to what appeared to be an agency recruiting workers for the UK for what she thought would be a first-class ticket to Europe. To begin with the transport, a minibus, was not too bad. Then more and more people got on board, and Blessing began to rethink her decision. 'I will do this many times,' she says. 'Many times. But you do not leave home unless a shark is after you and by then the shark was not only after me, it was travelling with me, armed with a gun. I found I was owing bad people too much money to be let go.' She continues with the stages of her journey in the same tone as Donna might describe a trip along the M1. Across Niger and they arrived at the Sahara Desert. They were forced onto a truck. No food and the minimum of water. Few stops. A woman died. They left her body behind. Here Blessing pauses. Only for a moment. Then she describes arriving in Libya. Another truck and they have to travel at night, only at night. They reach the coast somewhere near the border with Tunisia. Or maybe they have crossed over. None of them know where they are exactly. Then they must wait. In a makeshift camp. Hungry. Cold at night. Blazing heat in the day. No sanitary provision.

'I am regretting. I am regretting now,' says Blessing sadly. 'It is too late. I don't know how to get back. And on a clear day, we can see Europe. There is hope nonetheless.' Somehow she holds onto it and makes friends with a couple of the other women. They cheer each other on. She skims over the boat journey. It is too horrible to recall. One of her new friends fell overboard and Blessing saw her drown. This brings her to a halt again. She covers her eyes with her scarred hands. Hannah fetches her a glass of water.

The boat ran out of fuel, they took on water, they drifted, people were seasick to the point of pleading for death. Then they were saved. The Italian coastguard. 'I cannot tell you the relief. I thought I was going to be dead and then I am alive. I am being given a warm blanket, something to eat, something to drink. Someone with a white face is smiling at me.' This respite did not last long. The conditions in the holding centre in Sicily were desperate – dirt, lack of food, lack of privacy. But worst of all was the desperation of the people. 'So many people waiting so many months and still nothing is happening, they are going nowhere. Or they are going back. Now I am here, I think, I don't want to go back. Anyway, everyone says you are only taken to Libya. What do I want to go there for? No, I must go on.' And finally a girl says if Blessing waits at a particular roundabout on a particular day, she will be picked up and taken to work in an Italian city, secretarial work or cleaning. It sounded good. She went. She was picked up by a taxi. She handed over her passport as she was told it was needed for a work permit. She never held it again. It was always in the hands of another. First the driver's and then, after they stopped for a few nights in a town in the foot of Italy, in Felka's.

Felka said they were going to fly to the UK where there was work for them. The driver took them both to Rome and they did indeed get a flight to Manchester. But the work was not what Blessing imagined it to be. 'I would not, I would never work in a brothel,' she says, her voice strained. She clutches her fingers together and hunches over. She whispers, 'I had no choice. I had the shark at my back.' She is quiet. It is only after a while that Donna realises Blessing is silently weeping.

Again Hannah takes charge. Says they all need a breather. Theo suggests they can come back.

'No, no, no!' Blessing almost shouts. 'You need this information. I must give it. Now. Before it is too late for others.'

The problem is, she really has very little hard detail to give. She does not know where the brothel was in Manchester. She recalls little of the night she and Felka were moved to Scarborough. She thinks they were given sleeping pills.

Significant? Donna glances at Theo to see if he has clocked this. He has.

Blessing can describe Marius Badea – Felka's so-called boyfriend, by the way – but she hasn't seen him since Manchester. He called the man who brought her to Scarborough Mr T. He and their other guard in this town, a youngster, always wore a balaclava, a surgical mask and

130

latex gloves. They are both white for certain, shorter than Theo, taller than Hannah. The older is square (she makes the shape with her hands). The younger is scrawny. They have blue eyes. As for the customers, she tries not to notice them too much. 'In Scarborough it is better,' she says. 'There are fewer of them.' Even so she did not know how to escape until last night. The youngster left them for who knew how long, perhaps he was waiting just outside, but when she saw Hannah wave, she had to try. Blessing briefly touches Hannah's arm. 'She saw me. She saw me,' her hand goes to her chest. 'It made the difference.'

Hannah smiles shyly.

Talking has exhausted Blessing. 'I wish I could say more. It is not enough, is it?' she says, her tone drenched in sadness.

Donna assures her she has done more than they could have hoped.

'You have to stop them. Promise me.'

Transfixed, Donna and Theo nod, with more conviction than they ought.

Chapter 20

As Theo drives them both back to the station, Donna recalls parts of Blessing's story. Sometimes she wishes she could be inoculated against the sadness she encounters on a daily basis through her job. Even so, she suspects there would not be a vaccine strong enough. She knows her colleagues find ways of handling everything that gets thrown at them – or they don't, and they break or they become hard. A brittle hard. Or a brutal hard.

'When I was a kid, we didn't go back often to visit my dad's family,' says Theo slowly. He has previously told Donna his father came to Birmingham in the UK in 1964 at the age of twenty-two, staying to eventually train as a civil engineer and to marry a woman from Cardiff's well-established Cape Verde community. 'I'm not sure Dad wanted to go, after his parents died. His brothers were here. We were here. But when we did go, it was hot days by pools in a gated complex and being taken out to parks or amusements in air-conditioned cars.' Theo continues, sounding pained: 'To think all that happened in Nigeria.'

'It could happen anywhere. And she was basically enslaved in Sicily,' says Donna. Then remembers something, 'Didn't you say that's where Nathaniel Withenshaw set up his businesses?'

'There and Spain.'

A coincidence? Got to be.

Returning to the CID office envelops Donna in activity. She allows herself one small cup of coffee, hoping she won't suffer for it later, before joining Harrie and Theo in the DS enclave. Harrie gives her updates. The forensic reports on Abi's dress, plus on what was found at the house where Blessing was kept (which includes the pizza box dropped by the tearaway who may or may not be connected) are due Sunday or Monday. Abi has been told they will be seeking a warrant for her phone. Donna tells them that she has found Tony Finch on a hospital camera on Saturday 3 May, the day before she and Trev went to Abi's flat to retrieve her dress. Donna isn't certain whether she is repeating herself. From the interest being shown by Harrie and Theo, she reckons she isn't. She could kick herself for her – as she sees it – increasing forgetfulness.

'Doesn't put him in Abi's room,' says Harrie. 'Anyway, he's a fixer for Withenshaw who owns the flats. Not unusual for him to be in the vicinity.'

'He lied though, said he wasn't there,' says Donna. She's pleased Harrie's response indicates this has slipped her mind.

The final bit of information Harrie has to share is that Nathaniel Withenshaw was in the Territorials, in his twenties, however he didn't get paramedic training. 'Nothing beyond the basic first aid.'

'Maybe he likes to big himself up,' says Donna.

'It fits,' says Harrie. 'Had a bit of a conversation with

the lass who rang up as it goes. Tony Finch was in the Territorials at the same time as Withenshaw. Finch went into the army proper, had a tour in Northern Ireland.'

Theo says, 'Gives us the link between them.' He is perched on the window sill, supping from a very large mug of coffee.

'Still doesn't explain Stella Horsham and Withenshaw,' says Donna.

'Hardly relevant now,' Theo says flatly. 'We have two big ongoing investigations, we have to focus on them. Harrie, did the cavalry from the NCA arrive?'

Harrie nods and actually smiles. 'They went for a quick butty and brew. Shouldn't be long. Thought we'd meet in the family room. Ten minutes?'

Donna is glad of the respite to visit the toilets and tidy herself up. She is not bleeding today and is actually feeling quite perky. Her blue eyes are bright and she likes the way her cropped hair frames her oval face, as long as she ignores the flabbiness around her chin. She never wears much make-up, but she touches a bit of tinted gloss to her lips before giving herself a big smile. *Looking good!*

The family room is on the second floor. It's most frequently used for victims and their relatives or friends. It has the comfortable understated furnishings and decor to suit this purpose. However, the main thing is that it is big enough for the five of them. Donna is the last to come in and is introduced by Harrie to DI Lukasz Mazur and DS Parvez Khan. Both of them have toned physiques. The DI is older, perhaps in his fifties, salt and pepper hair and a pale square-jawed face atop a thick neck. DS Khan is maybe in his late thirties. He is tall, his features more delicate, his dark hair shaved back, his facial hair carefully barbered. He is wearing narrow-legged jeans and turquoise suede shoes. He has an accent Donna vaguely recognises. It turns out to be Mancunian and he and Theo swap some observations since Theo spent time on the force in that city. Parvez also remembers his family trips over to Scarborough when he was a child. Perhaps it is his obvious fondness for her town which has softened Harrie towards him.

Once they've got the introductions out the way, they sit down and Donna goes through the interview with Blessing. Mazur listens and Khan takes notes, both attentive and nodding at intervals. This kind of story is not new to them it's clear. Mazur confirms this by saying, 'The route from Sicily is well known. If this investigation can lead us to the main perpetrators that would be a win.' He turns to Theo, 'So what avenues of enquiry do we have?' His deferment to the local DI is also a win.

Theo explains about the wait on the forensics.

Though neither Mazur nor Khan do anything but nod, Donna senses a slight discomfort amongst her own colleagues. Would things happen faster in London? She glances around the room: does it look a bit shabby to people fresh from the metropolis?

Theo is continuing: 'Then there are the guards.'

'Who is Mr T?' Donna's thought comes out in words by mistake.

'Apart from a character in a rather louche 1980s TV series?' says Harrie.

The cultural reference passes Donna by and Harrie elaborates on it for her. Donna feels compelled to explain to Mazur and Khan she wasn't brought up in the UK and most of the late eighties she was becoming a mother. In order to contribute something useful, she says, 'T could be Tony, as in Tony Finch.' This leads to another round of elucidations.

'And you say Withenshaw had some haulage interests in Sicily?' asks Mazur. 'It's worth checking out. We can go through Europol.'

'There's the owner of the house Blessing was kept in,' says Theo. 'So far, all we've got is a company also based in Sicily.' He receives a nod. 'And we can see if we can track Tony Finch's movements in this town over the last few weeks.'

'What about the other guard?' asks Mazur. 'Your local intel will be crucial. A youngster like that could be indiscreet, let something slip.'

'Unless they've got him so terrified . . .' interrupts Khan.

'There's the pizza box,' says Harrie. 'If we get forensics and if it's linked, then it could give us a starting point.'

Mazur nods. He doesn't mention the whole bundle of 'ifs'. 'And the other woman, Felka Warszawska?' His pronunciation is as easy as Donna's had been.

Theo replies, 'Once she's up to it, we'll interview her.'

'Don't leave it too long,' warns Khan. 'It's not unusual for the women to go to back to their abusers. Fear or some kind of twisted emotional bond keeps them attached. Though I'm sure I don't need to explain all that to you.' His smile is for all of the local officers.

Does it linger for a split second on Harrie? Donna thinks maybe.

Harrie asks: 'What do you have for us? Do you know Marius Badea? Do you know this gang?'

'Badea is new to us,' says Mazur slowly. 'But this gang of traffickers, maybe. They are very good at covering their tracks, splintering, appearing and disappearing.'

'They pop up brothels for a short while in one area, then melt back into the shadows,' says Khan.

'Pop up brothels?' asks Harrie, obviously caught between mirth and horror.

'Yes,' says Mazur. 'As crazy as it sounds. And they are very good at blending in. The punters aren't likely to call them in, but nor do ordinary decent people notice them.'

'Or want to notice them,' says Khan.

'So it was excellent that you got the tip off.'

Khan goes on: 'It goes without saying, the people who get involved in trafficking have an over-inflated admiration of money and a very lowly respect for women.'

'Not so different from many men I've met then,' says Harrie with a twisted grin.

Khan smiles. 'You'd be surprised how many women are key operatives. Currently many of the trafficking gang members are Romanian. It has not always been so. It won't always be so. Trafficking is not nationality specific. No nationality is immune to exploiting other humans for money.'

'Ain't that the truth,' says Harrie.

Mazur says, 'We think this may have been a fragment from a bigger operation which moved out of Manchester before we could get to them in April. My question is why they came here? Which is where you come in with your local knowledge.'

'We have our fair share of prostitution and pimping,' says Theo. 'There're people known to us who we could bring in.'

'It's worth a try, they might have a whiff of something going off on their turf. However, I expect it won't be someone on your radar as yet – this is an international operation, the people involved have their sights set wider than a few streets in a small town. The statement from Ms Okokon about being given pills which put her to sleep. That's interesting, something we've not heard before – is it significant? Where could they have come from? Meanwhile, we will follow the money. They had started working again, they will have got the message out there somehow, there must have been posts on the internet and at least one mobile contact number. Services have to be paid for,' he says sardonically. 'Maybe we'll get lucky and someone used a bank card.'

A timetable for the tasks is agreed and Mazur and Khan are shown an office space they can use. It's not much more than a glorified broom cupboard, however, they seem satisfied with it. The NCA officers are then ready to book into their hotel. 'It would be great to have a tour of the town,' says DS Khan. 'Lukasz has never been here and I could do with a reminder – anyway, all I pretty much ever saw was the beach and amusements.' He's looking straight at Shilling.

To Donna's surprise, Harrie readily agrees with a wide smile. *Perhaps, I've finally nailed her sort*, Donna thinks and finds herself feeling vaguely like a mother hen.

Chapter 21

Felka comes home with Zlota on Friday night. Zlota creates a welcome meal and also brings out a bottle of red wine. 'Is it OK?' she asks Hannah tentatively.

When she moved in, Zlota was told the house was dry; Hannah skimmed over the reason. However, over the months, she has said more about her descent into alcoholism. She looks at the bottle and finds, to her surprise, no desire to have a taste. She nods. 'I don't know how good it'll be for someone who has had concussion.'

Zlota dismisses this. 'It is good for the heart. It fortifies.'

Though Hannah genuinely appreciates every bite – and says so – the dinner is not a success. The sisters bicker away in Polish. Or at least, Zlota does most of it. Felka gives curt and sparse responses. Hannah does not understand a word, but she is pretty sure she gets the sense of it. Zlota is once again trying to enforce her rule – Felka is to stay close and return to Poland as soon as they can organise it. Plus, Hannah suspects, Zlota is looking for an apology – for all the worry and fear she has felt over the preceding weeks (not to mention years) – though this probably remains, for the most part, unspoken.

The younger sister's expression barely changes from studied disinterest. For all she is smaller and slighter than her elder sibling, Hannah can see Felka is not going to easily give way to her. *Her tough carapace keeps her safe,* thinks Hannah. *She's scared of what might happen if she lets it crack. Of what's underneath.* Hannah takes another mouthful of *kołaczki,* thrilled by the mix of raspberry and poppy seed in its flaky pastry foldover. She drops her compliments in to interrupt Zlota's flow.

Felka eats less than she speaks, which is going something. However, she swiftly drains more than half the bottle of wine. Not unpredictably, this brings on dizziness and nausea. She says she wants to go to bed. Zlota puts an arm around her in order to help her up and Felka cannot stop herself from curving into the embrace. For a moment, the two of them are fused in a tender quiet.

While Zlota takes care of her sister, Hannah clears up the kitchen. Zlota had dressed the table by the French windows with a cloth, napkins and a small posy of colourful polyanthus. *Such caring attention,* she thinks sadly, because she doubts it registered with Felka. Hannah pours the last of the wine into Zlota's glass, so she can get rid of the bottle, and then gets on with loading the dishwasher and washing up.

By the time Hannah is finished, Zlota returns. She takes a large swig of her drink. 'I don't understand,' she says huffily. 'Is she crazy? Hannah, tell me, you are a counsellor, is she crazy? I offer her everything and she just turns her back.'

'She's feeling her shame,' says Hannah. The word suddenly makes her mouth dry for the crimson liquid going down the other woman's throat. To distract herself, Hannah puts on the kettle for a mint tea.

'She is embarrassed? Of course, she is embarrassed, she has been an idiot.'

'Shame is to embarrassment what a migraine is to a headache. You can't know how devastating it is until you've experienced it.' Hannah knows all about shame. She suspects Zlota does not.

'We make mistakes,' says Zlota, following her own train of thought. 'We learn and we go on.' She finishes the wine and Hannah finds she can breathe again. Zlota continues: 'I am not sure I can come tomorrow, to see Khalil. I don't like to leave her.'

Zlota changes her mind on this several times over the evening and into the next morning. Finally, over breakfast she says she will come if she can lock her sister – who has not yet appeared downstairs – in the house.

'Absolutely not,' says Hannah dumbfounded. 'What if there's a fire? Anyway, I don't think we can, there's no deadlock on the back door, only a bolt on the inside.'

Zlota looks gloomy. 'You will go anyway?'

'I have said I will.' They have already been round this particular loop several times.

'No,' says Zlota, with emphasis. 'Seeing him is important. He is alone. I will tell Felka she must stay in until we get back.' She smiles at Hannah. 'Trust, I must trust her, isn't that what you say?'

Hannah does not respond, though she rather thinks it is too late for that.

They have hired a car and Zlota drives. She takes the coast

road to HMP Hull as if it is a race track. The single carriageway slinks its way across the flatlands to the south of Scarborough. Hannah plants her feet on the floor and braces herself for every time Zlota decides to overtake with a restricted view ahead, which she does with terrifying frequency. Hannah attempts to focus out her side window. The sky is a bright eggshell blue, the white clouds scraped across it. The hedgerows are snowy with blossom and the wind turbines reach into the heavens, arms stretched in sacrifice. She is heartily thankful when they arrive at the prison car park in one piece.

She has visited a client on remand here before, so is aware of the slow, methodical process of entry. She has to persuade Zlota that any display of impatience could mean they are denied entry. 'This is worse than Russia,' Zlota says in disgust.

Khalil appears more delicate and gaunt than Hannah remembers him. Certainly he has lost his ready smile. He says he is doing fine, when she can see he is not. He says he still believes in the British legal system, when she can tell he does not. He says he had not, would never, hurt Mr Yates. She hears his conviction. She wants to tell him Theo would not allow a miscarriage of justice. But with Kelsey also in her mind, she is not as certain of his invincibility as she once was.

After attempting to paint prison life as if it is some kind of residential training course, Khalil covers his reluctance to talk by asking Zlota questions. She fills his silence with her worries about Felka. What has happened to her? Why won't she say? Could Zlota have done more to prevent whatever it is? What should she do now? The words – and even some tears – spill out of her. Will she ever be able to get her sister home, to Poland? 'Only there will she be safe,' she says. And, after a pause, she says, 'I am so afraid for her. She will disappear again. Pouf!' She gazes at Khalil as if expecting him to provide an answer.

He rouses himself, tells her about a device he has come across which can help people with dementia be traced if they wander off. It looks like a key ring.

This cheers Zlota. On the way home, with Hannah driving more sedately, Zlota insists they make a detour to an electronics store to buy one. She gets a pink one. 'Felka will never know,' she says, her mood much improved.

Chapter 22

She takes the turning almost without thinking. The opposite direction to Scarborough. Perhaps it is Blessing's story of broken family ties. Perhaps it is the last hour spent with Elizabeth in a room made stifling by loss. Perhaps it is merely the missed trip to Kenilworth last weekend. Whatever it is, sitting in the prison car park Donna has a yen to see Jim and her body acts on it when the car reaches the main road. The moors are burnt umber. There are patches of green where the rowan and hawthorn huddle together. The road clambers between the rolling earth and the vast cerulean sky. In small fields lambs investigate their environment penned in by grey stone walls. Donna watches one frisk into the air shaking its tail. It makes her smile. *It's going to be all right,* she tells herself. She hasn't warned him of her arrival, but Jim will be pleased to see her.

She is feeling decidedly less positive and energetic two hours later on. The route has taken her onto larger and larger roads until she's on the motorway, busy with traffic. She pulls over into some services and gets herself a tea and a ham sandwich. There are a few tables outside and she sits at one of them. The sun is warming. But the constant vrumm from the speeding cars, down the carriageway behind her, keeps the tension in her shoulders. She is an hour and a half from her destination (approximately). She considers whether to text Jim. Then she thinks, *And why shouldn't I just go? It's my house too. Since when did I have to make an appointment?*

It is late afternoon by the time she turns into the street where she has lived for twenty-five years. She recalls the first time Jim brought her here. They had been married six years. They were living in a terraced house which felt palatial to Donna, compared with what she was used to growing up, most latterly in East Berlin at the end of the 1970s. However, Jim always promised her 'better', as he put it. And this house, detached, sitting centrally on its plot, with bays on either side of the door, was the better already signed for. Donna remembers the paint sparkling that day and she was thinking they could not possibly afford it. But Jim assured her they could. And they did. Donna, always careful with money – a talent she learnt early – made sure they did. She sits in the car on the drive. *It's only a house,* she tells herself. And yet she is proud of it, of her, of her and Jim, for making it beautiful inside and out.

She exits the car and walks quickly to the front door. She opens it with her key and steps over the threshold, still marvelling that this is hers. *Mine and Jim's,* she reminds herself. The hall is square. A closed door on the left leads into the 'study' with its banks of bookshelves. To the right is the lounge which they had knocked into the back rooms to create a large space with kitchen and dining area opening onto the garden. In front of Donna are the stairs and above are the four bedrooms. Four. She had never had a spare bedroom before. It still feels such a luxury.

For a moment, her mind supplies noises. A young

Elizabeth playing her music too loud. A young Christopher shouting at his sister to turn it down as he is studying. Jim watching the golf on TV. Waiting. Waiting for Donna to prepare the dinner. This thought deflates her a little. Then she realises there are no sounds. Or are there? Something attracts her attention from above. 'Hello,' she calls out tentatively. What would Jim be doing up there at this time of day? *Perhaps he is ill?* This thought means she swiftly climbs the stairs. She rushes into their bedroom. Nothing.

Then it is unmistakable. A gasp, a giggle, a grunt, a grinding of headboard on wall. She crosses the landing and shoves the door to the guest bedroom. The carpet prevents it from swinging wide. Despite this, she can see enough. Two people under the duvet, so caught up in each other, they don't notice the intrusion.

'Jim?' she asks, as if there could be a doubt. There must be a doubt! She has to be wrong. Then she has to say his name more loudly to get his attention.

He turns his head, 'Donna? What the fuck are you doing here?' The woman yelps and hides herself under the covers. Even so, Donna recognises her. A friend. Or a 'so-called' friend as Elizabeth would have it.

The sense that this house never really belonged to her – was Jim's gift which he was permitted to retract – wrapped up in a fury and an embarrassment which knows no articulation, has Donna turning round and retracing her steps. She doesn't stop until she is back at her car, as if by rewinding, she can avoid what has just happened. She hears Jim shouting her name as she gets into her vehicle and drives away.

Chapter 23

There's been another row. This time the sisters were united, against Hannah. She told them that Blessing had spoken to the police and Felka would have to do the same. She offered to take her in, explained she knows the officers concerned and Felka would be treated gently. Felka said she would not do it. Zlota said it was too soon. Hannah said, ultimately, Felka would not be given a choice, it would be better to do it now and get it over with. This set off further fireworks from the elder sister, while Hannah could see the younger one was considering her options.

They are both upstairs. Zlota is giving Felka a haircut and manicure. Hannah does not feel entirely welcome in her own house. This annoys her. On the other hand, she thinks giving the sisters some time together might be a good idea. She decides to go out.

The refuge is only a few roads away and she drops in. One of the two workers on duty tells her there was an altercation at breakfast. Blessing was being friendly and helpful to the other women when one of them snapped at her to get lost and called her a black bitch. The abuser has been talked to and will have to leave. It's the rules. But both Hannah and her colleague know how vulnerable the woman is and that this is likely to send her back to drugs and unhealthy relationships.

Hannah goes up to Blessing's room and knocks on the door. 'It's Hannah,' she says when there's no response. Blessing says she may enter. The narrow bedroom is simply furnished with bed, side table, chair and wardrobe. The window overlooks the garden and a slender birch with a glistening snow leopard bark. Blessing is curled up on the bed. Her eyes are red and she makes a half-hearted attempt to hide them with her palms. Hannah asks permission to sit. 'Why do you ask?' says Blessing crossly. 'You own everything here.'

Hannah feels the punch of it. She sits and leans forward, elbows on knees. 'I don't own anything here,' she says. 'This is a charity, we raise money from individuals, get grants from government.'

'From the government?' Blessing says, suspicion seeping into her tone and expression. 'You do what they say then.'

'No. We are independent.'

'Huh.' Blessing closes her eyes.

After a moment, Hannah wonders whether the other woman has slipped into sleep. Then Blessing blinks. She slowly raises herself up, shuffling herself backwards to lean against the wall, arms across her body. She shakes her head when Hannah asks if she wants her to go.

Again Hannah leaves a pause, then says, 'I imagine it was very exhausting to tell the police your story on Friday.'

'I had forgotten it . . . No, I had it, you know, captured,' she moves her hands together as if they are a box and its lid. 'Now it is out again. I am thinking all the time. Even in my sleep. It's like I am there again.'

Flashbacks. 'We can organise counselling, it could help?'

148

Blessing shrugs. Then she rubs vigorously at her face. 'You are right, I am tired, I am tired of this room,' she snaps.

'Then let's go out for a walk,' says Hannah.

'I am allowed?'

'Of course, you can go out any time.'

They have to find some trainers and a coat from the cupboard downstairs where such donations are kept. Then they set off. Though Blessing's legs are longer, her pace is slower, and Hannah has to adjust hers to match. She leads them to a path which heads down to where a sea-water lido used to be. Hannah has seen railway posters celebrating its glory days. Fashionably turned-out crowds watch diving displays. The women are dressed in 1950s flounced frocks – which Hannah covets – the men in blazers and boaters. Since the pool was filled in, only the generous curve of it remains plus the pipes which once fed it. These now suck and glug with the waves as Hannah and Blessing come to a halt on the concrete rim.

'I used to love the ocean,' says Blessing. 'It was a special treat to visit the beaches near Lagos. It was where I learnt to swim. My mother insisted. She had too many pupils who had drowned. I never thought . . . I never thought I would be so scared of the water.'

Hannah watches the tremor spasm from Blessing's shoulders down her spine. Hannah feels again the weight of Blessing's story pushing on her abdomen. *Perhaps this was a bad choice of a walk?* she questions.

'This is not as beautiful as my ocean.' Blessing continues. 'But it is pretty.' She takes a breath.

Hannah is pleased to see a smile on the other woman's

face. They continue along the path which takes them past a stretch of tawny beach and exposed sandstone patterned like tiger pelts. Gutweed, bright green with the texture of a party wig, clings to the edges of rockpools and adds a tang to the air. Dinner-jacketed oystercatchers stab at it. Blessing points at them, even laughs a little at their antics and asks what they are called. Hannah tells her.

They walk on. Blessing says she does not want the woman who insulted her to be expelled from the refuge. Hannah explains that these are the rules. Blessing shakes her head. 'I know now what troubled is and she is troubled. Anyway it will be worse for me if she goes.'

They stop at the café to the back of the beach huts and Hannah gets them both hot chocolates and teacakes. They sit at one of the outside tables with an uninterrupted view to where sea and sky dissolve into each other. As she eats and drinks, Blessing becomes more talkative, or rather, interrogative. She wants to know whether Hannah thinks she has said enough to the police for her traffickers to be caught. 'I gave the police everything, I held nothing back.'

'That's good,' Hannah assures her. 'It's the only way if they are going to make any arrests.'

'If, yes, if. And if they don't, what will happen to me then?'

'You don't think the traffickers will come looking for you?'

Blessing shrugs.

'The refuge is a safe place, we have good security,' says Hannah quickly. Maybe she should talk to Theo about more?

'What about the others who went from Manchester? There was a young girl called Marianne. Will the police find her?' It is Hannah's turn to show uncertainty. However, Blessing is almost talking to herself. 'I don't know if I said too much,' she says softly. 'If I said it right. They weren't all mean all of the time. Mr T brought me books because he knew I liked to read.'

Hannah has heard other women at the refuge finding kernels of good in their abusers. She is surprised to hear it coming from Blessing. 'He put you to work, he held you captive,' she says sharply.

Blessing does not respond directly. 'And now I have given my witness testimony what will happen to me?'

'We are getting you a solicitor. You can claim asylum.'

'Yes, I can claim it, but will I get it?'

'We will do our best.'

Blessing smiles, 'I know you will. But will it be good enough?'

Hannah is perturbed by this question and how to answer it honestly.

Perhaps this shows. Blessing pats Hannah's arm, 'I am sorry, I have become too used to only trusting myself.' Her gaze shifts to the horizon. 'What type are they?'

Hannah looks to where white birds hover and swoop. 'Gannets,' she says. Then one folds its wings and plummets, making a splash like a tennis ball as it hits the water. Others follow. It is a dizzying display.

'They have faith, do they not, Hannah?' says Blessing. 'Look how they drop knowing they will catch fish and the sea will not harm them. Yes, they have faith. As did I.'

Hannah considers how Blessing's faith has been so ruinously misused and then the scraps spat back into her face. No wonder she has none to hold onto now.

Chapter 24

Donna wakes. She can't believe she slept. Nor can she believe she drove all the way back to Scarborough last night. Without stopping. Clutching the steering wheel as if it was a lifebelt. Even at the time she knew it was dangerous and she was lucky not to have caused an accident. Or to have been stopped for speeding. As she left Kenilworth further and further behind, she began to question what she had seen. Then it would hit her – wumpf – in the abdomen. As it does now. *I must have dreamed it,* she tells herself. *A nightmare.* The crumpled pile of clothes by her bed. And the three missed calls and two texts from her husband tell her otherwise. All he says is various versions of: 'We have to talk.' But the volume of attempted communication is evidence she did not imagine the scene in her guest room. *Oh Jim!* She rolls over and pulls the duvet over her head.

She might have stayed like that. She wants to. But, of course, she has to get up to use the bathroom. Then she feels thirsty and gets herself a tea. She slumps at the tiny table in her small square kitchen. Out of the window, blue tits and blackbirds busily make or mend nests. *Oh Jim, why?* Immediately she comes up with reasons and they are all to do with her. Since entering the peri-menopause she has put on weight around the hips, her moods have been changeable.

I am no longer attractive, she tells herself. Then there is her insistence on coming to Scarborough. Jim did not even want her to be a police officer. *Did it all start that far back?* Misery engulfs her and she cries.

It is only after this release of tension, as she mops up tears and snot, that she thinks, *How could he? How could he betray me like that? And with her?* It would be easier to understand – maybe almost excusable – if the her in question were younger, more slender, more beautiful than Donna. But she is not. Even at her worst moments – and this moment is the ultimate in worsts – Donna knows she outshines the woman Jim was romping in bed with. *Romping? Scheiße! Perhaps that's it, we haven't done enough romping in a while? I'm always bleeding or too tired or away.* Up until now, she didn't think Jim was bothered about their lack of a sex life. *Looks like I was wrong.* Dullness settles on her once again.

Dull would be Elizabeth's verdict on her parents' life together. Yet Donna had craved the ordinariness of it. Over a couple of years after leaving Ludlow she took on something of a peripatetic bohemian life, sofa surfing, living in squats or camping in the good weather. She worked whatever job she could get and threw herself into the causes of the 1980s – Reclaim the Night; anti-Thatcher; anti-racism; CND. She loved the energy of it all. She loved being part of something, a team focused on a goal. It's why she enjoys the camaraderie of working for the police. She takes a sip of tea and reflects, with a grimace, that it might be a hangover from growing up in a communist regime. *Jeder nach seinen Fähigkeiten, jedem nach seinen Bedürfnissen. From each according to his ability, to*

154

each according to his needs. Supposedly. And then Jim walked into the bar where she was working. It was a low point. She was camping and the weather was awful. There had just been a huge argument in her circle of female friends about one of them taking up a post at an investment bank. She was tired of jobs which didn't stretch her intelligence. Jim was good looking, he was charming and he did not immediately want to take all her clothes off. It was amazing how many men in the campaign groups she belonged to thought sex without strings was a tenet of socialism and wooing was the worst part of the capitalist hegemony. Jim courted Donna. She did not even know she wanted to be courted. But she did. She wanted to be cared for. When she had run away from home, she had been forced to rely on herself. How lovely to let some of that go and sink into Jim's secure and predict-able world. She wanted a nice house. She wanted material comfort. She wanted things, things which had been in short supply in her childhood.

Now, as she sits in this small town tossed up on the edge of what used to be known as the German Ocean, she finally thinks back to the girl she was and the name she had thrown away: Erika Neuhausen. Erika had strained against the restrictions of her life. She had been brave once or twice. Where had Erika gone? Where was she in Donna? The notification of a text coming in punctures her thoughts. She reads it: 'Donna love give me a call J x'

Love? He talks of love? The spurt of anger gets her to her feet, into the shower and dressed. In her work clothes. Somewhere along the line she has lost grip of what day it is. Sunday. She decides to go into the station anyway. She can check on a few things. And just maybe it will distract her from the confused tumbling in her head.

The CID offices are not busy. Greetings come her way, but no one questions why she is there. She finds two messages for her. She does the easy one first: the taxi driver who was in Stella Horsham's street early on the morning of 27 April. He has been on holiday, hence not being in touch sooner. He explains his dashcam overwrites itself every seven days unless he stops it, so the footage from the twenty-seventh is gone. He does remember a car parked a few doors down from his drop-off. He can't give a registration, however, he gives a make, model and colour. It doesn't take long for Donna to confirm it matches that of Stella Horsham's car. Without the information from the licence plate, it is not conclusive. But is it good enough to put her back at the house?

She calls the next number on her list. Abi's sister answers the phone and, with some reluctance, hands it over to Abi. She also does not sound pleased. When Donna confirms they are seeking a warrant for Abi's phone, she says; 'I don't believe you are harassing me like this. I am the victim here. I am telling you there is nothing on it. Why isn't that good enough for you?'

'You are withholding information about the man you were to meet,' explains Donna, keeping her voice calm.

'He had nothing to do with this.'

'Neither of us really know this,' says Donna firmly.

There's a pause, then Abi says, 'OK. I will come down Tuesday and tell you everything you want to know. Then will you leave me alone?'

Donna thanks her, and quickly, before the connection is cut, asks her if she told Stella Horsham about being raped.

'Stella?' Abi sounds vague. 'My sister rang personnel to say I would be off and why. But Stella wasn't there. Her mum's died or something?'

'When did your sister call?'

'Not sure.' Donna hears her have a conversation in the background. 'The Tuesday after the Bank Holiday.'

'Are you sure?'

'Yes,' snaps Abi. 'Why must you grill me on everything?' She clicks off her end of the line and Donna is left with fuzz.

She rubs at her forehead. A fog – from too little sleep and the never-ending litany resulting from seeing Jim in bed with that woman – is threatening to foreclose. She pushes on through. She begins to gather more information on Stella. She finds her biography on the hospital website. It tells her Stella has worked there for the last thirty years and has various qualifications in human resources and management. She is also a trustee for a local charity which works with adult survivors of childhood sexual abuse. Her hobbies are listed as baking (Donna is unconvinced having seen the kitchen) and theatre. Donna cannot find Stella on any social media. However, she does turn up an obituary in *The Times* for Stella Horsham's father from June 2002.

A theoretical physicist who spent his life at Oxford University, Professor Prometheus Horsham retired to Scarborough with his wife so they could be close to their only daughter. The professor has a catalogue of books to his name and was revered for his theorising on the 'folding' of time. He doesn't seem to have been concerned with making his work popular or particularly accessible, but his sharpness of mind and wit are praised by one colleague. Nothing is said about his private life, apart from the existence of his wife and daughter. There is a photo of Professor Horsham, in an academic gown and mortar board. He's handsome – Donna can detect the same bone structure which gives Stella's face its grace. All at once, she recalls the lack of photos at the Horsham house. *No remembrance of Daddy or Mummy?*

Boots, no, belts and braces: she does a quick search of police databases and finds a case number attached to Stella's name. Dated 1984, its details are not part of the computerised archive, so Donna puts in a request for it.

She goes to make herself a cup of lemon and ginger tea. Stella Horsham could not have told Nathaniel Withenshaw about Abi being raped. Stella Horsham could have been at her house at about the time when Abi was being raped. The kaleidoscope has been shaken into a new configuration.

'Hey Donna, didn't know you were on duty.' It's Trev. 'I've just had a call from Gordon Yates. Want to come with me? No emergency, finish your drink.'

Outside Donna is cheered by the spring weather. Inside her is so desolate, she had forgotten about warmth and green things. She sets Trev off talking about his grandchild, so she doesn't have to say anything. Will she ever have grandchildren? *There's time.* Aged twenty-six, Trev's daughter is younger than Donna's two children. Though five years older than Donna was when she had Elizabeth. *Was I too young? Did I drag Jim into being a father before he wanted to be?* It's not how she remembers it. However, what she saw last night puts everything in question.

As they leave the graveyard on the approach to Yates's house, Trev asks how things are with her.

'Fine,' she says, something clenching at her heart.

The outer door of the porch is open, but the inner one is firmly locked. They don't have to wait long for Gordon Yates to let them in. He greets them warmly. The bruising has just about gone. His skin looks more like tissue paper, pouched under his eyes. Using a walking frame, he leads them to the sitting room at the back. 'I saw you coming,' he says.

This makes no sense. Donna wonders if the attack has permanently affected his faculties.

Apart from the sun streaming in, the room is little changed from the last time Donna saw it. Gordon's chair is still at the centre, all the accoutrements of his daily life within easy reach. He drops into it with a grateful 'u-oof'. 'Hate that thing,' he indicates the frame. 'They said I had to have it to be able to stay home. Now, lass,' he fixes her with a gaze from under drooping lids, 'if you and PC Trench want a brew, you know where the kitchen is.'

Donna glances at Trev. He grimaces. 'I can do that, Mr Yates,' Trev says. 'If you want anything?'

'No, son. My daughter-in-law will be by soon with my tea.'

'Well, perhaps we should get on,' says Donna. 'So we're done before she arrives.'

'That's for you.' Gordon points at a box on the carpet about a metre from his feet.

Donna gets her disposable gloves out of her pocket and crouches down. The box has been opened. With as little disturbance as she can manage she investigates what is inside.

159

There's a bundle of silver spoons wrapped in a plastic supermarket bag and some currency in an envelope. She looks up.

'Aye, the spoons are mine,' says Gordon with satisfaction. 'And the money is all there apart from twenty quid.'

She stands, feeling the creak in her knees as she does. 'Can you tell us what happened?'

'Aye, lass, it was left not two hours ago in the porch. I rang the station and spoke to Trev here, as soon as I saw what it was.'

'Left? Not delivered? Did you see who left it?'

Gordon's smile broadens. He indicates they should gather round him. There is a device on the table by his chair. And all of a sudden, his earlier remark makes sense. 'My lad got this all sorted,' says Mr Yates. 'Cameras on the front and at the back, and I can watch the comings and goings from here. Now let me see.' He takes a moment to change his glasses and stares closely at the screen. He talks himself through the procedure and, after a few attempts, gets up what he wants. 'Clear as day,' he says. Indeed it is. A youngster pushing the box into the porch. Donna cannot immediately identify him. But she does recognise the young man standing by the front gate watching. She looks at Trev for confirmation. He nods.

Chapter 25

'Donna? I didn't know you were in today?' Donna does not bother answering Harrie's enquiry. She could ask Shilling the same thing, it is her day off too. Instead Donna explains what she and Trev have discovered. They are standing in Gordon Yates's front garden, its borders abloom – presumably the show is the result of Khalil Qasim's work. Is this phone call the first step to having him released? Donna hopes so. What Harrie tells her surprises her. She cuts the connection and says to Trev: 'We're to go back in, he's already in the cells.'

The CID offices look particularly dismal after their walk through the verdant graveyard. They find Harrie and DS Khan in the DS's alcove. It is a bit of a squeeze with Trench's bulk, which may explain the close proximity between Harrie and Parvez. Though Donna does not think it looks coincidental. Shilling brings them up to speed. A condom found amongst the debris taken from the corner of the park where Abi was raped has yielded some DNA which has given a hit on their systems.

'Are they sure?' asks Donna. She can't quite make the person fit with the crime. Jayson Smith is in his twenties, a local crim known for fraud, theft, receiving stolen goods. But rape?

'Don't say he's not the type,' says Harrie fiercely.

Donna might have been tempted to. She closes her mouth.

Harrie continues, 'To be clear, we know who ejaculated into the condom. Its outside is too contaminated to have any information about who Jayson was having intercourse with. Plus, same DNA on the pizza carton. Smith was caught on CCTV at the takeaway on Castle Road the night of the eighth of May when Ms Okokon and Ms Warszawska were discovered at the address on Queen's Terrace. And now you have him returning stolen goods to Mr Yates?'

'Not exactly.' Trev has the footage on his phone and shows it to Harrie and Parvez.

'Do you know who the young 'un is?' Harrie asks Trev. He shakes his head. 'Nor do I,' she says. 'Another question for Mr Smith. We've got officers searching Smith's home address. Trev, will you liaise with them and let us know if something comes up? Also get on with finding an ID on Jayson's delivery boy. Donna, you and I will interview Smith. OK?'

Adrenalin or something is keeping her upright and she'd rather be focused on the nefarious doings of Jayson Smith than those of her husband. She nods.

Harrie continues: 'Given Smith's possible connection to the trafficking investigation, Parvez will be watching on video link.'

Parvez? Does Donna detect a bond coursing through Shilling's and Khan's stances? If so, it quickly evaporates.

A brief review of Jayson Smith's previous shows Donna how he has gone from sallow youth to a young man in his mid-twenties who took up pumping iron during a short stay in prison. He also got himself a fine array of tats on his forearms: a rose briar on one, a grinning, contorted skull on the other. Although his teeth are still yellowed and crooked, his skin has a healthier colour than the police photos of his younger self.

Jayson has the duty solicitor sitting next to him. Despite being hardly more than thirty years of age, strands of white are creeping into his dense crop of dark hair, maybe as a consequence of his job. The harsh overhead light shows up the cheap sheen of his suit.

Harrie has agreed Donna should start with what happened at Gordon Yates's. If Smith gives up the name of the other boy, then Trench can get on and bring him in. However, Jayson watches the snippet of video impassively and decides on 'no comment' to all Donna's prodding. She sits back for Harrie to continue.

She begins, 'A young woman was raped at between ten-thirty p.m. and eleven-thirty p.m. on Saturday the twenty-sixth of April at the corner of Park Avenue and the A170. What can you tell us about it, Mr Smith?'

Jayson shrugs, he leans back, his arms resting on his thighs, 'Nothing. I don't know nothing about it.' He sounds unflustered. Donna watches carefully as Harrie shows Jayson a photo of Abi and receives another shrug. Maybe his demeanour is cagey. Perhaps this is merely the result of having a record.

Harrie asks: 'For the tape, do you not recognise the woman in the photo or are you saying "no comment"?'

'Whatever you like, love.' His grin is cocky.

'DS Shilling to you, Mr Smith. Which is it?' Harrie waits.

Finally Jayson says, 'Don't know her, OK.' He sounds bored.

Shilling continues with: 'Where were you on the evening of the twenty-sixth of April?'

His gaze whips to the ceiling and back. 'No comment.'

'You have chosen to go to "no comment" when you were being so helpful?' Harries says sardonically.

His glare says, *And what're you going to do about it?* while his solicitor bestirs himself to point out his client's rights.

'Mr Smith,' Harrie leans slightly forward. 'You do realise how serious rape is, don't you?'

Jayson stares at his hands now clasped in his lap.

'Mr Smith, we have found your DNA on a condom at the site of the rape.'

The impact is immediate. Jayson crosses his arms, lurches upright, 'It wusn't me, must be a set up, I wouldn't put it past you lot—'

His solicitor shakes his head, says wearily, 'And this condom was definitely used in the rape?'

'If it wasn't, then maybe Mr Smith would like to explain what it was doing there?'

The solicitor looks at Jayson, who squeezes his eyes closed.

'Where the fuck did you say it was found?' he asks in a taut voice.

Harrie repeats the location and then helpfully adds its connection to the park.

'Well why the fuck didn't you say so in the first place?'

says Jayson, everything about him wired. 'I was there with a lass, the other evening, just hanging out, then things got, you know, interesting.'

'You were there with Abi Davis on the twenty-sixth of April and things got out of hand and you raped her,' Harrie's voice is commanding.

Jayson blinks several times. 'No, no, you've got me all wrong, I wouldn't . . . I don't need to, if you get my meaning.' His grin arrives and then disappears quickly as he realises its inappropriateness. Jayson sets his elbows on the table. 'Look, I feel right sorry for this lass, Abi is it? But it wusn't me and that's the truth.'

Harrie says, 'We need to speak to this girl you say you were with.'

'I can't,' he shakes his head. 'We were just messing, but we weren't meant to be messing if you know what I mean.'

Harrie moves her elbows to the table as if she is about to start arm wrestling with their suspect. She says softly, 'Rape is serious, Mr Smith. I would suggest causing some discomfort in relations amongst your entourage is minor compared to being charged with rape. Where were you on the twenty-sixth of April?'

Jayson throws up his hands, 'I told you I wusn't there—'

'Prove it,' Harrie cuts him off.

Jayson pushes his chair back until it hits the wall behind him. He crosses his arms. He views Harrie through slitted eyes. 'No comment,' he says clearly.

Shilling also sits back and after a moment nods at Donna. She says, 'Mr Smith, what were you doing on the evening of Thursday the eighth of May around seven-thirty p.m.?'

His attention dragged onto Donna, Smith initially appears a little bewildered. 'I don't know, Detective Constable.' He continues in a slightly poshed up tone: 'I'd have to check my diary.'

'We have CCTV of you buying pizzas on Castle Road and then coming up to Queen's Terrace. Where were you going?'

'To see a mate.'

'Address?'

He shrugs.

'You don't know where your mate lives?'

'Maybe I don't want to tell you. GDPR or summat?'

'Not in a police investigation.' Donna holds up a pen as if ready to note down the information she guesses won't come. It doesn't.

'No comment,' Smith says to his chest.

'I put it to you, Mr Smith, you were going to a house on Queen Street where trafficked women were being held. What can you tell me about that?'

If possible Jayson slumps further.

Donna can feel every muscle in her body on alert. *He knows something*. 'When you arrived to find the police at the house, you scarpered.' After a beat, she adds: 'Mr Smith, I saw you.' Then: 'You can be identified.' This is a stretching of the truth agreed with Harrie.

Jayson puts a hand to his face. Mutters something, it sounds like bitch or possibly bitches.

'Mr Smith, did you call me bitch?'

Nothing comes from the drooping head. The room has grown overheated and there is the hint of sweat pervading.

A lorry huffs and puffs at the traffic lights outside, diesel wafts in through one of the windows, high in the wall, which has an ill-fitting frame.

The solicitor moves as if to get up. 'OK, I think we need a break and I need to speak to my client.' He looks from one detective to the other.

Both Harrie and Donna know they will be unlikely to get anything further from Smith after his solicitor has talked to him. However, they also know they cannot refuse the request. Harrie says, 'I do hope common sense will prevail and Mr Smith will see it is in his interests to cooperate. Meanwhile I would like to remind you both, we have officers searching Mr Smith's address for corroborating evidence on his whereabouts on the twenty-sixth of April and eighth of May.'

Jayson Smith shifts uneasily in his seat. 'Can I go now? I'm dying for a piss,' he says angrily.

Chapter 26

Hannah is surprised when Felka says she is ready to go to the police. 'It has to be now,' she announces. 'I only have nerves now.' Being with Blessing has had an emotional toll and Hannah would rather have some time to herself, to read or listen to music. However, she knows Felka's statement is important and putting it off even a few hours (judging by her countenance) could mean it never gets done. Therefore, she takes the two sisters down to the police station. She is glad when it is DC Donna Morris who appears. She had previously found her attentive and perceptive. Today she is dressed in a rather unbecoming waist-less dress and appears hot and tired. Even so, she greets the three of them with a smile and leads them up to a room with comfortable furnishings. Felka and Zlota sit on a sofa. Hannah and Donna take an easy chair each.

When invited to, Felka tells her story. She describes growing up with a father slogging to make ends meet and a sister toiling equally hard to make up for the absence of their mother. The small town felt oppressive to the young Felka. She did not excel at school, opportunities were limited and all she wanted was to get out. She began waitressing at a small bar serving food. It was here one night Marius Badea walked in. With his smart suit, polished shoes, flashy watch and seemingly endless cash, he was what Felka had been waiting for. He said he owned restaurants in Sicily and could give Felka a job. She went with him without telling her sister or father, because she knew they would object. It turned out Badea did not own anything. However, he did get her work in a bar owned by an associate. It was a bit seedier than the one Felka had left, no food and a sleazy floor show, but she was somewhere new. 'It was exciting, you understand. Marius had lots of friends. He showed me a good time. And he never . . .' Here she pauses to swallow. She says softly, her gaze sideways at her sister, 'He never made me do anything I didn't want to do.'

She didn't keep in proper contact with her family back in Poland. 'Marius said best not to, my sister would only try to stop the fun.' Again the sliding look at Zlota who is studiously examining her carefully polished nails. Felka explains this situation went on maybe six months, then Marius told her he has a new venture in the UK, in Manchester, and he wants her to come with him. In the end he went on ahead and she was told to come after with another woman. This was when she met Blessing. Marius instructed Felka she must see Blessing through passport control at Manchester and she was given (by one of Marius's associates) documents for her. 'An Italian passport. I knew Blessing was not Italian. I was scared.' She rubs at her arms as if she is cold. 'But I want to see Marius and he is in this place Manchester. So, of course, I go. And I am so anxious, I am almost sick. But it is easy, so easy.' Another swallow and she asks for some water. Donna suggests a break for tea or coffee. Felka shakes her head, 'I must say it now.' She takes a long draft from the glass Donna brings her.

The room is warm and feels close now, like the story is drawing them together and holding them fast in its net. Hannah is glad that the detective constable has thought to provide everyone with water. Its coolness is a relief to her throat – lifting her arm to get the drink to her lips allows some tension to ease from her shoulders.

Felka goes on. 'Everything changes in Manchester. I am kept in this horrible house with other girls. They work, you know, are working girls. I am not.' She sits up straight. 'I help clean, make food, that sort of thing. Marius would not expect me to . . .' She stops. 'It is not for ever, he says. Just for a little while.' She sounds tearful. 'When I hear from my sister, it is good. I think maybe of leaving.' Zlota touches her arm. 'Yes, I think maybe of going back home.' She takes a breath. 'But then it is all turned upside down.' Her version of the night of the move to Scarborough is very similar to Blessing's. 'Mr T makes me work, like Marius never would.' She slumps over. 'I don't hear of Marius any more. I don't know where he is.'

Donna gently asks her various questions that could elicit information which would identify the two guards. At each one Felka shakes her head. When Donna asks whether she has her own mobile or email account or any contact information for Badea, Felka says: 'No, no, no.' Then she pushes herself upright against the back of the couch, 'I tell you I don't know any more. I have nothing more to say.' Zlota adds that she will take her sister home now.

After this, Donna thanks Felka for coming in and being

so cooperative. She hands over her card, says either sister can be in touch at any time. Then she shows them all out again.

Once on the street, Felka smiles widely and says she wants a drink. Zlota agrees to take her to a pub. Hannah wants desperately to be in her own house and on her own, to be alone with her thoughts. As she leaves them she can't help but think Felka's narrative all sounded rather rehearsed. But then, why wouldn't it be? If the young woman had been getting up the courage to speak, she would have gone over it in her head to get it straight. Though getting a story straight does not guarantee the truth of it. And Hannah reckons there is something off with Felka's version, if only what she said about her role in the brothel in Manchester. *So she is protecting herself, or her sister,* Hannah disparages herself. *It doesn't mean everything else is false. And DC Morris was satisfied, so it must be OK.*

Chapter 27

Donna returns to the CID offices to find Theo has joined Parvez and Harrie. They are discussing the interview with Jayson Smith. The NCA officer is being surprisingly upbeat. 'You did well to push him,' Parvez now includes Donna in his praise. She notices Harrie's pleased expression. Parvez continues, 'He's rattled. Rattled people make mistakes. And now we've got this link with Hull.'

Theo answers Donna's enquiring look with the information that a torn-up train ticket has been found in Jayson's bin. If he used it, he went to Hull on 26 April. DS Spinelli would be following up. A house-to-house has also yielded neighbours saying Smith had been coming and going at odd hours, though this is not unusual for him.

Donna reports back on Felka's statement. Theo catches onto her disquiet. Donna explains the young woman was economical with the truth when talking about what she did in Manchester. Does this mean she wasn't wholly accurate about other things?

'It would be unusual if she told us everything first time around,' says Parvez. 'Sounds like she's in deep. We will have to keep an eye on her and keep pushing. We can't treat her as merely a victim.'

This does not alleviate Donna's discomfort. Does he

mean she didn't try hard enough in her questioning?

The others have moved on to the big news. The young lad caught on camera making the delivery to Gordon Yates has been identified as Kyle Geraty. He has been picked up and fingerprinted. He is currently being interviewed by Trench and a colleague.

Donna is able to grab a sandwich and a fruit tea before the interview with Jayson Smith is reconvened. His solicitor has a written statement: 'If Mr Smith did say "bitch" it was not directed towards DC Morris. However, he apologises if any of his language has offended anyone. He has already explained why his DNA may be on a condom found in the area of interest to the police. And is willing to provide the name of the witness—'

'Yes?' Harrie interrupts.

The solicitor looks at Jayson who reluctantly gives a woman's name and a mobile number. The solicitor reads on: 'He knows nothing about the rape of Ms Abi Davis. On the eighth of May he procured a pizza and was going to the Castle Dykes to eat it. He has no knowledge of people trafficking. He has no more to say.' Both Jayson and his solicitor sit back in their chairs.

'You were going the wrong way for the Castle Dykes,' says Donna.

'No comment.' The response is almost a sneer.

Donna feels her irritation rising. It's been a long day. She is exhausted from keeping thoughts of Jim at bay. An image comes to her of Abi in her hospital bed, her white, pinched face, her fingers plucking anxiously at the sheets.

She practically killed herself for Chrissake. She's not going to recover quickly. And what of Blessing and Felka? Nor are they. Women harmed by men. Her fury about Jim reignites. *And Jayson, you know something.* Annoyance weighs into her tone: 'Where were you on the twenty-sixth of April and the eighth of May?'

'No comment.'

Harrie says, 'We have a train ticket for Hull dated the twenty-sixth of April found in one of your bins. Will we find you travelled there?'

There's half a beat before the flat 'No comment' comes.

He is worried about something. Donna relaxes a tad. She picks up her pen, a sign to Harrie that she is taking over the questioning. She tempers her voice, makes like this could be a friendly chat. 'You've experienced prison, Jayson, you're bright enough not to want to go back there. Abi Davis, Blessing Okokon and Felka Warszawska, they've all been badly hurt. Won't you help us to find out what happened to them?'

Jayson lets the tip of his tongue run along his yellow teeth and dry lips. He has a sidelong glance at his solicitor.

'Come on Jayson,' Harrie says encouragingly. 'Drop the "no comment", tell us what you know.'

Jayson's gaze goes to the floor. It's his solicitor who replies, 'Mr Smith has every right to stick to "no comment". He's already responded to your questions as best he can. He has no more to say.'

'I think he has a lot more to tell us,' says Donna. She noticed Jayson's greater discomfort when Blessing and Felka were mentioned. Abi's name and photo meant nothing to him. *But maybe he didn't see her? Maybe he didn't know her name?* She picks up on a thread she and Harrie had agreed they might use if nothing else worked.

'Mr Smith, where were you between eleven-thirty and midnight on November fifth, 2012.'

He's about to shrug and give the stock rejoinder, then something stills him. He gazes up at Donna without moving his head. He is reminded by his solicitor that he doesn't have to answer and Jayson nods slowly. Then he says, 'It was the night our lass Kelsey was raped and you fuckers have done nowt about it.' He sounds genuinely upset.

'You know Ms Geraty?'

'Her mum and mine are like sisters. If you think I'd have done anything to hurt her, you're more cracked than I thought.' Jayson Smith has his hands in fists. The roses on his arm bloom while the skull bloats. A coiled cobra-ness insinuates into his frame. 'You had 'im, you had the fucker and you let him go. Just cos I don't have a posh accent like him, I'm stuck in here and he's free to do it again. You're gobshite.'

It takes a moment for Donna to digest all of this. At least it explains one thing. 'Which means you know Ms Geraty's brother and can explain why you accompanied him to Gordon Yates's house to deliver a box of stolen goods?'

'No comment.' Jayson has gone limp, his attitude and tone is back to can't-be-bothered.

'Would you like to add something to your statement?' asks Donna, aware once more of the fetid air in the room and the traffic noise outside.

'No comment.' Then he juts his chin upwards: 'Can I go now?'

'No,' Harries says firmly. 'We may be gobshite, Mr Smith, but it'll be you who is staying in our cells until we get some more answers. And if that means we have to extend your custody time, we will do so.'

There is a quick exchange of glances between Jayson and his solicitor. Then Jayson shrugs, grudgingly stands and slowly walks out of the room to be handed over to the custody sergeant.

Chapter 28

Donna rolls into bed as soon as she gets home, exhausted. At 4 a.m. she is wide awake and there is a chiselling headache threatening. She pulls on joggers and a fleece, and goes to the kitchen. Through the small square window the sky is already a deep indigo, the hinterland between night and day. She takes painkillers and makes herself a cup of lemon and ginger tea.

Jim was her first thought on waking, however, now her mind strays to sisters. Felka and Zlota. Abi and hers. Donna never had a sibling. Would it have been different if she had? Like Felka she fled a situation she found suffocating to follow an unsuitable man, who, luckily for her, was no Marius Badea. Donna paces the kitchen, opening cupboards.

She doesn't know what she is looking for until she starts to gather the ingredients for a *makowiec*. Her mother was (*is?*) a fine cook and, growing up near the border of East Germany and Poland, this was something she would frequently bake. Of course, she had the wherewithal because she toed the line, didn't question the regime. *She did it for me*, Donna now thinks. She understands the lengths a mother will go more than she did as a teenager. *I wish I had been more considerate then.*

She quickly realises she does not have the crucial poppy seeds. She reassesses her options. All last autumn, her next-door neighbour, Rose, kept her supplied with the produce from her garden and allotment, especially berries. And like Donna's mother, Rose bottles and preserves for the lean times. Donna devours all she is given; consequently what she is left with are two overripe bananas. She changes her plan to making a bread with them. The familiar actions of measuring, chopping and mixing soothe her. Once the tin is in the oven, she goes into her lounge and opens up her laptop. She spends some time prevaricating, searching, wording, deleting and then rewording, until she has put a message on a Facebook group for former residents of East Berlin. She presses enter as the timer pings to tell her the banana bread is ready.

Once it is cooling, she curls up on the sofa, meaning only to doze as it is too near getting up time to sleep. She is shocked to find herself dragged from a deep slumber by what she thinks is her alarm bell. It is not. It is the land-line she had forgotten she even had connected. Who has she given the number to? Jim, she realises too late as she lifts the receiver and hears his voice. Her instinct is to crash the handset down again. Instead she clenches her fist around it.

'Donna, love, is that you? At last, I was getting worried. I have been trying to get hold of you. I guess you have been busy. I wouldn't have bothered you so much, only it's about Christopher . . .'

Her stomach plummets.

'Nothing serious . . .'

'What's happened?' she barks.

'Fell off his bike, silly boy, just a graze and a twisted ankle. I thought you should know.'

She can't work out whether to be relieved or cross. 'Why didn't he ring me?'

'I said not to worry you. He's fine. He only told me because we were talking about the business anyway.'

Now the conversation has started down this track, Donna is finding it hard to steer it otherwise. 'Well, thanks for letting me know.' *He's managed to get me to be grateful?*

'And he's coming up here next weekend. I thought maybe you'd like to come over. I know it's your weekend without Elizabeth.'

He's carrying on as if nothing has happened? Maybe nothing did? It's like she has slipped into a parallel universe. 'And will she be there?' Donna says softly. 'Will Wendy be there?'

'Oh I don't think so – why should she be? It'll just be the four of us. Chris's wife of course will come. We had a good time at Christmas didn't we?'

Why should she be? 'Jim, I saw you with Wendy,' Donna forces the words out of her mouth. 'It can never be like it was at Christmas.'

'Now Donna, there's no reason to take on so. We're still a family.'

'At least apologise, James,' shouts Donna. 'At least show a little contrition.'

'What for?' he says blandly. 'You sound upset, love. Is it all your health problems flaring up again? I thought the doctor had got you sorted?'

'It's not my bloody womb that's the problem here, it hasn't

179

affected my eyesight.' She's screaming and hates herself for it. 'It's you shagging my friend, my ex-friend.'

'No love . . .' he starts. 'You've got it all wrong.'

She slams the phone down before he hears the wail which wrenches itself free. Unaware of the time, she goes upstairs, flops into bed and pulls the duvet over her, tears flooding out of her along with hiccupping sobs. *It can't be, he's not just going to ignore it, deny it?* When thoughts can form, it is disbelief and anger which predominate.

It must be a good forty minutes before she rouses herself enough to look at the clock. *Mein Gott!* She is already an hour late into work.

She is clumsy and slow getting ready and it is mid-morning before she reaches the CID offices, her banana bread held in her hands like a peace offering. Immediately she is pulled into a vortex of activity. There have been developments, explains Theo, hardly pausing to greet her, ask her if she is OK and receive her assurance that she is fine. Gus (or DS Spinelli as Theo calls him in front of DI Lukasz Mazur, who is also present) has discovered what Jayson Smith was doing in Hull on 26 April. A mix of CCTV and good old-fashioned talking to the locals has confirmed he arrived off the Scarborough train at eight-thirty in the evening and met with a couple of local taxi drivers. He handed over packages to them. Then he went onto several pubs until at least midnight. It is unclear what he did there – he's seen talking to people, buying rounds, nothing incriminating. On the following Monday, the taxi drivers paid in one thousand pounds each in takings at two local banks for which they gave Gus suspect explanations. DS Khan and Harrie are re-interviewing Smith. Donna is told to grab a tea and join Theo and Lukasz to watch the video link.

Grateful not to have received any scrutiny and to have something else to think about, Donna does as she is bid, supplying the others with slices of her banana bread for good measure. She is gratified both Theo and Lukasz make appreciative noises when they taste it and they all settle down to watch the screen.

Harrie is explaining to Jayson that they have confirmed his story of impulsive sex in the park with the woman concerned and they also know he was not in Scarborough on 26 April, so he is no longer arrested on suspicion of rape.

He makes to push himself to his feet. 'I told you I had nuthin' to do with it. I'll be going then.'

'Not so fast. We are rearresting you on suspicion of money laundering and people trafficking.'

'This sounds like a fishing expedition,' the solicitor objects.

'I think you will find Mr Smith has some questions to answer. For instance, Mr Smith, what were you doing in Hull on the evening of the twenty-sixth of April?'

'No comment.' Jayson dips his head and fidgets. As Harrie takes him through what Gus has discovered about his schedule on that night, he continues to answer, more and more monotonously, 'No comment.'

Donna would have thought he had stopped listening, except for the rigid set of his spine.

Harrie persists in her methodical way, going on to his involvement in trafficking. She suggests each time Jayson

181

was noted as being absent from his house by his neighbours or caught on CCTV in Castle Road, he was going to the house on Queen's Terrace. His response remains the same. Finally she says, 'You do realise, Jayson, we've had forensic officers crawling all over the Queen's Terrace address. If your DNA or fingerprints are there, we will find them.' She pauses, then adds: 'Every contact leaves a trace, you know that better than some.' Another beat before she leans forward, 'Come on, Jayson, we know you were working for someone else. Why take the rap for them?'

Smith does not react immediately. Donna can see he is considering what Harrie has said.

Perhaps Parvez does not intuit this when he adds: 'You're a minnow in this, Jayson, we just want the sharks.'

At this, Donna can see Jayson bridling. *He doesn't like being called small.*

'No comment,' he says with a sneer.

'Fuck,' says DI Mazur.

Jayson's solicitor intervenes, also leaning in. 'Stow your trawling gear, officers,' he says, like he's a local fisherman confronting the bigger boats which threaten his livelihood. 'My client's custody time is about up.'

'He won't be getting bail,' says Harrie quickly. 'A flight and intimidation risk.'

The solicitor is on the verge of objecting when Jayson raises his hands and shrugs.

Maybe he does fear the sharks, thinks Donna.

'One more thing, Mr Smith,' says Harrie. 'My colleagues have been talking to Kyle Geraty. He has admitted to robbery and common assault on Gordon Yates. He doesn't have your facility with "no comment", plus his fingerprints match a partial lifted from the back door.'

'And you are telling my client this why, DS Shilling?' asks the solicitor, sounding weary.

Harrie keeps her gaze on Jayson. He meets it. She goes on: 'He said you persuaded him to return the stolen goods. What's that about, Jayson? Suddenly got a conscience?' Smith does not say anything. Harrie continues: 'What about the trafficked women? Don't they deserve your compassion?'

The solicitor says quickly, 'Mr Smith has denied all knowledge of trafficking. Now are we done?'

As he rises, Jayson says softly, 'Mr Yates is one of ours.' He juts out his chin. 'We don't work over one of our own.'

Harrie does not get a chance to give a retort to Jayson as his solicitor practically shoves him out the door into the arms of the custody sergeant. Probably a good thing – her glower as she and Parvez return to the CID offices reveals how she might have chewed him out.

DI Mazur also appears unhappy. 'I think we missed a trick there,' he says to his DS, who shrugs.

Donna reckons Parvez knows his senior means the 'we' to be 'you'.

Lukasz goes on: 'We'll get out of your hair. We've still got our Europol query on the Queen's Terrace building and now we'll get on with chasing the money trail.'

'Two thousand pounds,' says Donna. 'And perhaps more if Jayson did meet with other contacts in the pubs. It can't all come from the proceeds of the brothel?' She doesn't want to think about what this might mean Blessing and Felka went through.

Lukasz shakes his head. 'There'll be the income from other businesses. Car washes, nail bars, cleaning. And then more if they are bringing the people into the country, as they probably are. For a lorry, the fee can be six hundred pounds per person, ten people per lorry, two lorries a night, we're talking twelve thousand pounds seven days a week.'

The relief Donna feels at the beginning of the DI's explanation quickly dissolves into new horror.

The two NCA officers appear unperturbed as they disappear into their broom cupboard.

There's a pause amongst the local officers before Theo quietly asks Harrie to follow-up on enquiries into the activities of Tony Finch as well as Jayson Smith. 'We know from the security team at the nightclub, Finch has not been around as often recently. So where was he?'

Once it is just the two of them, Donna regains her voice to tell Theo about Abi coming to talk the next day. She also explains what she has learned about Stella, including that she could not have told Nate about the rape.

Her DI takes a moment to consider all this information. 'So Stella could have returned home on the twenty-sixth and Nate knew about the rape without being told?'

'Without being told by Stella, when he said it was her who had given him the information,' clarifies Donna. 'I'd still like to know what has brought Withenshaw and Stella Horsham together.'

'Me too.'

'Will we talk to him again?'

Theo nods. 'But let's wait until we've seen Ms Davis. And what about that red dress? Chase it up will you, Donna?' As she turns, he adds: 'You must be pleased.'

'What about?'

'As soon as I get onto the DCI, Khalil Qasim will be released, hopefully today.'

She smiles for the first time for ages it feels like. 'Aren't you glad?'

'Yes, Donna, I am. Very.'

Chapter 29

Theo suggests they walk and get a sandwich on the way. Donna is relieved to escape the stuffiness of the CID offices. From the top of the South Cliffs gardens, the sky is the crown of a lapis lazuli Fabergé egg. The sun its gilding. They take the path down through beeches, birches and oaks bursting with foliage and the chitter of small birds. The café sits on a balcony with a view across the bay to the harbour. They order and find an exterior table. The sea is a spread of parachute silk, RAF blue. *There's a term for the quality of this air*, thinks Donna. *Like vodka? No, gin. Gin clear.* They drink in the view while they wait.

They've both ordered ham, cheese and mustard toasties. As they tuck in, Theo asks Donna how she is doing. 'It's been pretty full on these last few days. And you were in for the whole of Sunday weren't you?'

'I'm OK,' she says carefully, not wanting to spoil the uplift in her mood.

'Has something happened?'

When he watches her like that with those dark eyes behind his metal-rimmed glasses, Donna feels the compulsion to speak the truth. She wonders whether he has the same effect on suspects in interviews. Like them, she wishes she has the option of 'no comment'. There's no way she wants to share the images of Jim and Wendy, which still return with the power to knock the breath from her chest. Instead she says, 'I've been considering the DC vacancy.' She hasn't. 'I think I will apply for it.' She only makes up her mind as she speaks.

'You've discussed it with your family?'

She nods. She hasn't. Not even Elizabeth. This is a decision she's taking for herself, by herself. The last time she did this was over thirty years ago. *And look where that got you?* a snarky voice inside her says. *Made yourself, to all intents and purposes, an orphan.* She flashes back, *Made myself a new life with two gorgeous children.* Deliberately leaving aside the husband for the moment. *I am good at leaving,* she reminds herself. *No long goodbyes.*

Abi and her sister are staying at a bed and breakfast in a tall Edwardian house on one of the quiet streets just back from the Esplanade. When Donna and Theo arrive, Una leaves to go shopping. Given no one with Newcastle on their doorstep is likely to find Scarborough shops particularly fascinating, Donna understands this is Abi manoeuvring her sister out the way. *Perhaps she feels she has to in order to be more open?* Donna thinks hopefully.

They are in a gracious lounge at the front of the building which has an impressive, tiled fireplace filled with a spray of dried flowers. Cornicing and other evidence of its elegant past adorn the room. Abi sits on a big sofa, her feet tucked under her, while the officers take the large easy chairs.

Abi appears more anxious than ever. She is wearing a long chunky cardigan wrapped round her like a blanket. She fingers its edge as if it's a keyboard. 'You keep saying you need to know who I was meeting that night.' Her tone is snappy. 'I don't know why. How will it help you find out who raped me?'

Donna begins to say, 'I understand it's difficult—'

'Do you? Do you really?' Abi's whole posture tautens. 'Do you know what it's like to be hit and hit again and thrown down and for it to happen when you don't want any of it, dog shit in your mouth, up your nose. He, he pushed me, he threatened me, he hurt me . . .' The words bang out of her until she runs out of breath.

Briefly disconcerted, nevertheless Donna attempts to pick out a strand which could move them forward. She asks if Abi heard her attacker's voice.

'No, no, no.' Abi looks miserably at her jerking hands. 'He didn't say anything, but I knew, I knew if I didn't do as he said, he'd kill me. I can't tell you any more.'

'Ms Davis,' Theo says gently. 'Please tell us about the man you were going to meet.'

'Because you are going to find out anyway when you take my phone.' If anything, her expression becomes even more wretched. 'It was Nate, Nate Withenshaw.'

The atmosphere around Donna suddenly seems to harden, as if the oxygen has solidified. For a moment, her mind and mouth won't act together.

Luckily, Theo's self-possession doesn't desert him. He asks Abi to tell them more.

'Like what?'

'Like how did you meet him?'

This is an inspired choice of a way in, as the memory

brings the tension down in her body and allows her to speak more fluently. 'I met him at the Christmas party at work, end of last year. You know what it's like, drinks, nibbles, music, a chance to let your hair down a bit. And Nate was . . .' She pauses. 'He was just nice. Attentive. Not pushy like some of the blokes. We chatted about stuff. He has lived in Sicily. I've always wanted to go to Italy. It sounded so, so glamorous.'

'Who invited him?' asks Theo into the gap she leaves.

'What? Not sure. He owns the accommodation by the hospital, maybe . . . No, actually, I think Stella Horsham from HR invited him.'

Nate and Stella? Again? Donna ponders this strange twosome.

Theo encourages Abi to go on. She describes roses coming in the New Year. More on Valentine's Day. *Aren't we over that?* Donna wonders at how these romantic gestures still have such meaning to a woman of the younger generation. *Obviously not.* There was coffee in the hospital café, then a few in town. A trip to the cinema. As she goes along, Abi does get more cagey. Is it just as she gets closer to the failed date in April? Donna does not think so. There is something else. When Abi comes to a halt again, Donna prompts her, 'And what happened on the twenty-sixth of April?'

Abi looks down. Her dark hair curtains her face. Her fingers restart their scales. 'We were going out to dinner. Our first proper date, well I thought it was.'

'You got a lovely new dress and everything,' says Donna softly.

Abi nods. She finds a tissue to dab at her pinkening nose. She says firmly, 'I told you what happened. He didn't turn up. I phoned him. He said he didn't think it was a proper arrangement. I went home. I was raped.' She gasps air in. 'Why aren't you looking for my rapist?' her tone is shrill. 'Instead of asking me these stupid questions? Nate was looking after Stella Horsham's mother that night. He told me. And anyway, anyway, he wouldn't, he would never . . .' She puts her face in her hands.

The two officers wait. Donna suggests a break and a cuppa.

Abi shakes her head. 'I just want you to go,' she mutters.

'A few more questions,' says Theo. 'Then we will leave you in peace.'

'I get no peace,' says Abi grimly. With an obvious effort, she wipes herself up until her reddened eyes glare out at them from her white face framed by her raven-wing mane.

Before the meeting, they agreed Donna would ask once more about the pills. She is not certain how it fits here, however, Theo indicates she should go on with the question. 'The pills, Abi, which you took. Where did you get them from?'

'What?' She appears disoriented. She says slowly, 'Didn't I say before? I took them. I work in a hospital, for Chrissake. Pills are everywhere.'

Then, from nowhere, something occurs to Donna: 'Did someone ask you to get them?'

'What? No.' Her voice wobbles. Abi really is a terrible liar.

'They were dated the nineteenth of February 2014. That is several months before you were raped. Were you already

190

considering suicide?' She knows the words sound harsh, but she feels the necessity of following this thread. She gauges Theo's approval through his concentration on Abi.

'No,' she says. Then reassessing her answer, 'I mean . . .'

'Abi,' Donna says firmly, 'why did you take those pills?'

'Ah,' her hands fling themselves upwards. 'What does it matter? I've thrown away my career. I really loved my job.' She plummets forwards, her elbows on her knees, her fingers in her hair. 'No one, no one will ever employ me as a nurse again.'

Donna feels caught by the younger woman's sadness as if by a riptide.

'I got them for him, for Nate. He said Mrs Horsham, Stella's mother, was having trouble sleeping and asked for my advice. Of course, I told him to go to the GP first. But he said Stella was dead set against getting her mother onto more prescription drugs and then he said Mrs Horsham was really suffering.' Her voice goes small. She shrugs. 'I thought I was helping.'

'So you took, what? Two tubs of temazepam?'

'It just happened that way. They had been prescribed for two different patients. One sadly died. The other got moved on, more quickly than expected. Only a couple of pills had been used from each tub and I should have returned them to the pharmacy. Instead I filled in the paperwork to say one had gone with the patient and the other had got lost. It sometimes happens, they get swept up with the deceased's effects.'

For a moment, Donna can see the competent nurse.

As Abi continues, she disintegrates. 'I kept the pills.

Nate had only asked for one tub, so I gave him it. I held onto the other because . . . Oh I don't know, I suppose I thought it might keep him coming back?' She looks up, wide-eyed. 'Stupid, stupid. I have been so stupid.'

Both Theo and Donna lean back, like they've survived a storm which is passing.

'Are we done?' Abi pulls herself into the corner of the sofa, her knees drawn up, her thin arms clasped around them. 'That's Una coming in.'

All at once, Donna can hear sounds exterior to the room, one of them being the front door, the tap of heels in the hall and the call of 'hello.'

'There was his smell,' says Theo quietly. 'Last time, when I mentioned smell, something occurred to you about the man who raped you.'

She hesitates, then shakes her head vehemently, 'You are mistaken.'

Even as Una brings a new energy in with her, the vigour of the outside world, Donna is jolted not just by this, but by the question of a man's smell.

Chapter 30

Wednesday morning and Nate Withenshaw is seated in one of the interview rooms. Donna contacted him after the conversation with Abi. He appears to have been expecting a party on a yacht; he is dressed in a polo shirt, chinos and deck shoes, his hair is shining, his skin tanned. And there is nothing off-the-peg about his glossy solicitor. Both are relaxed, Nate with an easy smile, which he bestows equally on Theo and Donna. She recognises how she is meant to feel consecrated. Instead, she feels faintly oily.

Theo explains (for the tape) that Mr Withenshaw has agreed to assist them further with the investigation into the rape of Abi Davis.

'I don't know how I can,' says Nate. 'I am not acquainted with the young woman personally. And I certainly did not rape her. I don't rape women.'

'Ms Davis has told us you do know each other,' says Theo. 'Indeed were developing a relationship. We already have corroborating evidence from her phone. And I am sure we can get more by asking around, however careful you both were about keeping it quiet.'

'I wouldn't call it a relationship,' says Nate, not missing a beat. 'She's a shy young woman who does a fantastic job as a nurse. I gave her some flowers every now and again. Bought her coffee.'

'You've just said you did not know her,' says Theo.

'She wasn't keen on being gossiped about. I respected her request for privacy.'

'Let's make one thing clear, Mr Withenshaw, this is an investigation about a serious crime. Withholding information is not an option, whatever the reason.'

Nate puts his arms in the air as if Theo had drawn a gun. His tone and expression are grave, 'Of course, Detective Inspector. My mistake.'

Theo continues, 'You have given us your account of what you were doing on the twenty-sixth of April. Is there anything you would like to add to it?'

'I don't think so,' Nate says slowly.

'How about Stella Horsham arriving home sometime before eleven-thirty?'

His forehead rucks. 'Is that what she says she did?'

Donna is pretty sure this is off-script for Nate. Neither officer allows anything to come into their bland expressions.

'Maybe she did and I was not aware,' Nate continues. 'I am a pretty heavy sleeper.'

'Not a great trait for someone caring for a frail, elderly woman,' says Theo.

'I would have heard Eileen's bell, of course I would,' Nate says quickly. He leans forwards and rests his clasped hands on the table, as if to emphasise his earnestness.

'So you were not aware of Stella returning home on the night of the twenty-sixth of April?' says Theo. 'And you stayed at the house all night?'

'That is correct, Detective Inspector Akande.' He continues to look puzzled.

Donna suspects he is doing a good act. 'Ms Davis says you had arranged to meet with her.'

'She was mistaken.'

'She rang you, though. Did you also forget to mention this previously?'

'We may have spoken.' Nate's tone continues to be calm.

'We've seen her phone,' she says. 'You spoke twice. You rang her back at around ten-twenty. Why did you do that?'

Nate narrows his eyes, a caricature of someone trying to recall something. 'She seemed upset when we spoke earlier. I wanted to make sure she was OK.'

Damn you, that's the last thing you were worried about. Another man not taking responsibility. Donna's irritation pushes her into swampy ground, 'I think you were checking where she was. When she told you she was going home, you got yourself over to the pub, followed her until you arrived at your favourite spot for rape—'

The solicitor pounces, 'DC Morris. My client has never been charged with that offence.'

A glimmer of a smile appears on Nate's face.

Theo doesn't leave a gap: 'You asked Ms Davis to supply you with temazepam. Why was that?'

Nate's fingers twitch. His lips appear to freeze, giving them a ghoulish quality.

'Mr Withenshaw, don't answer that,' the solicitor says. 'Detective Inspector, my client agreed to come here to help,' she stresses this word, 'your investigations into an incident of rape.'

195

An incident of rape? Donna notices how this phrase usefully minimises and distances the terror of the act.

The solicitor continues: 'If you are also investigating your complainant's dealings in controlled substances then that is a whole different set of circumstances. I would need to consult with my client as to whether he has anything he could usefully contribute to such an inquiry.' She glances sideways. Nate's head shakes as he dips it forwards. She returns her gaze to Theo. 'Perhaps you have something more than Ms Davis's testimony that connects Mr Withenshaw to the said temazepam? Has he ever been discovered with any in his possession, for instance?'

Theo sits back, as does the solicitor. It is the tactical withdrawal of troops.

Donna moves in. 'How did you know about the rape of Abi Davis?'

Nate turns to her. Though he continues in a measured tone, his posture is showing the strain. 'I'm not sure, if I'm honest.'

'You previously said it was from Stella Horsham, is that correct?'

'It must be correct that I said it, I trust you Detective Constable Morris, but I have forgotten how I heard.'

His solicitor intervenes: 'I think we should call this meeting to a close. My client has already been as open as he can be.'

Donna very much doubts it. 'You told me Ms Horsham informed you of the rape the day before she could have known herself.'

'DC Morris, I said we are done,' the solicitor says firmly.

'Or do you have enough to arrest my client?' She pauses, her carefully made-up visage questioning. 'No, I thought not.' She begins to pack her notebook into her neat leather briefcase. 'Mr Withenshaw, shall we—'

Nate speaks over her, leaning in towards Donna. 'Why would I rape Abi Davis? She would have given me anything I wanted.'

His solicitor's protests are background as Donna meets his glare: 'Rape isn't about sex. It's about power. You got a taste for it with Kelsey Geraty.'

'Enough, DC Morris,' says the solicitor. 'Mr Withenshaw—'

Again Nate ignores her. 'I will tell you something, Detective Constable, that's the person you need to be watching, Kelsey Geraty. She's following me around everywhere I go. Last time she had a baseball bat. I'm the victim here.'

'Do you want to make a formal complaint?'

He shakes his head. 'Just telling you who you should be watching.' He jabs his finger in the direction of her eyes and, despite herself, Donna flinches back.

'Mr Withenshaw,' his solicitor says with greater insistence. 'Shall we go?'

Nate bestows one last smile on both Theo and Donna before exiting the room.

Donna takes a lungful of fuggy air. As Nate came ever closer, she got the full onslaught of his aftershave. It was unmistakable. Donna is certain that, despite her qualms, Abi does know who her rapist is. *If only she would admit it to herself. And to us.*

Chapter 31

It seems as if the amount of clothing Kelsey wears increases in proportion with the growing warmth brought by the spring weather. This Thursday she is dressed in black combats with a matching shirt and brown lace-up boots. 'Military' is the word which comes to Hannah's mind. The outfit is loose, Kelsey's bosom is no longer as noticeable. And her mood has taken a dip. Hannah felt it as soon as she let her client in. Kelsey had been referred because of depression, but there'd always been a fizz of energy, a fizz from her anger, which gave it the quality of storm clouds laden with thunder and lightning. Today is different and Hannah is wondering why that is. She is also wondering what Kelsey is avoiding telling her.

The session began slowly, Kelsey finding it difficult to pick her words, hesitations and silences punctuating her speech. Her brother is in trouble with the police and she believes it is her fault. She's taken too much of their mother's attention. He got lost somehow. She is not doing well on the course she started, eventually admitting to not attending regularly. She doesn't think she can manage it. 'I'm too stupid.' The word 'stupid' returns several times, especially as she begins to talk about the rape. She had been stupid to go with Nate. Stupid to let him do what he did. Stupid to lead him on like she did. Stupid to call it rape. Stupid to trust the police.

Hannah feels as if she is being buried under the weight of 'stupid'. She begins to think herself stupid for not being able to burrow her way out. *Powerlessness,* the notion flits through her mind. *I have to hold on to my own power.* She takes a deep breath, plants her feet firmly on the carpet and pulls herself up straight. In doing so she notices her client is slumped down, her breathing is shallow. She gently breaks into Kelsey's flow, inviting her to take a moment away from the torrent of 'stupid's, to become aware of what her body is doing, of how she is inhaling and exhaling. While going through these exercises, Hannah considers her options. The easiest route would be to discuss some practical solutions to support her client in her studies. Hannah is tempted to ask Kelsey who is calling her stupid. But then there's the intangible, whatever it is Kelsey is skirting around. They are in their usual room, with its high ceilings and cornices. The tall windows are behind Hannah; the sun's rays have reached through the glass and nets to touch her shoulder. There are other therapists working around the building; she can hear a door clang, some chatter from the kitchen, a kettle clicks off. In the end, Hannah allows the quiet between her and Kelsey to settle.

After having found a more comfortable, less beaten down, posture, Kelsey now begins to fidget. Finally she says forcefully, 'Aren't you going to say anything then?'

'What do you want me to say?' Obviously the anger is back, this time it's the clink of flint sharpening on granite.

'You're paid to know, you're paid to tell me, put me right.

Make me feel better. Intya? Get me well. So earn your fucking money.'

'You're angry . . .'

Kelsey starts to clap slowly. It's the same mocking applause Hannah has heard from groups of (frequently male) teenagers when they are trying to intimidate. Their eyes shuttered in case empathy might slip through. A similar zombie-look has taken over Kelsey's features.

She's been perfecting this, the thought troubles Hannah. *To help her feel powerful and better about herself, for a time at least.* 'I can't make you feel anything, no one can – you are in charge of your feelings.'

'What a crock of shit you are. So Withenshaw didn't make me feel like I was nothing, like I was worthless, he didn't make me feel pain.' She's trying to contain her emotion, though her eyes are becoming glassy pools and pink is infusing her chalky face.

'I didn't mean that.'

'What did you mean then?'

Yes, what did you mean, Hannah? She struggles to find an adequate response. 'Nate caused you a great deal of pain and hurt, psychological and physical, as did the subsequent police investigation. And nothing we do here will change this, we can't change reality. However, what we can do here is find a way for you to live a life with that reality in it.'

Kelsey sits back, she's rubbing her arms as if cold. 'I need to get over it, that's what they say.'

'Who does?' For the first time this session, there's something of the connection which they had been building over previous ones.

'They, they, everybody. Everybody's sick of me moaning on.'

'I'm not sick of you and I don't hear you moaning. I'm here to listen.'

'It's been eighteen months, how much longer is it going to hurt, Hannah?' she looks up, vulnerability etched across her face.

Yes. Hannah is glad when she experiences her client allowing this intimacy. *However,* she cautions herself, *there is still something she is not telling me.* 'We find a way for you to live your life with the pain in it,' she says bringing her attention back to Kelsey's body and her movements, her hands sliding from her elbow to her shoulder joint. As she does so the sleeve cuffs shift revealing the wrists underneath. And Hannah sees it. She sits forward slightly. 'Kelsey, have you hurt yourself?'

Kelsey's gaze skitters about, then she drops her head down, letting her hands fall open and still in her lap, 'No.'

Hannah has to force herself not to grab at her client's arm. She remembers her own denial and wonders what would have helped her then. She says quietly, 'I know you are hurting, you don't have to harm yourself to prove it to me. I know it feels like a release short term, but it isn't a long-term solution.'

'You know, you know.' Kelsey glares at her. 'You fucking know nothing.'

Hannah meets her gaze steadily – she has a split second to decide, what would be most supportive to Kelsey? She says evenly, 'I have experienced being sexually violated and I chose at one time to use self-harm as a way of dealing with the hurt. I know it can seem like a good option for a while, but the effects wear off and then escalation can occur. It's like taking drugs.' She holds her breath, was this the right thing to say?

For a moment, there's a softening in Kelsey's expression. Then she crosses her arms, and her face becomes chipped rock. 'I am not self-harming, OK?' She looks theatrically at her watch, 'Now are we done here? I've got places to be.'

'We have ten minutes, I would like you to stay, but you can choose to leave.'

'Ten minutes, OK, so tell me something useful.'

Hannah would have liked to spend the ten minutes in silence or challenge Kelsey in another way, but another part of her is scared she has done the wrong thing and wants to answer Kelsey's criticisms. They spend the final minutes talking about what Kelsey can do to get her studying back on track. Afterwards, when reviewing the session, Hannah is sure this is the least valuable part of the hour. She remains conflicted on whether she took the right course sharing a part of her story. She hears her supervisor saying, if you keep your client's needs paramount there is no right or wrong. *But was it for Kelsey or for me? Was I trying to prove something? Or worse, eliciting her sympathy?*

Chapter 32

Donna hopes the briefing will be mercifully brief. With both investigations stalling, she is exhausted and out of sorts. Yesterday, after the encounter with Withenshaw, Theo gave his mantra that no interview is ever wasted. He doesn't look as upbeat now. They are with Harrie and the two NCA officers in a corner of the CID section. Shilling is using a map to show Mazur and Khan the plethora of ways an individual might get to Queen's Terrace without being detected: through Royal Albert Park or the Castle Dykes or the back streets of the Old Town. She goes on to say that forensics on the house haven't produced a solid lead. Not because everything was wiped clean. Quite the opposite. There is a soup of DNA and a glut of fingerprints. Given the precautions the guards took, these are likely to be punters or previous occupants of the building. She glances at Donna and she offers up the results of her afternoon's work. Books found at the property were obviously secondhand, so she did the rounds of the charity shops. No one could say who had bought them, nor identify Tony Finch as a customer when shown his photo. 'We still do not know if our Mr T is Finch,' she says. 'The T might not even refer to his name. He could be a Gordon or a Prometheus.'

Harrie arches a tweezered eyebrow. 'Prometheus? Where did you get that from?'

She's not really expecting an answer and doesn't get one. However, the atmosphere has lightened a tad. She turns to Lukasz, 'Have you anything?'

'We've got access to the Hull taxi drivers' accounts,' he replies. 'They have made one large cash deposit previously and, as we would expect, they move it on relatively swiftly into several other accounts and so it goes on, until the funds are consolidated again. But it's a bit like following *Alice in Wonderland*'s white rabbit down his burrow at the moment. We have verified the house is owned by a shell company based in Sicily. It'll take more digging to find out the people behind it.'

'A shell company is an inactive one,' says Parvez. 'In this case it will be being used solely for financial manoeuvres.'

Whoops! Donna can tell this bit of 'mansplaining' has gone down badly with Harrie. Maybe she hasn't forgiven his misstep with Jayson either. Or the fruitless day has left her feeling sour.

Theo has been leaning against a desk, arms crossed. He pushes himself to his feet. 'I suggest we won't get any further now. Let's reconvene tomorrow.'

Mazur nods. His DS says brightly, 'We'll be grabbing a bite to eat. Anyone want to join us?'

Aw bless. Donna clocks his hopeful glance at Harrie.

She doesn't see it or ignores it. 'An early night for me,' she says. 'Want a lift, Donna?'

For once, Donna is grateful to forego her walk home. After hasty farewells, she scurries after Harrie.

Once she is driving away from the station, Harrie says, 'Do blokes always have to be so disappointing?'

Two weeks ago, Donna might have said, *No, though nobody is perfect.* Now she says simply, 'Yes.' And Harrie grunts her approval.

After such a troubling session, Hannah desperately wants to go straight home. However, she did promise to meet Zlota at the care home to help her carry the weekly food shop back to the house. Plus Hannah hasn't visited her mother for over a week. She hopes it can be a quick in and out, but her plans are thwarted when Zlota says she can't leave for another ten minutes.

Val Poole is sitting on a sofa in the lounge area. Beside her is Stella Horsham. Between them is a tray of tea and cake. They appear deep in conversation. Hannah considers turning round and waiting for Zlota in the lobby. She is too late. Stella has spotted her. *Sharp eyed that one,* thinks Hannah, preparing her smile for joining the little party.

Her mother doesn't bother to hide her displeasure. Firstly at Hannah's absence for the last ten days. Then at her presence. 'Stella and I were having such a lovely chat,' she says.

'Don't let me stop you,' says Hannah. She helps herself to a cup of tea, which she finds to be stewed. The slice of lemon drizzle she tastes is sublime.

'Hannah must be very busy with her work,' says Stella in her tinkling tone. 'I am sure she comes as often as she can.'

Val humphs. But she has some gossip to impart and Hannah is a new audience. She can't help herself, she blurts out: 'You'll never guess what Stella has just told me.'

'I'm sure I won't,' Hannah takes another bite, perhaps enough sugar will keep her sweet. She almost chokes when her mother divulges the tale. Hannah never expected to hear Nate Withenshaw's name in this context, as prodigal brother to Stella.

'It's all very *Long Lost Family*, isn't it, Hannah?' Val continues. 'I do love that show, don't you, Stella? I sometimes dream of a new daughter coming in through that door. One I didn't know about.'

Maybe the gin has finally addled her mother's brain. How would she not know about a child she gave birth to?

'What, sour puss?' Val looks over at Hannah.

She addresses Stella: 'Did you know about him all along?'

Stella shakes her head. 'Mummy wasn't very well when I was little. She had to go away. I was, oh, about seven. She, well . . .' She dips her head. 'She met someone and fell in love. Only it wasn't to be. And, obviously, she wanted to come back to me. So Nate was brought up by his father and his wife. It was all very cordial. Nate tells me he had a very happy childhood. And I did too, of course.'

Hannah finds all this hard to believe. Eileen Horsham leaves her husband and child because she is ill, but is still healthy enough to have an affair? She gets pregnant and happily hands the child over to her lover and his wife, before returning to her husband and daughter? Then keeps it all secret for forty-odd years. She wonders how she can drill down to get to the truth. Or whether she's even got the energy for it. Before she can try, Stella is asking her about whether she has heard about 'a truly awful attack on a nurse? I know her, of course, poor Abi. Such a wonderful nurse, really an angel.'

Hannah is now regretting the cake, saccharine overload making her feel slightly nauseous.

'You don't know whether they have arrested anyone do you, Hannah?' asks Stella.

'Me? Why should I?'

'Your friend, what was his name? Detective Inspector Akande. Such a nice man. Thank you so much for putting in a word with him about Mummy. I do appreciate it. I can start organising the funeral. Along with Nate, of course.'

As Stella takes a breath, Hannah says, 'I didn't say anything to DI Akande. And he certainly doesn't share with me the state of his investigations.'

'Doesn't he?' Stella looks sad. 'I am surprised they haven't made an arrest, that's all.'

With Kelsey not far from her thoughts, Hannah says, 'Perhaps they don't have enough evidence.'

Desperate not to be left out, Val says, 'But you could talk to him, couldn't you Hannah, ask him about the nurse? It would put Stella's mind at rest.'

'No, Mum, I could not.'

Val *tsks* and apologises for Hannah's manner while Stella says of course she understands confidentiality.

Hannah is relieved to see Zlota waving from the doorway. As she says goodbye, she advises Stella to try the local paper's website for any update on an arrest. After this she quickly retreats.

Once out into the evening air, both women maintain a sprightly pace despite the number of shopping bags. Hannah wonders if Zlota has rather over-compensated the amount of food needed for her sister's presence in the house. She doesn't say anything. Instead they exchange news. When she mentions Stella, Zlota says the older woman called up earlier in the day enquiring when Hannah would be there.

'Why would she do that?' asks Hannah.

'Perhaps she likes you,' responds Zlota.

Even this notion does not dampen Hannah's pleasure at being away from her mother. And Zlota appears in a good mood too. The ambience of the house has improved over the last few days, with Felka being happier and their welcoming of Khalil back to Scarborough. It is a surprise, therefore, that when they reach the front door, they find all is in darkness. And when they step into the hall and call out, there is silence.

Christopher rings when Donna is already undressed for bed. Her delight at speaking with her son is dampened when she realises he is on a mission, a mission to get her to Kenilworth at the weekend. Perhaps he was always closer to his father, though the business they have together buying and converting a rundown warehouse in Birmingham has certainly cemented their relationship.

Do you know how much Jim has hurt me? Donna cannot quite put the thoughts into words. Is it for her to spoil her son's view of his father? He's an adult, but still.

Or maybe he already knows and is OK with it. At this notion her insides shrivel. She did not bring Christopher up to be OK with betrayal. *Did she?* He did not seem overly bothered when he learned about the misinformation she fed him over years about her own childhood.

Does he think what Jim did is some kind of just deserts? She doesn't want to get into this kind of discussion. She keeps her tone easy as she makes certain Christopher knows she is interested in him and pleased to hear from him. But she avoids making any commitment to return to the house she shares with Jim, which she is having difficulty thinking of as home.

After the phone call, Donna lies for a while staring at the ceiling of her square bedroom in this square house at the back of town. If she is going to apply for the DC vacancy, she must do it soon. If she gets it – a big if, she tells herself – she decides she will move, find somewhere to live where, when she opens the window, she can hear the sea.

Hannah has slept several hours. However, in her dreams she's been rushing around trying to clear up a mess which just gets bigger and bigger, so it's as if she's had hardly any respite. She's in her room up in the attic, there are the usual ticks and creaks from the house below. Through the skylight the sky is a fathomless expanse. It is the colour of peeled overripe plums speared by diamante skewers.

She sits up in bed, turns on the light and finds her journal. Last night she wrote about her day. As usual, she avoided more than a sentence about her mother, not wanting to sully the pages with her and the more baffling Stella. Now she does not edit. The word forgiveness comes up several times. *What does it mean?* She's heard all the platitudes and notes them: 'Forgive and forget.' 'Move on.' 'You only hurt yourself by not forgiving, by holding on to all that anger.' *But how do I forgive?* It is a puzzle whose solution has long eluded her. Hannah gets up and opens the window. The cool dampness greets her skin, flushed from not enough rest. Hannah takes lungfuls of the tart air. *We don't forgive. We don't forget. We just find a way to live with the hurt, so it becomes like a limp we accommodate.*

She is pleased with this conclusion and gets back under the duvet to add it to her reflections in her journal before closing it. She is still not ready to sleep. She picks up the book from her bedside table, a poetry anthology of local authors. She finds one to read at random: 'Knitting' by Eta Snave.

> There came a moment of inattention,
> I think I was trying to make sense of my own design,
> when it began to unravel.
> I dropped stitches,
> felt the yarn untwist then knot between my fingers.
>
> There came that moment of inattention,
> when my own fashioning began to seem unwieldy,
> and I purled instead of plained
> and our glorious pattern looked
> awkward, unworked, unbeautiful.
>
> There came this moment
> when I saw what I had done
> and cried.
>
> Then there came another moment
> when together we scooped up the sorry mess

and wove

a variation on what we had before

but more brilliant.

This feels like forgiveness, Hannah decides. She is about to turn to another page when there is tapping at her door. 'Hannah, are you awake?' Zlota whispers.

Hannah invites her in and she comes to sit beside her on the bed. She is wearing pjs and a fleece, even so her feet are bare and Hannah brings her under the duvet. Zlota rests her head on Hannah's shoulder, 'I am very worried about her.'

Hannah puts an arm around her shoulder. On finding Felka gone, Zlota had immediately tried to ring her – on the phone that Felka had denied having to the police, and which Hannah only in that moment discovered existed. Zlota got the answerphone, she left a message and they waited. Hannah suggested going to the police. Zlota would not hear of it. 'It is them she is running away from.' Hannah did not argue, though she considered Felka may be running from her sister, or even towards someone else. Hannah and Zlota agreed they would wait until morning before deciding what to do.

Now Zlota continues: 'Why does she not call back, just to say she is OK? It's not much to ask, is it?' Her sadness is shot with exasperation. 'I don't know why she has gone again. She seemed happy, don't you think, Hannah?'

Hannah agrees.

'What are you reading?'

She shows Zlota the poem. 'I don't know how to knit.'

'It's not really about knitting,' Hannah says. 'It's about building relationships.'

Zlota seems unconvinced. She turns a few pages. 'This one is very long,' she says and puts the book down. 'I taught Felka to cook. We had fun, making cakes, putting, what do you call them? Sprinkles? She always wanted too many.' Zlota chuckles. 'Did Val teach you to cook?'

Hannah shakes her head. 'She wasn't that interested.' *Or maybe I wasn't?*

Zlota is continuing with her own memories, about how, when Felka was upset or ill, Zlota would tend to her, would stay up with her all night.

Hannah notices a queasiness growing in her chest. This is what mothering is about, she knows this, yet descriptions or demonstrations of it can still illicit a wince of envy.

Zlota suddenly sits up straight. 'I have to know where she is.'

Thinking Zlota is going to call Felka again, Hannah suggests leaving it. 'Maybe she just needs a bit of space.'

'From me?' says Zlota, outraged. She is working on her phone, then she shoves it under Hannah's nose. 'Look, the key ring, I gave it to her and it is transmitting.'

There's a pulsating red spot on the road Hannah recognises as leading up the coast north of Scarborough. It is basically in the middle of nowhere.

'We will go there.'

'Zlota, it's the early hours of the morning, how will we get there?'

'Taxi, we will get a taxi.' She throws off the covers. 'Hannah, she might be in trouble.'

'Then we get the police.'

'No!' Zlota stands. 'I go on my own.'

Hannah grabs her arm, 'Wait.' She scrabbles to check the time, it is 4.30 a.m. 'An hour, Zlota, it will be light in an hour. Then we go.'

The other woman droops. Reluctantly she agrees and slides back into the nest Hannah makes for her.

Chapter 33

Donna has slept better. Maybe it was the thought of a room with a view of the sea. When she gets into work just after nine, she receives the handover. Nate Withenshaw's car was vandalised last night between 10 p.m. and 11 p.m. in his club's car park, which is woefully deficient in CCTV. Withenshaw can be so precise about the time because he only went into the bar for an hour to check out a new member of staff. He is utterly convinced he saw Kelsey Geraty scarpering from the scene and is insisting the police arrest her.

The duty detective sergeant looks weary. Nate apparently gave her more than an earful when she suggested waiting for the collection of other evidence, threatening to make a complaint against her for inaction. 'I'm off now,' she says to Donna. 'You decide the best course of action. But I would have a word with Ms Geraty. Chances are you can clear it up one way or another pretty quickly if you do.'

Donna agrees with this rationale and PC Trev Trench is more than willing to come with her to the neat terrace on the Barrowedge estate where the Geratys live. It is Kelsey's mother, Jude, who answers the door. She doesn't look old enough to have a twenty-year-old daughter. She's thickset with dyed blonde hair. 'What do you want, Trev?' she says in a not unfriendly tone. 'Haven't we had enough of you lot recently?'

214

Trench introduces Donna and explains they need to talk to Kelsey. Jude reluctantly lets them in and leads them to the back of the house, calling up the stairs for her daughter. The kitchen is cluttered with crockery, folders of what could be bills and magazines on every surface. Everywhere is spick and span, though, and this is despite a large hairy dog snoring in a basket in the corner. Jude offers beverages and makes coffee for her and Trev, while Donna has a glass of water. Kelsey's mother asks several times what the visit is about, but Trev says they will need to wait for her daughter. She eventually arrives. Donna immediately sees the family resemblance, Kelsey is short and stocky, currently enveloped in layers of fleeces with some trackie bottoms. She accepts a coffee from her mother and then both women sit at the table with Trev and Donna.

'Mr Nathaniel Withenshaw's car was vandalised last night—' begins Donna.

'Right and it has to me,' interrupts Kelsey belligerently. 'Well it wusn't, OK? What would I want with attacking the tosser's car anyway?' She sits back in her chair. Her features tense. Her mother clamps her hand over Kelsey's arm and looks fiercely at the two officers.

Donna says peaceably, 'Would you mind telling me where you were last night, Ms Geraty?'

'Yes, I bloody would. And yous lot would fit me up like you did Kyle whatever I said anyway.'

'Now, love,' says Jude softly, 'you know Kyle did what he did to Mr Yates and it was wrong. I should never have let him stay all those years with his father. It changed him.'

Donna recognises the expression of resignation, almost defeat, which washes over Jude's face. It is one she has worn herself, as a mother realising she's not done enough to stop her child getting into trouble.

Trev says, 'Come on, Kelsey. If you tell us where you were we can clear this up and get out of your hair. You can trust me, can't you?'

Jude nods and gives her daughter's arm a squeeze.

Kelsey sighs. 'I was at the theatre in York. Yes,' she glares at Donna. 'You're surprised, ain't you, that a lass like me would go to the the-a-terr? Well I went OK. It was a performance of *The Merry Wives of Windsor*. Yes! Shakespeare! My mate was in it and they made it all modern with mobiles and stuff. My ex-English teacher from school, the only one who gave a flying fuck about me, she organised an outing for her class. And she had a spare ticket.' She pauses as if something has occurred to her. 'Or maybe she got me a ticket. Anyways, that was where I was. And after the show we got a pizza. Weren't back here before midnight. Here,' she flourishes her phone. 'Got some photos and this is miss's number if you want to check with her.' As Donna takes down the information. Kelsey continues, 'And I'll tell you another thing, I've done nothing to Nate fucking Withenshaw, but he deserves to have his balls cut off for what he did to me.' Her mother nods vigorously. 'And you,' Kelsey points at Trev, 'you know your lot didn't do right by me.'

Donna feels his discomfort. He reaches down to caress the ears of the dog who has been shaken awake by the pitch of Kelsey's voice.

'Thank you, Ms Geraty,' Donna says. 'You have been very helpful and we have everything we need now. We'll be on our way.'

Kelsey snaps her gaze round. She looks like she might find a harsh retort. Then she lets her chin fall to her hands on the table and begins to chew on the skin at the edge of her thumb. It is already ragged.

'Leave it, love,' says her mum. 'Don't spoil your nails, you've just had them done.'

And indeed they are smooth and painted a bright pink.

By the time Donna and Trev return to the police station, Donna has corroborated Kelsey's story with the teacher. She updates the log and ponders who else might want to smash up Nate's sleek motor. *Abi?* She can't imagine the young woman having the strength. For some reason, Stella comes to mind. *But why? Tony Finch pissed off with his boss?* Her thoughts are interrupted by a phone call from Ethan Buckle, crime scene manager. He has sent her an email and asks her to open the attachment. It is an image of a black woollen hat. It was found under the front seat of Withenshaw's car. It rang bells with Ethan, because he was also CSM on Abi's and Kelsey's rapes. He is going to send it for analysis.

Donna thinks this is maybe worth sharing with Theo and she goes to his office. She knocks and enters, though she does not hear him say come in. He is standing with DI Lukasz Mazur looking at a mobile phone screen. 'And you were going to tell me you are running a covert surveillance op on my patch when?' asks Theo crossly.

'Do you know them?' Mazur asks.

'Yes, yes I do. At least I know one of them. That's Hannah Poole.' He realises Donna has arrived and shows her the screen.

She nods. 'The other one is Zlota, Felka Warszawska's sister.'

'Fuck,' says Mazur. He talks into the phone: 'We've got civilians in the parish.'

Donna hears Parvez echo his boss's expletive.

Chapter 34

They slept beyond dawn. They were woken by Zlota's phone, a text from Felka, saying she is fine and will be back soon. Zlota spent the morning circling the rooms in the house, one after another. She reminded Hannah of a lioness separated from her cub. By 11 a.m., Zlota could wait no longer. She insisted they go to the house the key ring was transmitting from. 'We go, we make sure she is okay, we leave,' she promised.

Several times, on the taxi ride over, Hannah reviewed her decision not to call Theo. His presumed work overload and Zlota's aversion the main stumbling blocks, even though Hannah knew it would be the right thing to do. As they swung off the main route north to Whitby onto the narrower road which meanders back towards a more isolated part of the coast, a volunteer from the refuge rang. Blessing had gone. This increased Hannah's agitation. She picked up her phone to very definitely dial Theo's number and noticed she had just lost her signal.

'Here you are,' says the taxi driver cheerfully.

Hannah steps out of the car with Zlota and immediately thinks better of it. Where they are is at the start of a driveway swallowed by huge leylandii hedges on either side.

Across the road are fields dipping towards the beading of cobalt sea, fastening land to the lighter blue sky. There are some sheep in the distance. No human life. Crowding round whatever the hedges conceal are trees swathed in a dazzling variety of greens.

Zlota has already paid the fare and the taxi does a quick three-point turn to take him off towards town again. Zlota links arms with Hannah and firmly takes her up the gravel path. They pass a board which announces this is a holiday rental called Beech Copse. Zlota misreads it and Hannah corrects her. She hopes there won't be a corpse at the end of this, but now the idea has inveigled its way in, it won't let her alone.

They are headed towards a two-storey cottage made of grey stone through a garden where goldfinches and blue tits twitter in the bushes. *It should be picturesque*, Hannah tells herself. But there is a stillness about the place which increasingly unnerves her. Suddenly there is a clatter and a screech. The two women grip each other. Hannah's heart thumps into her throat. 'Bloody fuck,' says Zlota. 'What is that?'

Seeing the bejewelled tail of a pheasant as it escapes into the woodland does nothing to calm Hannah's jitters.

Then a man appears from the side of the house, holding an axe.

Theo insists on a full explanation from Mazur, which he gives even as they both scramble to talk to the DCI and assemble some back up. The NCA were watching both Blessing and Felka. Standard practice apparently. They know both were picked up last night – it seems they went willingly – and were taken to a property to the north of Scarborough. Felka has since departed with a man they established is Marius Badea when both were detained at Manchester airport trying to board a flight to Sweden. Blessing remains in the cottage near Scarborough with a man. When Mazur reveals his image to the local officers, Harrie names him as Tony Finch. 'Our Mr T, then,' says Mazur.

'And you didn't intervene because?' asks Theo.

'Finch isn't the boss. We are waiting for him.'

'You know who he is?'

Mazur glances away. 'Nate Withenshaw. Everything appears to lead to him. The shell company, the laundered money.'

'And when did you confirm this?' asks Theo sharply. Then holds up his hand, 'No, don't tell me. I don't want to know how long you've been undermining our supposedly joint investigation.'

'It's all supposition so far,' says Mazur forcefully. 'You've seen how careful he is. We need to catch him with dirt on his hands.'

'And Ms Okokon is bait?' asks Donna.

'She made her own decision.'

Did she though? thinks Donna. *What kind of choices did she feel were left open to her?*

'And now Hannah and Ms Warszawska are in danger,' says Theo flatly.

'That was obviously not in the plan,' retorts Mazur.

'Well, we'd better improve our plan this time around,' fires back Theo.

'Hello ladies,' says the man with the axe. His body is broad and his T-shirt reveals developed biceps. His black hair is thick. His grin appears wolfish to Hannah. She begins to say they made a wrong turning and are sorry and will be going, when Zlota says abruptly, 'We are here to see Felka. Where is she?'

The man shakes his head. 'You've got it wrong love, no Felka here.' He holds the axe across his abdomen. The sun glints off its blade. Perhaps he sees Hannah staring at it. 'Been chopping wood,' he says. 'Don't need it at this time of year, of course, but I like to keep in shape. Anyway, you'll be on your way, good to have met—'

'We're not leaving,' says Zlota. She pulls out of Hannah's grip and steps forwards. 'Felka is here. I will see her.'

The man shakes his head. He also takes a pace towards them. 'No, love. Now off you go, this is private property.'

A movement from an upstairs window catches Zlota's attention. 'She's there, I can see her.'

Hannah glances up. It is not Felka. It is Blessing. She snaps herself back from the glass. Zlota runs for the front door. Hannah pulls out her phone, praying for a signal. Only to have it grabbed from her hand by the man, who drops it on the ground and smashes it with the axe.

For a split second Hannah is mesmerised by the violence of it. She is aware of the man with his beefy shoulders and meaty hands. She is aware of Zlota looking back from the locked front door, her face echoing Munch's *The Scream*. Hannah is aware of the little birds flitting and chirping in golden sunshine. For a moment she cannot make herself move. Then she turns, slips on the loose stones, begins to run and stops. *What about Zlota? What about Blessing?* As she hesitates, her arm is grabbed, pulling her round, and something large and heavy clouts her on the side of the head.

The stab vest is like a corset over Donna's light summer blouse. It is also too warm – she can feel the sweat already starting under her arms. She opens the window a slit. She is in the back of Mazur's car. Theo is up front and Harrie is beside her. Once the NCA officers identified the property where Blessing and Felka were taken the previous evening, cameras were set up for the surveillance as an officer sitting in a vehicle would be too conspicuous. Parvez has been monitoring the feed as well as the road leading to the cottage from his car parked in a side lane. They are going to rendezvous with him now. He radios in to say he has spotted 'target A'. Lukasz nods when Theo asks if this is Nate Withenshaw.

Someone has thoughtfully put her in the recovery position. She feels the weave of the carpet against her cheek before she opens her eyes and sees the stretch of dove-coloured fluff ending in white-painted wood. She tries to stretch her legs and arms out and realises they are pinned behind her back by twine which cuts into her wrists and ankles. She moves her head and immediately wishes she hadn't as acid burns into her mouth. She groans. Because movement is painful and nausea inducing, it takes several attempts to right herself. She is in a room with a pleasant view of the crests of trees. She rests her throbbing head back against the bed. She sees a squirrel through the glass scampering along a branch and asks it what the fuck is she going to do? She tries calling out: 'Zlota? Blessing?' She finds she can only croak. Her chin slumps to her collarbone and she croaks a sob.

Below she can hear some moving about. People coming into the room underneath the one she is in. Two men, she realises, arguing.

'Your tour in NI left you more cracked than I realised,' says one. 'I thought you'd killed her.'

'I had to stop her,' says the other. Hannah thinks it is the man with the axe, though his voice sounds a whole lot less friendly. 'She'd seen my face.'

'And how many times have I told you not to damage the merchandise? What got you revved up? Did she reject your charming advances?'

Hannah can hear water being poured, a kettle beginning to boil. *They're making bloody tea*, she thinks. She suddenly realises how dry her mouth is. She runs her tongue across her lips and finds them cut and sore. Like every other part of her face.

Axe man does not respond. His companion goes on, 'We could probably use the Polack – who is going to notice if she goes missing? But the white bitch, that's a bigger problem.' There's more evidence of drinks being prepared with a fridge door opening and closing. Then axe man's friend says: 'Well, it's your mess, you can clear it up. You find a way to despatch her without leaving a trail. Didn't you get used to that sort of thing when you were dealing with the IRA?' He laughs.

He's actually laughing. It doesn't quite compute.

He adds: 'You've still got your gun, right?'

Axe man grunts in agreement.

Hannah begins to shake, despite the warmth of the room.

The armed response team look otherworldly in their heavy black jackets, trousers, helmets and visors. If Donna passed them in the corridor out of uniform – as she may have done – she would not recognise them. Their superior and Mazur are coordinating things. For now as much information as possible is being collected by officers carefully checking the perimeters, as well as by a silent drone with a telescopic lens.

'We want to know who is there and where they are. We want visuals on everyone before we go in,' says Mazur. He sounds worried. Or annoyed.

Either way, his tone does not fill Donna with confidence. Plus she has nothing to do and this makes her fidgety. Not to mention the weaponry. Like everyone here, she's had firearm training, however, she's never wanted to take it any further. Recently, she's begun to wonder if this is because it brings back difficult memories of her upbringing in East Germany. The guns the Volkspolizei carried. The revolver she herself held when she was almost eighteen and pointed at a boy from her school. She turns her gaze away from the hedges concealing the cottage towards the glitter of waves rimming the cliffs. She would have much preferred to have been left behind in the office. *What good am I doing here?*

It hasn't been more than ten minutes, though it feels like an age, when Mazur quietly communicates the plan. The women are upstairs. Finch and Withenshaw downstairs. There are two weak points at the rear with French windows leading into the lounge and a back door judged to be relatively flimsy. These will be used to gain access and 'neutralise' the two men before they have the chance to get upstairs and it becomes hostage situation. All this will be swiftly achieved by the armed response officers. Donna is more than relieved to hear her role is to stand back and be ready to receive the women when required.

Time is elastic. It could be two minutes, it could be ten. Hannah hears something, a hoarse whisper. She manages to half slither, half crawl – her joints screaming at every awkward shuffle – to the wall. 'Yes?' she says to the discreetly striped wallpaper.

'Hannah? It is me, Blessing. I have to say sorry. I am sorry. I should not have gone with Tony.'

She raises her gaze to the windowsill. She sees the keyring Zlota gave to Felka, obviously naively continuing to transmit its position. 'Why did you?'

'He promised me my passport, to help me get home. He told me his name. He brought me books.'

Hannah feels the misery of what Blessing's life had been reduced to. So bereft of kindness, Tony's actions – most likely meant as a bribe – took on the shape of generosity.

'He said he did not like what the others did to me. He was lying. He tried to do the same.'

'I am so sorry, Blessing, for everything you have gone through.' She is finding it hard to talk, her throat sore and tense. Finally she manages. 'I wish you could have trusted me.'

'I do trust you, Hannah, I just don't trust the process.'

'The system, Blessing, you don't trust the system,' Hannah says too quietly for the other woman to hear. 'And who can blame you?' However, for a moment, Blessing's mistake elicits a stinging smile. *Trust the process, it's what we all say in therapy. It's not easy to do.* She rests against the wall, closing her eyes. *I am so tired.*

Time is elastic. It could be two minutes, it could be ten. Then all hell breaks loose.

Donna watches her colleagues doing what they have been trained to do. She and Harrie stand together in silence. Theo is with Mazur. Parvez remains between the couplets as if unsure which one to join, moving uneasily from foot to foot. Donna has the feeling Harrie is ignoring him. Though at this moment, everyone is focused on the black-clad officers edging carefully between the hedges and up the drive.

The first shot cracks into the tranquillity. But what really makes Donna jump is a pigeon launching itself from a nearby tree, its wings clapping like a football rattle. There's further gunfire along with smashing of glass and smoke. Who would have thought there would be smoke wisping into the clear cerulean sky?

Donna has to force herself to stay rooted. Harrie takes a couple of steps forward and Donna would follow her.

'Keep back,' shouts Parvez. Both Donna and Harrie freeze.

Time is elastic, it could be two minutes or ten, then Mazur finally gets the call through the radio: 'All secured.'

Now, thinks Donna, *I can do something useful.*

***

Hannah has never heard guns going off in reality. At first, she hears what she thinks are the pop of several beechnuts being stamped on. Once she realises what is going on, her body automatically shoves itself into the corner as if this would protect her from what is coming. Heavy boots on the stairs. A sci-fi stormtrooper in black with a gun held ready. Hannah shrieks. Bends herself double. Prays to a god she does not believe in. She hears a woman shout: 'Clear.' Then the terrifying entity becomes a person, a female, with a soothing voice, 'It's OK, you're safe now.' She begins to unfasten Hannah's bindings.

It is almost as painful to have all her limbs unbent. She hiccups and retches as the officer helps her to her feet. 'I'm sorry,' she says, seeing the flecks of vomit on the pristine uniform.

'Don't you worry, honey. I've had worse. Let me check you over. Do you think you can walk?'

Hannah stumbles stiffly down the stairs. The hall is full of activity. There's the after-smell of sparklers. It is weirdly mixed with the scent of lavender. A large candle has been toppled, its fluted glass holder smashed.

Hannah practically falls over the front step. Then she sees him coming towards her. She tumbles thankfully into Theo's embrace. 'I've got you,' he says. She could bury herself into his chest. Then she remembers. 'He's got a gun,' she says. Does he hear her? She must try harder.

It's an outsized ants' colony with the armed response officers purposefully going about their work. They have Withenshaw and Finch corralled to one side. Hannah comes out through the front door and drops into Theo's arms. Harrie and Donna move forward together. There are Zlota and Blessing, who might need help. As Donna passes Hannah she hears her rasp, 'He's got a gun.'

Who? All secure they said?

Then there's a thud. Finch slams himself through the human cordon. He makes it to a lean-to neatly stacked with wood and grabs something. Donna hasn't a moment to work out if it is a gun before she hears it fire, a snap of a leather strap. A body barrels into her, knocking her backwards. Parvez shouts: 'Take cover.'

Donna dives to the ground, her training kicking in. Tentatively lifting her head, she sees Finch shot and disarmed. She rolls over. Harrie has also taken cover, it seems, face down, prone on the gravel drive. Donna says to her, 'It's OK, they've got him.' Harrie does not reply. Donna reaches out, pats Harrie's back. Still no response. Donna's hand comes back wet. *Fuck, fuck.* On her knees now, she lurches forward, screeching: 'Officer down. Officer down.'

Chapter 35

The injured Anthony Finch is in hospital and, in the divvying up of responsibilities, under the jurisdiction of the NCA officers. But Nathaniel Withenshaw is theirs. For now. Because of the ongoing inquiry into the rape of Abi Davis. If they can't make that charge stick, however, Nate will go to the NCA. Donna watches him being taken down into the bowels of the police station to the holding cells. For the first time in her professional life, she can imagine taking a suspect into a dark hole and punching them until their blood runs like a river.

Theo insists they need time out before questioning Withenshaw. He is curt when Donna tries to protest. She doesn't think she will be able to rest or to function normally again. Yet, once home and in bed, she plummets into sleep as if off a precipice. The next morning, she even manages a relatively sane conversation with Jim and Christopher. She will not be joining them this weekend. She has work to do. She does not fill in the detail. She promises she will set a date for a visit soon. They are more peeved than she thinks is reasonable. They would have cancelled on her because of their jobs without turning a hair. She cuts the connection, twists into the back of the sofa and pummels the cushions, screaming her inarticulateness. Unfairness is the least of her agonies.

Donna and Theo reconvene in the CID office. It has the atmosphere of a phantom wreck. The officers who are in avoid them as if they are cursed. Perhaps they are. The blight of an officer down.

'How are you?' asks Theo with an intensity only he can manage to inject into those three words.

She shrugs. If she says, she might start to cry again. 'You?'

'Gus has come to stay. I don't know what I would do without him. But you're on your own up here. Do you need to go home? Back to Kenilworth? We can manage—'

'No!' She cuts him off. 'It helps to keep busy.'

He nods. 'Let's get on then. I'll review the intel from the NCA. There's an email from Ethan concerning Ms Davis's rape, info on her dress and about a woollen hat. You look at it. We'll aim to bring Mr Withenshaw up in an hour. I want us to go in hard. I want to nail him.' Donna has never heard such steel in Theo's tone before. But then, nothing is as it was.

There is a degree of satisfaction in seeing a night in custody has rubbed the sheen off Nathaniel Withenshaw. He is wearing the kind of washed-out grey tracksuit given to detainees when their own clothes are required for forensic analysis. His eyes are dull, sunk into paunches. His sleek solicitor is not with him. Maybe she does not work Sundays. Or she isn't interested in lost causes. Reggie Harvey, of course, doesn't turn his nose up at them. He is as spruce as ever, his bow tie a silky navy and green stripe. He keeps his composure as Theo reels off the charges – human trafficking, keeping a

231

brothel, being landlord to premises used as a brothel, money laundering, kidnap, false imprisonment – and on into the minutiae of the offences allowed by the Crown Prosecution Service. Donna is almost soothed by the rhythmic cadence of Theo's voice. Almost. The economical legal jargon almost smooths over the agonies of the actuality. Almost. Donna tastes the sour burn of her rage. She takes a sip of water. Nothing will douse it.

Withenshaw is slumped in the moulded plastic chair, his forearms on his thighs, his hands clasped. His head is tilted slightly to one side. His gaze is to the floor. The only charge he reacts to is the last. 'I did not rape Abi Davis,' he growls quietly. 'I don't need to rape women.'

Harvey says calmly, 'My client will be making no comment during this interview.'

Though it is no surprise, the embers in Donna's stomach glow a smidge hotter. She expects it is the same for Theo. Nonetheless, he matches Harvey's tone when he says directly to Nate: 'That is your right, Mr Withenshaw, however, you might like to consider that our colleagues at the National Crime Agency are interviewing your colleague Anthony Finch as we speak.'

This causes a tightening around Nate's jaw and a flattening of his lips.

No winning smiles today then, thinks Donna. As agreed, she begins. She shoves a photograph of Abi's stained and torn red dress across the table. 'Do you recognise this?' When Nate does not respond, she says, 'For the tape, is that a no or a no comment?'

Nate sits back, his legs sprawled wide, his arms crossed.

232

He glares at Donna from under his distinctly greasy thatch of blond hair. *How quickly those eyes can turn from charming to malicious.* She keeps herself steady as she stares back. He slowly lifts his shoulders and then lets them fall.

'It belongs to Abi Davis. There are traces of semen on it. They have been matched with the DNA sample we have for you on file from the investigation into the rape of Ms Geraty.'

Reggie Harvey leans in and says conversationally: 'It does not look in great condition. Where did you find it? In a bin? I do hope we are talking a secure evidence chain.' His conjecture shows up the weakness in their suppositions.

Donna says firmly to Nate: 'Explain how your semen got on this dress belonging to Abi Davis.'

Harvey's attitude is equally implacable. 'Are you sure the semen got on the dress the night Ms Davis was raped?'

'She was wearing it when she was raped.'

'That's not what I am asking.'

Donna produces another photograph: 'And this black woollen hat? Do you recognise it, Mr Withenshaw?'

Nothing beyond the searing gaze.

'It was found in your car. And guess what? It has your DNA on the outside and Ms Davis's on the inside. When Ms Davis was raped, she was blindfolded by having this hat pulled over her head.'

'This hat or another one like it, DC Morris?' Harvey's voice of reason hardly penetrates the furnace raging between Donna and Withenshaw. She maintains her poise even as she feels, in addition, the heat whipping itself up internally. She expects her face has gone the colour of beetroot and she senses a slight relaxation in Nate. *He thinks he's winning,* she thinks miserably. *Why now? Why fucking now?* she berates herself.

Then he twists his lips into something like a smile and says, 'So we had sex, and she was wearing that dress. Or she could have been, I didn't really notice. And you know what? Little Miss Prim Davis likes it a bit kinky. She suggested the hat over her head. She wanted it rough. She liked it rough.'

'Nathaniel Withenshaw,' Donna says, her anger seeping into her tone. *Too much, too much.* It's making her voice shake. She dials it back, 'Nathaniel Withenshaw, on the twenty-sixth of April this year, you followed Abi Davis to a deserted corner of the park, you pulled this hat over her head, you forced her to the ground, you hit her and you raped her.'

Despite Harvey's advice to say nothing, Nate leans forwards and says almost gently, 'I did not, DC Morris. We had sex, yes, but not on the twenty-sixth – I was caring for Eileen Horsham and I was there all night.'

She can smell him, unwashed and slightly sweaty as he is, there's still the distinctive undertow. 'What is the aftershave you use, Mr Withenshaw?'

Reggie Harvey attempts to intervene are again brushed aside, and Nate's smile regains some of its brilliance, 'Sauvage, DC Morris. Do you like it? Perhaps you'd like to get some for your husband? Remind you of me. Bring some excitement back into the bedroom.'

'Personal comments like that to my officer are completely unacceptable,' says Theo brusquely.

Withenshaw shrugs and sits back. But at least his licentious gawp is no longer drilling into Donna's forehead. She tries to ease her rigid spine and shoulders into the curve of the back of the chair. Clamminess is caught beneath her breasts and in her underarms. She would like to ask for a break. But Theo won't want to let the pressure lapse. *He will want his punches to land, unlike mine.*

Theo begins as if the story he is telling is an everyday one. Donna fears it is. 'In December last year Blessing Okokon arrived as a refugee into a holding camp on Sicily. In February of this year, she is picked up by a taxi and taken to the Italian mainland. Her passport is taken from her. On the third of March this year she is flown with another woman, Felka Warszawska, from Rome to Manchester. There she is held prisoner and forced into prostitution. On the twenty-third of April, or thereabouts, she and Felka are given sleeping pills, probably temazepam. They are driven to Scarborough where they are once again held against their will and forced to perform as sex workers. They were released from this on the eighth of May. Unfortunately, shortly afterwards they accompanied Anthony Finch to a holiday let called Beech Copse near Staintondale. Ms Warszawska left with a man called Marius Badea. They have since been detained. Ms Okokon was held prisoner and sexually and physically assaulted. When friends of hers, Hannah Poole and Ms Warszawska's sister, arrived at the house, they were kidnapped and physically assaulted. What can you tell me about all this, Mr Withenshaw?'

There's a pause. Reggie gives his client a sidelong look and Nate breathes: 'No comment.'

'Interesting, because we have found connections to you threaded all the way through. The premises in Manchester were let to a shell company owned by your haulage business. This same company owns the house in Scarborough where the women were held. Lorries from your haulage business are on a watch list drawn-up by UK Border Force because they have been stopped so many times and found to contain people attempting to enter this country illegally. We know you asked Abi Davis to supply you with temazepam. And we have found this in your portable filing cabinet.' He moves several photocopied sheets across the table. 'Accounts from a business which clearly states that Ms Okokon and Ms Warszawska are earning money for you.'

Theo had told Donna there was an account book. She could hardly credit it, but Nate did keep accounts, hiding his illegal activities in amongst his legitimate ones. However, now she sees the pages, she realises she recognises the handwriting gracing each page. She wonders if it is important enough to interrupt her DI's flow. She decides not.

'Plus, we note you were paying for much of the maintenance and renovation of your properties in Scarborough in cash. Not to mention the money you got young Jayson Smith to distribute to taxi drivers and the like in Hull, which we will prove eventually finds its way into your account. Then there is your presence at Beech Copse. What were you doing there, Mr Withenshaw?'

Nate's lips are in a grim line. He has crossed his arms across his chest. He mumbles his 'No comment.'

'I would like to remind you, Mr Withenshaw, we have testimony from Ms Okokon, Ms Poole and the two Ms Warszawskas. And, now that you and Finch are in custody, Mr Smith appears ready to be more expansive, as is

Marius Badea. However, of more concern to you, I am sure, Anthony Finch is telling his version of events. Wouldn't you like to give us yours?'

Withenshaw rubs a hand over his face. His fingernails are immaculately manicured, but there must have been grime on his palm as it leaves a stain across his cheek and nose. His chin looks jowly as the vigour drains from its muscles. He takes a deep breath, then puffs it out.

Reggie senses a change in his client and says quickly, 'Mr Withenshaw, my advice is still to say no comment.'

'What do you know about anything?' Nate blasts out.

For the first time in Donna's experience, the solicitor appears to grit his teeth and half hunch his shoulders.

'Anthony Finch, Tony, Finchy, Mr T,' Nate begins slowly. 'Don't you know he's as mad as a hatter? Five years a soldier during the troubles in Northern Ireland did it for his sanity and his conscience. Yes, maybe I helped him out every once in a while, we were mates. I helped him secure the property in Manchester and let him use the one here. But I didn't know what he was doing with them. He owes me, Inspector, big time. I mean, I got him out of financial debt years back, he gives me cash to pay it off, I use it for my property business.' He has let his arms drop to his sides and has moved a fraction towards the table. He is focused on Theo now, his voice is wheedling, 'It was just plain bad luck my lorries got infested with those illegals—'

Infested. Donna feels the word stab at her chest. She had come to this country with false papers. She had run from a situation she found intolerable.

'No charges were ever brought,' Withenshaw continues. 'And I went to the holiday let to stop Finch doing his worst.'

'That's not what Ms Poole overheard you saying,' says Theo, his tone sharp.

Withenshaw shrugs. 'I don't know this Ms Poole, but whoever she is, she must have got confused. I was trying to calm things down.'

'I believe Ms Poole's witness statement will stand up in court and so does the CPS.' Donna hears Theo's concern for Hannah in his snappiness.

Again Withenshaw shrugs, but he has slumped in his chair now.

'And these accounts?' says Theo. 'How are you going to explain those away?'

'They're not mine,' he says, not looking at the sheets on the table. 'Finch asked me to store an accounts book for him, I didn't ask what it was for.'

'Funny, your fingerprints are all over the pages and there are details of your letting and property businesses here too.'

'It's not my writing.' It's like he has run out of breath.

'No,' interrupts Donna. 'It's Stella Horsham's.'

Theo keeps staring straight at their detainee, however, the slight twitch in his neck suggests he wants to turn to Donna and ask: *What?*

'There you go,' says Nate. 'Ask her what she was up to.'

'We will, Mr Withenshaw,' says Donna. 'Are you so very sure she is going to cover for you?'

This time something like a groan escapes.

Obviously not then, thinks Donna with some satisfaction.

238

Nate bends over until his elbows are on his knees. 'I'm done,' he says. 'I've nothing more to say.'

Reggie Harvey visibly gathers himself; maybe he has been overawed by the extent of Withenshaw's wrongdoings. Far beyond the usual crims he finds himself defending. 'You heard my client, Detective Inspector, this interview is at an end.'

Theo nods. Both he and Donna watch Withenshaw shuffle out of the room. They both feel as exhausted as he looks. But both know they are not going to rest now there is more to do.

Chapter 36

The freight of sadness hits them front and centre on entering the CID offices when they realise (again) she is not there, eager for their debrief. The only way is to keep going. Like everyone else who was there, they will be interviewed about the shooting at Beech Copse. However, they should have already typed up their recollections. The DCI has interrupted his Sunday to insist they get on with it. And they must not confer while doing it.

Donna does her best to detach herself as she sets down the bald facts. Even so, afterwards she has to take herself off to the toilets for a brief weep and to splash her face with water. On her return, to distract herself, she goes through her emails and then turns to a folder which was delivered to her desk the day before. A folder with an old case number on it. After reading it, she makes a call to Eileen Horsham's neighbour who turns out to be a damn sight more clued up than the police. Donna sits back. The kaleidoscope has finally settled into a pattern which makes sense.

When she goes to find Theo to update him, he insists they go out. 'I don't think I can sit in here a moment longer,' he says. He scowls at the squash of the four walls and the porthole of a window which never truly captures the light. The 'without her' is left unsaid.

They get sandwiches, and Donna allows herself a real coffee, to take to a bench on North Bay. Despite the sun and the lack of wind, the water is choppy, flecks of white on the wave crests like snow on distant mountain tops. It reminds Donna that the sea has its own pulse set by the moon, regulated by currents and weather patterns far beyond the shores of North Yorkshire.

As they settle, Theo says, 'I hope you are going to tell me why Stella Horsham is keeping accounts for Nate Withenshaw and how you knew.'

'I saw her handwriting when we visited her the first time. And the why is something of a long story.'

'I'm listening.'

After several shots of caffeine she begins: 'When Stella Horsham moved to Scarborough to take up the job at the hospital she came to the police with the accusation that she had been sexually abused by her father as a child of seven.'

'Don't tell me it was never investigated,' says Theo gloomily.

'It was. Only both parents vehemently denied it and said their daughter was a fantasist. And in those days, this was enough for it to be dropped. Roll forward thirty years and Nathaniel Withenshaw arrives in Scarborough.' She pauses to take a mouthful of egg and cress. She hadn't been able to tolerate breakfast. Now the creamy mix tastes good.

'And for some unknown reason becomes best mates with Stella.'

'He's her brother.'

'What? How?'

'Eileen told her buddy next door that she married her

241

husband late. She was thirty-six and he was thirty-eight. They didn't think she would have children. But she had Stella two years later. Seven years on and things aren't going well in the marriage. Note the age Stella was at this point.'

'Seven?'

'Indeed. Mrs Horsham leaves her husband and daughter for a married man on the basis that he would ditch his wife.' Donna works hard not to let an image of Jim intrude. She continues: 'He didn't. Eileen found she was pregnant. She was well into her forties by then, she didn't expect another pregnancy. Apparently, the lover wasn't that interested until the child comes out a boy. Then married man went back to his wife and persuaded her to adopt Nate.'

'And Eileen lets him?'

Donna shrugs. She would have fought for her children until her fingernails were torn off and worse. 'The way Eileen told it to her buddy, she thought Nate better off with two parents than just her, and she wanted to get back to Stella. It seems she was able to return to her husband and they carry on as if nothing has happened. She did keep up with Nate on and off, which is why he knew how to find her when he was ready.'

'Then he swans back in and everyone is happy?'

'Yes, according to the neighbour, despite not knowing about her mother's illicit affair, Stella welcomed Withenshaw with open arms.'

Theo has finished his food and screws up the paper bag. He takes a gulp of coffee. 'Bit strange?'

'I think they were useful to each other. Stella started doing Withenshaw's accounts, so she must have known what he was up to.'

'And accepted it?'

This sits uncomfortably with Donna. Women betraying women. 'I suppose.'

'And how was he useful to her? It has to be more than sitting with Eileen an evening every few weeks.'

'Yes, he gave her an alibi for the night she came back and suffocated her mother.'

'He was complicit in her killing their mother?'

'He wasn't there. He didn't know anything about it. Maybe still hasn't realised it. Though he looked like he was putting two and two together and making five when we told him Stella came back on the twenty-sixth.'

'If he wasn't there, why didn't he say? He almost got caught up in a murder inquiry.'

'But he didn't. And maybe he was willing to risk it because he didn't want to be in the frame for the rape of Abi Davis.' She wraps up the last of her sandwich. She can't finish it. However, another taste of coffee is good. 'The DC checking the CCTV on the night Withenshaw's car was vandalised came up with something. She sent me the clip of someone coming out of the club's car park in the right time-frame. The image is fuzzy and indistinct. However, I reckon it's Stella Horsham. She planted that woollen hat where we were going to find it.'

'She wanted him arrested for Abi's rape? Why? It might have backfired on her.'

'She has the death certificate. The neighbour has the funeral invite. Maybe Stella thinks she is safe.'

'Maybe she is. For her mother's death at least. But maybe she knows something about the rape of Abi Davis. And

243

there's still her writing in the accounts book. I'll talk to Mazur about who brings her in.'

It is agreed Theo and Donna should speak with Stella Horsham. A PC fetches her, keeping the reason as vague as 'helping with ongoing investigations'. Risking a migraine in favour of staying alert, Donna accepts the coffee her DI makes her, while Stella is left to wait in an interview room. Time to unsettle her a bit.

Not that Stella looks unsettled. She is smartly dressed as if she is going to a concert, her sleek white hair held back in a grip decorated with a velvet bow. She is sitting up straight as she waits for them. Waiting doesn't appear to bother her. If they are right about her, she is skilled at waiting.

As arranged over their cuppas, Donna takes Stella through her story for 26 and 27 April. An inordinately long time passes for very little information to be imparted. Another of Stella's skills: after a while people might well stop paying attention.

However, Donna is focusing on Stella's expression when she is telling the story she wants them to hear. After she finally halts, Donna says, 'What happened when you drove back to your house sometime before eleven-thirty on the twenty-sixth of April, Ms Horsham?'

Yes, there is a change in her features, it is subtle, a slight hardening around the jaw, a brief nibble at her lower lip, several rapid blinks. Then she smiles, 'I'm sorry, Detective Constable?'

'I think you heard me.' The irritation gets the better of Donna. 'Are you having difficulty deciding what lie to go with?'

'Oh, DC Morris,' she takes a lacy handkerchief out of her sleeve and dabs at her mouth. 'You'll have to excuse me, I haven't been quite myself since Mummy passed. I thought maybe I misheard your question. I have told you I did not return home until the morning of the twenty-seventh.'

'It's what you told us. But it's not true, is it?' says Donna. 'We have a taxi driver who saw your car parked outside your house on the twenty-sixth.'

'If he has said that, and I believe absolutely what you are telling me, DC Morris, your taxi driver must be mistaken. I was not there. And Nate was.'

'But you know he wasn't, Ms Horsham. You'd already discovered that on previous occasions Mr Withenshaw put your mother to sleep and left her. Perhaps she mentioned him giving her tablets from the temazepam tub and you came back to investigate? Once you had worked out what he was doing, you used it for your own purposes.'

Stella sounds indignant. 'DC Morris, that is too awful to contemplate. I would never, ever have done such a thing. How can you even think it, let alone suggest it?'

Donna glances at Theo. He shifts his head slightly. They will move on. For whatever reason Eileen Horsham did not protect her daughter, so some might call Stella putting a pillow over her mother's face rough justice. However, in any case, the coroner would need more than what the officers have to reopen a natural causes verdict.

Theo takes over. 'Ms Horsham, what do you know about these?' He shows her the images of the accounts book.

'Nate's financial records, I believe,' Stella says vaguely.

'And do you recognise this handwriting?'

'I did copy out a few pages for him, Detective Inspector. Oh,' she puts her fingers to her throat. 'You can't think I knew anything about what he was doing? No, no, no. I would not have had anything to do with that.' She is most emphatic.

'Where were you last Thursday night between ten and eleven?'

She smiles. 'Why at home, of course, I don't like being out late, even now Mummy is gone and I am not needed. There was a rather good concert on Radio 3.'

When is there not? Donna moves the CCTV image across the table. 'Ms Horsham, this is you, is it not?'

Stella hardly looks at it. 'I don't think so, dear, though how could you tell? Not even a person's mother would recognise their child from that.'

'Ms Horsham, you vandalised Nate Withenshaw's car last Thursday and put a black woollen hat under the front seat. This – as you hoped or expected – has yielded DNA evidence connecting Mr Withenshaw to Abi Davis. What do you say?'

'That poor girl, she is such a gentle soul,' Stella says, genuinely upset. 'I had a long conversation with her sister Una, it quite distressed me to hear what happened to her.'

'Una told you about the woollen hat. You found a similar one in the room where Mr Withenshaw stayed. You knew Mr Withenshaw had a relationship with Abi. You knew he was out when she was being raped. You made the connection. Why? Because you already knew he had raped Kelsey Geraty.'

'I knew no such thing. I have no idea who this Kelsey Geraty is.'

'Suspected then. And you know Abi Davis, she is one of your staff – it gets more personal.' Donna has the sense of wading through treacle towards Stella just as she is continuously getting further away.

'Rape is a disgusting act,' Stella says imperiously. Her narrow frame is so tight, it appears to be vibrating. 'I hope you catch the man who raped Abi. Even if it does turn out to be my half-brother.' She puts a heavy emphasis on 'half'. She goes on, seemingly getting control of the quiver in her voice, 'But I did not go out last Thursday and plant evidence. I would not do such a thing.'

'What about the other women?' Theo's question takes Donna by surprise. His tone, though low, is dangerously heated.

'The other women?' again Stella sounds vague.

'Blessing Okokon and Felka Warszawska? You noted down their earnings in Mr Withenshaw's account book. You must have known and you did nothing.'

She shakes her head vigorously. 'No, Detective Inspector, of course I did not know.' She pauses and pats her top lip with her handkerchief. 'Though we mustn't judge too quickly, certain women make certain choices, you have to agree. Where they come from, they have cultures quite unlike ours. Abi Davis, well, she's only from just up the road. It's quite different.' She seems satisfied with her explanation. 'And anyway, if not Nate, then who? At least he treated them well.'

Rage courses through Donna. *From only just up the road? You mean Abi's 'like us'. You mean she's white. And can she really believe Withenshaw looked after the women?* An urge sweeps her away, her fingers around Stella's scraggy neck, how good that would feel.

She sees Theo is also struggling to restrain himself. His hands and jaw clenched. His body turned to reinforced steel.

Into the silence, Stella once again smiles. 'Well, Detective Inspector, Detective Constable, if that will be all?'

Donna says hastily: 'Are you sure it was Mr Withenshaw who asked you to write in the accounts book?'

Stella nods. 'Of course, it was Nathaniel. Who else would ask me?'

'Mr Finch.'

'No, no, no, Anthony never did anything without Nathaniel's express instructions. I think Anthony was a bit afraid of him.'

Withenshaw was right, his sister – his half-sister *– is prepared to throw him to the hyenas. The NCA boys will be pleased.* This knowledge brings a certain satisfaction which means both Donna and Theo manage a relieved grin once Stella Horsham is off the premises. Then they both miss, almost in unison, an acerbic comment from Harrie. And the gloom descends again.

Chapter 37

They discuss calling it a day. However, a phone call tells them Abi will only be at the bed and breakfast in Scarborough for a few more hours before returning to Newcastle. They need to have one more try. She reluctantly agrees to see them.

Stopping at a supermarket on the way, they arrive at the B&B, to be shown into the lounge by Una who says she will be just upstairs if anyone needs anything. Abi is curled up in one corner of the sofa; the long cardi once again wrapped around her body, which appears to be more diminutive, more bony than before. She has an afternoon tea tray by her side. The food is untouched and a cup is half drunk.

Donna starts with the red dress.

'I bought it for the date with Nate,' she mumbles. 'The date which never was.'

'On Saturday, the twenty-sixth?'

She nods. 'Why is it so important?'

Theo keeps his voice gentle to soften the bluntness of his question: 'Abi, we need to be sure. Did you and Nate have sex before the twenty-sixth and were you wearing your red dress?'

'Is that what he told you?' she asks, looking down at her fingers twisting at a loose button on the end of a thread.

'That we had sex? Are those the words he used?' outrage permeates her weak voice.

'Did you?' asks Theo.

'No. No we did not.'

Theo continues: 'We have Mr Withenshaw's semen on your red dress and his DNA on the exterior of a black woollen hat, which also has yours on the interior. He says you had sex previous to the twenty-sixth, you were wearing the red dress and asked to have the hat pulled over your face.'

Abi drops her gaze, shaking her head.

Donna has second thoughts about her idea. The young woman is too fragile. She glances over at Theo – he gives a slight tip to his head and shrug of the shoulders. *My call.* She thinks about leaving it, then about the other women Nate is going to rape. She takes a deep breath: 'I know you recognised the scent used by the man who raped you.'

Abi's hands tremble as they continue with their worrying.

Donna holds out the cloth she has doused in the aftershave Sauvage they have just bought. She continues gently, 'It's the scent which alerted you. I know you know who he was.'

Abi turns her head away, her hand over her mouth and nose. 'It wasn't him. It wasn't Nate,' she whispers. 'He didn't need to. He wouldn't have.'

Theo talks quietly, as if he is afraid a loud noise will make the young woman shatter: 'The DNA evidence says different.'

Abi looks from Theo to Donna and back. 'Is this what it's going to be like? Talking about when I had sex? Turning it all dirty? Bullying me to say things I don't want to?' She jumps to her feet, stands behind the sofa, as if it is a shield or a prop. 'I won't go to court. I won't talk about this in front of all those people. I won't be pulled apart. I won't go through it over and over. Why do you keep making me go over it again and again? I want to forget, don't you understand?' Her voice rises in pitch and volume.

'We understand,' says Donna. 'But Nate needs to be punished. He needs to understand he can't treat women in this way.'

'And going to prison will teach him a lesson? Hah!' Abi wraps her arms around her thin shoulders.

'What about other young women who are at risk if—'

'No, no, no,' Abi yells. 'You're not laying that on me.' She turns away. 'I'm not brave. I've never been brave. I can't do it. I can't say this to anyone else. I can't do it any more.'

'Abi—' Donna begins. Theo shakes his head. Maybe he is feeling what she is, that they are doing more harm than good.

Theo gets to his feet. 'OK, OK. No more,' he says.

She turns her gaze on him – her eyes, already inflamed pink, are wet. 'For now?'

'Ever. If that's what you want, Abi?'

She shakes her head. 'I didn't want any of this. I was a good nurse. I worked hard. I got on with people. I've got a disciplinary hanging over me because of those damn pills. I probably won't work again as a nurse. I thought,' she pauses and swallows, 'I thought he loved me. Nothing about this is what I want,' she finishes with emphasis.

'I'm sorry, Abi,' Theo says. His sorrowful tone heartfelt and, Donna suspects, already close to the surface.

They leave defeated. Abi Davis will become just another statistic. She will join the yearly toll of over fifty-one thousand survivors of rape who never see anyone charged.

Somehow they drag themselves back to the police station, bracing themselves for the gust of absence which could well completely overwhelm them this time. But in the near deserted CID room, they find Gus. He doesn't hesitate to give Theo a hug which lingers. Then he puts a comforting arm around Donna and holds them both. 'I have news from the hospital,' he says.

Donna is glad she is in his embrace or she fears she might fall.

He continues: 'Harrie's awake. She's out of danger.'

Chapter 38

Time is elastic. It stretches and contracts. A minute feels like a day. A day like a minute. It's been ten days and twenty-two hours and fifteen minutes since it all happened. Hannah's brain knows this. But sometimes it is as if she is still in the middle of it. She smells the strange mix of cordite and lavender. She hears the cracking, as if twigs are being crushed under heavy boots. From the inside it felt like chaos. Not just chaos, but dangerous. Not just dangerous but life-threatening. Her body freezes. There must have been a plan, she tells herself. It takes more than a while before she can unpick herself from the ice again.

At least she has her therapist, friends and colleagues. One of whom has taken on her clients. Except for Kelsey who has refused to see anyone else. She wants to carry on with Hannah when she is better. Kelsey sent a card via the therapy centre, saying she is determined to start again on her college course in the autumn and she has a funded placement at the theatre in York over the summer. 'It's sick,' she wrote. 'The new Kelsey is ready to burst out of the old.' It cheers Hannah no end to read these words, which she does often.

Hannah is cognisant that she is lucky to have her support network, her cheerleaders as she thinks of them. It has been harder for Zlota who has so far declined to speak to anyone. She circles aimlessly round the rooms in the house. A lioness now injured as well as cubless. She did not get beaten as Hannah did. Even so, her psychological scars are deep. She has stuffed fennel seeds in keyholes. A talisman against evil spirits, she says.

Today Hannah is recruiting Khalil to her campaign to bring Zlota some comfort. Hannah checks in her mirror. She can still see the yellow and purple staining on her face, though it is fading. Knowing it is the consequence of axe man's combat PTSD doesn't take away the ache. She attacks the tangled nest on her head, then gives up and wraps it in a colourful scarf. It's the best she can do.

She goes downstairs to find the kitchen is already drenched in appetising odours. Khalil is cooking a rich vegetable broth, followed by a kind of pancake with cinnamon and dates accompanied by a zesty yoghurt dip. Hannah has bestirred herself to make a Victoria sponge which she now finds is cool enough to fill with jam and cream.

Zlota is sitting morosely at the table, a mug of cold tea in her hand. Hannah suggests she comes and offers advice. But Zlota isn't biting.

'She isn't coming back,' she says bitterly once they are all seated with the soup in front of them. It has become an almost daily litany.

Khalil assures her Felka will want to return to her sister one day. 'You are family,' he says simply as if this is reason enough.

'You don't think so.' Zlota points her spoon at Hannah.

'I don't know. How can any of us know?' says Hannah

cursing her decision to be truthful with her friend. 'But give her time and maybe she'll come round.'

'Maybe,' says Zlota.

The despondency in her features and tone adds further to Hannah's aches. She quotes: 'Then there came another moment when together we scooped up the sorry mess and wove a variation on what we had before but more brilliant.'

'I told you I don't knit,' says Zlota crossly.

Khalil looks at Hannah as if she has gone slightly bonkers, quickly offering second helpings.

After lunch Hannah manages to speak to Blessing on the phone. She is at an unspecified address in an unnamed city. 'DI Mazur tells me it is a safe house,' says Blessing. 'I don't feel safe.'

Hannah cannot in all honesty give her any reassurance.

Blessing does not seem to be looking for any. She continues: 'He says they will do everything they can to assist my case with the immigration. I do not believe they will be successful.'

She tails off and Hannah knows she has to tell her. Information conveyed by Theo. About a woman called Marianne. She was found at the house in Liverpool set up as a brothel by Badea. Hannah hesitates.

'She is well?' asks Blessing. 'Tell me she is well.'

'I am very sorry, Blessing, she is not.'

'They killed her? That bastard killed her?'

'No,' Hannah gathers herself. 'She hanged herself. She left a note saying "Sorry Blessing" with a scarf.'

'A dhuku. The half of my dhuku I gave her. I promised her we would be together again. I would come and find her.'

Hannah can hear the tears with the words. The line hums and clicks into the gap.

'It's not your fault,' says Hannah.

After a moment, Blessing says, 'I am tired, Hannah. I am tired of being here. I am tired of not making my own choices. You understand?'

'What do you want to do?'

'I want,' Blessing stops, breathes, goes on: 'I want to speak to my sister. Maybe we can mend something. Maybe I can go home.'

'Can't you call her?'

'I don't know where she is. She could be with my parents. But she was moving out, to go to university. I am not ready to speak to my mother.'

Hannah understands this reluctance. She wonders if Theo can help. She says she will speak to him.

For the first time, Blessing sounds less than hopeless. There's even a kind of chuckle in her voice, 'The man from home? He is a good man, Hannah?'

'Yes, he is a good man.'

'A man worthy enough for you to marry?'

Hannah laughs then. 'He's not interested, he's got a boyfriend.'

'A boyfriend?' Blessing is quiet for more than a moment. 'I see.'

'It doesn't change that he is a good man, Blessing,' Hannah says firmly.

'In my country . . . Well, you probably know.'

'Yes.'

Blessing breathes heavily. 'And I have changed my mind

about many things since leaving my country. I have learnt that a person's kindness, it, how do you say? It trumps everything?'

'Yes, Blessing you are right.'

Later that day, Hannah walks down the path to the South Bay lido to meet Theo. Even though he assures her they are no longer noticeable, she is not ready to reveal her bruises to a café audience and she perches on the concrete rim of the filled-in pool. Theo comes with the takeaway hot chocolates.

Beyond the railings, the tide slops over the concrete wall, as if to take the land by stealth. A froth like melted ice cream fills the walkway. A herring gull lands. Its feet pink dinner plates. It fixes them with its orange eye and chortles.

At Theo's prompting, Hannah tells him about Blessing. He agrees his father, who is making a trip to Nigeria, might be able to assist in her search for her sister. And he wants to know the latest on Khalil, still concerned about him, though he is no longer of interest to him professionally. He is relieved when she tells him she has linked the young Syrian with a solicitor who will work pro bono on his immigration case.

Then it is her turn to ask him. Firstly about his complaint against the racist traffic officer on the Humberside force. Theo's displeasure seeps into his tone as he responds. The man has been allowed to 'leave the service'. Hannah protests, this cannot be. Theo shrugs. 'It's one step on from not even investigating and allowing him to stay.'

Their attention turns to Harrie, now in a centre where she can receive rehabilitative care. Anthony Finch's bullet

– made wayward by the armed response officers' attempts to disarm him – had avoided the stab vest to lodge between her collarbone and spinal cord. No one is certain whether she will regain the use of her legs. 'She's so depressed,' says Theo sadly. 'Not surprisingly, obviously, but the staff say having a more motivated attitude would really help. I wish I could do more.'

Hannah puts her arm around his shoulder and – as he has done so often for her – gives him a hug. 'What?' she notices his smile.

'She's had several bunches of flowers sent to her.'

'Who?'

'DS Parvez Khan. And he came to see her the day before yesterday.'

'Was she impressed?'

'Not in the slightest. That was the best, to see a bit of the old Harrie coming through.'

Chapter 39

The midsummer dawn breaks a yolk across the turquoise cloth. There's not a wrinkle on the giant's table, flat to a horizon smeared with raspberry-soaked cirrus.

Donna is no longer in the full wetsuit. She has treated herself to a natty swimming costume, scarlet striped, with short legs and a scrap of a frilled skirt. She is with Rose and a couple of doughty companions she does not know. She steps into the water. It retains the chill of winter. The flick of a breeze speaks of far-off continents. She stands for a moment as hushed as if she is entering a church. She walks on, the creep of cold rising from ankle to shin to thigh to hip to waist. Without effort she allows the buoyancy of the tide to embrace her.

She feels her misgivings roll from her shoulders. She is shriven. Shriven of the snap of a leather strap which meant Harrie could not get up again. Shriven of the guilt that they nearly jailed the wrong man. Shriven of her past wrongs. Of leaving her parents without a word for all those years. Of not being a good enough mother to Elizabeth. Shriven. Is she? She dips her head under the waves. Shriven of a husband who – despite his clamour – no longer cares. She would forgive him if only he would ask for forgiveness. Would she?

She rolls onto her front and stretches into her strokes. In front of her the lighthouse dazzles. The dilapidated castle keep on its mound has a sapphire eye. From this distance the Grand Hotel regains its former dignity.

The water carries her. It is silk down her back. She can forget how her body lets her down. How she becomes drained of her life force along with her blood. She feels strong and, *yes Elizabeth*, just a little brave.

She paddles her way back to the others and joins them on the beach. There is chat now. One of the other swimmers asks Donna if she is local. 'Yes,' she replies gazing at the simple curve of the bay. 'This is my home.'

Acknowledgements

Thank you to Krystyna Green, Amanda Keats and all the crew at Constable/Little, Brown for making this happen. It is quite literally a life-long dream. Thanks go to Howard Watson for his sympathetic copy editing. Any errors which remain are mine. Thanks go to my husband, Mark, my sister, Ros, and all my lovely friends – readers and writers alike – who supported me with my writing. It's been a long road travelled, but generally a good one.

Thank you very much for reading my novel, I do hope that you have enjoyed it. Please feel free to come and find me on Facebook or Instagram. Or sign up to my blog at my website www.scarboroughmysteries.com to get writing tips, be introduced to new writers and hear the latest news on my novels. Thank you.

Author's note

This is a work of fiction. While attempting to create a sense of reality, there are no doubt mistakes, and all which remain are mine. Scarborough, North Yorkshire, exists and the vast majority of settings I have used are real. On the other hand, HMP North Yorkshire is not a genuine institution. There is no prison slap bang in the middle of the Yorkshire Moors, though it sometimes feels as if there might be.